TRAVIS McGEE

An astute and outspoken commentator on 20th-century life . . . a man of intelligence, wit, and compassion . . . a modern-day philosopher whose observations chronicle a changing world. With each book, McGee gets older, wiser, and more cynical . . . but always better at adapting himself to a world he both renounces and respects.

Get to know one of fiction's most enduring heroes by reading the twenty Travis McGee novels in order . . . right up to his latest smash best seller, *Cinnamon Skin.*

THE DEEP BLUE GOOD-BY

NIGHTMARE IN PINK

A PURPLE PLACE FOR DYING

THE QUICK RED FOX

A DEADLY SHADE OF GOLD

BRIGHT ORANGE FOR THE SHROUD

DARKER THAN AMBER

ONE FEARFUL YELLOW EYE

PALE GRAY FOR GUILT

THE GIRL IN THE PLAIN BROWN WRAPPER

DRESS HER IN INDIGO

THE LONG LAVENDER LOOK

A TAN AND SANDY SILENCE

THE SCARLET RUSE

THE TURQUOISE LAMENT

THE DREADFUL LEMON SKY

THE EMPTY COPPER SEA

THE GREEN RIPPER

FREE FALL IN CRIMSON

CINNAMON SKIN

JOHN D. MacDONALD

THE LONG LAVENDER LOOK

FAWCETT GOLD MEDAL • NEW YORK

A Fawcett Gold Medal Book
Published by Ballantine Books

Copyright © 1970 by John D. MacDonald

ISBN 0-449-12965-9

Manufactured in the United States of America

First Fawcett Gold Medal Edition: October 1970
First Ballantine Books Edition: December 1982
Fourth Printing: March 1985

When I play with my cat, who knows but that she regards me more as a plaything than I do her?

—MICHEL EYQUEM DE MONTAIGNE

ONE

LATE APRIL. TEN O'CLOCK AT NIGHT.
Hustling south on Florida 112 through the eastern section
of Cypress County, about twenty miles from the intersection of 112 and the Tamiami Trail.

So maybe I was pushing old Miss Agnes along a little
too fast. Narrow macadam. Stars above, and some wisps
of ground mist below. But not much of it, and not often.

The big tires of the old blue Rolls pickup rumbled along
the roughened surface. Big black drainage canal parallel-
ing the road on the left side. Now and then an old
wooden bridge arching across the canal to serve one of the
shacky little frame houses tucked back in the swamp and
skeeter country. No traffic. And it had been a long long
day, and I was anxious to get back to Lauderdale, to
Bahia Mar, to *The Busted Flush,* to a long hot shower and
a long cold drink and a long deep sleep.

I had the special one-mile spots turned on. They are
bracketed low on the massive front bumper. Essential for
fast running through the balmy Florida nights on the
straight narrow back roads, because her own headlights
are feeble and set too high.

Meyer, beside me, was in a semidoze. We'd been to the
wedding of the daughter of an old friend, at the fish camp

he owns on Lake Passkokee. It is a very seldom thing to be able to drink champagne, catch a nine-pound bass, and kiss a bride all within the same hour. Meyer had been giving me one of his lectures on the marital condition.

So I was whipping along, but alert for the wildlife. I hate to kill a raccoon. Urban Florida is using the rabies myth to justify wiping them out, with guns, traps, and poison. The average raccoon is more affable, intelligent, and tidy than the average meathead who wants them eliminated, and is usually a lot better looking.

It is both sad and ironic that the areas where the raccoon are obliterated are soon overrun with snakes.

I was alert for any reflection of my headlights in animal eyes in the darkness of the shoulders of the road, for any dark shape moving out into the long reach of the beams.

But I wasn't prepared for the creature of the night that suddenly appeared out of the blackness, heading from left to right, at a headlong run. At eighty, you are covering about a hundred and twenty feet per second. She was perhaps sixty feet in front of the car when I first saw her. So half of one second later, when I last saw her, she was maybe ten inches from the flare of my front right fender, and that ten inches was the product of the first effect of my reaction time. Ten inches of living space instead of that bone-crunching, flesh-smashing thud which, once heard, lingers forever in the part of the mind where echoes live.

And I became very busy with Miss Agnes. She put her back end onto the left shoulder, and then onto the right shoulder. The swinging headlights showed me the road once in a while. I could not risk touching the brake. This was the desperate game of steering with the skid each time, and feeding her a morsel of gas for traction whenever she was coming back into alignment with the highway. I knew I had it whipped, and knew that each swing was less extreme.

Then a rear tire went and I lost her for good. The back end came around and there was a shriek of rubber, crashing of brush, a bright cracking explosion inside my skull, and I was vaguely aware of being underwater, disoriented, tangled in strange objects, and aware of the fact that it was not a very good place to be. I did not feel any alarm. Just a mild distaste, an irritation with my situation.

Something started grabbing at me and I tried to make it let go. Then I was up in the world of air again, and being dragged up a slope, coughing and gagging, thinking that it was a lot more comfortable back under the water.

"You all right, Trav? Are you all right?"

I couldn't answer until I could stop retching and coughing. "I don't know yet."

Meyer helped me up. I stood, sopping wet, on the gravelly shoulder and flexed all the more useful parts and muscles. There was a strange glow in the black water. I realized Miss Agnes's lights were still on, and she had to be ten feet under. The light went off abruptly as the water shorted her out.

I found a couple of tender places where I had hit the wheel and the door, and a throbbing lump on my head, dead center, just above the hairline.

"And how are you?" I asked Meyer.

"I'm susceptible to infections of the upper respiratory tract, and I'd like to lose some weight. Otherwise, pretty good."

"In a little while I think I'm going to start being glad you came along for the ride."

"Maybe you'd have gotten out by yourself."

"I don't think so."

"I'd rather think so. Excuse me. Otherwise I have to share the responsibility for all your future acts."

"Do I ever do anything you wouldn't do, Meyer?"

"I could make a list?"

That was when the reaction hit. A nice little case of the yips and shudders. And a pair of macaroni knees. I sat down gently on the shoulder of the road, wrapped my arms around my legs, and rested my forehead on my wet knees.

"Are you all right, Trav?"

"You keep asking me that. I think I will be very fine and very dandy. Maybe five or ten minutes from now."

It seemed very very quiet. The bugs were beginning to

find us. A night bird yawped way back in the marshland. Vision had adjusted to the very pale wash of starlight on the road and on the black glass surface of the drainage canal.

Miss Agnes was down there, resting on her side, facing in the direction from which we had come, driver's side down. Sorry, old lady. We gave it a good try, and damned near made it. Except for the tire going, you did your usual best. Staunch, solid, and, in a very dignified way, obedient. Even in extremis, you managed to keep from killing me.

I got up and gagged and tossed up half a cup of swamp water. Before he could ask me again, I told Meyer I felt much improved. But irritable.

"What I would dearly like to do," I said, "is go back and find that moronic female, raise some angry welts on her rear end, and try to teach her to breathe under water."

"Female?"

"You didn't see her?" I asked him.

"I was dreaming that I, personally, Meyer, had solved the gold drain dilemma, and I was addressing all the gnomes of Zurich. Then I woke up and we were going sideways. I found the sensation unpleasant."

"She ran across in front of us. Very close. If I hadn't had time to begin to react, I'd have boosted her with the right front fender, and she would be a piece of dead meat in a treetop back there on the right side of the road."

"Please don't tell me something."

"Don't tell you what?"

"Tell me she was a shrunken old crone. Or tell me she looked exactly like Arnold Palmer. Or even tell me you didn't get a good look at her. Please?"

I closed my eyes and reran the episode on my little home screen inside my head. Replay is always pretty good. It has to be. Lead the kind of life where things happen very quickly and very unexpectedly, and sometimes lethally, and you learn to keep the input wide open. It improves the odds.

"I'd peg her at early to middle twenties. Black or dark brown hair, that would maybe have been shoulder length if she wasn't running like hell. She had some kind of ribbon or one of those plastic bands on her hair. Not chunky, but solid. Impression of good health. Not very tall. Hmm. Barefoot? I don't really know. Maybe not, unless she's got feet like rhino hide. Wearing a short thing, patterned. Flower pattern? Some kind of pattern. Lightweight material. Maybe one of those mini-nightgowns. Open down the front and at the throat, so that it was streaming out behind her, like her dark hair. Naked, I think. Maybe a pair of sheer little briefs, but it could have been just white hide in contrast to the suntanned rest of her. Caught a glint of something on one wrist. Bracelet or watch strap. She was running well, running hard, getting her knees up, getting a good swing of her arms into it. A flavor of being scared, but not in panic. And not winded. Mouth closed. I think she had her jaw clamped. Determination. She was running like hell, but away from something, not after it. If she started a tenth of a second earlier, we'd be rolling east on the Trail by now. A tenth of a second later, and she'd be one dead young lady, and I could have racked Miss Agnes up a little more solidly, and maybe you or I or both of us would be historical figures. Sorry, Meyer. Young and interestingly put together, and perhaps even pretty."

He sighed. "McGee, have you ever wondered if you don't emit some sort of subliminal aroma, a veritable dog whistle among scents? I have read about the role that some scent we cannot even detect plays in the reproductive cycle of the moth. The scientists spread some of it on a tree limb miles from nowhere, and within the hour there were hundreds upon hundreds of . . . . "

He stopped as we both saw the faraway, oncoming lights. It seemed a long time before they were close enough for us to hear the drone of the engine. We stepped into the roadway and began waving our arms. The sedan faltered, and then the driver floored it and it slammed on by, accelerating. Ohio license. We did not look like people anybody would want to pick up on a dark night on a very lonely road.

"I was wearing my best smile," Meyer said sadly.

We discussed probabilities and possibilities. Twenty miles of empty road from there to the Tamiami Trail. And, in the other direction, about ten miles back to a crossroads with darkened store, darkened gas station. We walked back and I tried to pinpoint the place where the girl had come busting out into the lights, but it was impossible to read black skid marks on black macadam. No lights from any house on either side. No little wooden bridge. No driveway. Wait for a ride and get chewed bloody. So start the long twenty miles and hit the first place that shows a light. Or maybe get a ride. A remote maybe.

Before we left we marked Miss Agnes's watery resting place by wedging a long heavy broken limb down into the mud and jamming an aluminum beer can onto it. Miracle metal. Indestructible. Some day the rows of glittering cans will be piled so high beside the roads that they will hide the billboards which advertise the drinkables which come in the aluminum cans.

Just before we left I had the final wrench of nausea and tossed up the final cup of ditchwater. We kept to the middle of the road and found a fair pace. By the time our shoes stopped making sloppy noises, we were swinging along in good style.

"Four miles an hour," Meyer said. "If we could do it without taking a break, five hours to the Tamiami Trail. By now it must be quarter to eleven. Quarter to four in the morning. But we'll have to take a few breaks. Add an hour and a half, let's say. Hmm. Five-fifteen."

Scuff and clump of shoes on the blacktop. Keening orchestras of tree toads and peepers. *Gu-roomp* of a bullfrog. Whine song of the hungry mosquito keeping pace, then a *whish* of the fly whisk improvised from a leafy roadside weed. Jet going over, too high to pick out the lights. Startled caw and panic-flapping of a night bird working the canal for his dinner. And once, the eerie, faraway scream of a Florida panther.

The second car barreled by at very high speed, ignoring us completely, as did an old truck heading north a few minutes later.

But a good old Ford pickup truck came clattering and banging along, making the anguished sounds of fifteen years of bad roads, heavy duty, neglect, and a brave start on its second or third trip around the speedometer. One headlight was winking on and off. It slowed down as if to stop a little beyond us. We were over on the left shoulder. I could see a burly figure at the wheel.

When it was even with us, there was a flame-wink at the driver's window, a great flat unechoing bang, and a pluck of wind an inch or less from my right ear. When you've been shot at before, even only once, that distinctive sound which you can hear only when you are right in front of the muzzle, is unmistakable. And if you have heard that sound several times, and you are still alive, it means that your reflexes are in good order. I had hooked Meyer around the waist with my left arm and I was charging like a lineman when I heard the second bang. We tumbled down the weedy slope into the muddy shallows of the canal. The truck went creaking and thumping along, picking up laborious speed, leaving a smell of cordite and hot half-burned oil in the night air.

"Glory be!" said Meyer.

We were half in the water. We pulled ourselves up the slope like clumsy alligators.

"They carry guns and they get smashed and they shoot holes in the road signs," I said.

"And they scare hitchhikers and laugh like anything?"

"The slug was within an inch of my ear, old friend."

"How could you know that?"

"They make a little kind of thupping sound, which would come at the same time as the bang, so if it was further away from my ear, I wouldn't have heard it. If he'd fired from a hundred yards away, you'd have heard it, too. And if it had been a sniper with a rifle from five hundred yards, we'd have heard a whirr and a thup and then the shot."

"Thank you, Travis, for the information I hope never to need."

He started to clamber the rest of the way up and I grabbed him and pulled him back. "Rest awhile, Meyer."

"Reason?"

"If we assume it is sort of a hobby, like jacking deer, he is rattling on out of our lives, singing old drinking songs. If it was a real and serious intent, for reasons unknown, he will be coming back. We couldn't find where the young lady busted out of the brush, but we didn't have headlights. He does, and he may be able to see where we busted the weeds. So now we move along the slope here about thirty feet to the south and wait some more."

We made our move, found a more gradual slope where we didn't have to keep our feet in the water. Settled down, and heard the truck coming back. Evidently he had to go some distance to find a turnaround place. Heard him slow down. Saw lights against the grasses a couple of feet above our heads. Lights moved on beyond us, the truck slowing down to a walk. Stopped. The engine idled raggedly. I wormed up to where I could part the grasses and look at the rear end of the truck. Feeble light shone on a mud-smeared Florida plate. Couldn't read any of it. Engine and lights were turned off. Right-hand wheels were on the shoulder. Silence.

I eased back down, mouth close to Meyer's ear. "He better not have a flashlight."

Silence. The bugs and frogs gradually resumed their night singing. I held my breath, straining to hear any sound. Jumped at the sudden rusty bang of the truck door.

I reached cautiously down, fingered up a daub of mud, smeared my face, wormed up the slope again. Could make out the truck, an angular shadow in the starlight, twenty feet away.

"Orville! You hear me, Orville?" A husky shout, yet secretive. A man shouting in a whisper. "You all alone now, boy. I kilt me that big Hutch, right? Dead or close to it, boy. Answer me, Orville, damn you to hell!"

I did not like the idea of announcing that there was nobody here named Orville. Or Hutch.

Long silence. "Orville? We can make a deal. I got to

figure you can hear me. You wedge that body down good, hear? Stake it into the mud. Tomorrow you call me on the telephone, hear? We can set up a place we can meet and talk it all out, someplace with enough people nearby neither of us has to feel edgy."

I heard a distant, oncoming motor sound. The truck door slammed again. Sick slow whine of the starter under the urging of the fading battery. Sudden rough roar, backfire, lights on, and away he went. Could be two of them, one staying behind and waiting, crouched down on the slope, aching to put a hole in old Orville.

I told Meyer to stay put. Just as the northbound sedan went by, soon to overtake the truck, I used the noise and wind of passage to cover my sounds as I bounded up and ran north along the shoulder. I had kept my eyes squeezed tightly shut to protect my night vision. If anyone were in wait, I hoped they had not done the same. I dived over the slope just where the truck had been parked, caught myself short of the water. Nobody.

Climbed back up onto the road. Got Meyer up onto the road. Made good time southward, made about three hundred yards, stopping three or four times to listen to see if the truck was easing back with the lights out.

Found a reasonably open place on the west side of the road, across from the canal. Worked into the shadows, pushed through a thicket. Found open space under a big Australian pine. Both of us sat on the springy bed of brown needles, backs against the bole of the big tree. Overhead a mockingbird was sweetly, fluently warning all other mockingbirds to stay the hell away from his turf, his nest, his lady, and his kids.

Meyer stopped breathing as audibly as before and said, "It is very unusual to be shot at on a lonely road. It is very unusual to have a girl run across a lonely road late at night. I would say we'd covered close to four miles from the point where Agnes sleeps. The truck came from that direction. Perfectly reasonable to assume some connection."

"Don't upset me with logic."

"A deal has a commercial implication. The marksman

was cruising along looking for Orville and Hutch. He did not want to make a deal with both of them. He knew they were on foot, knew they were heading south. Our sizes must be a rough match. And it is not a pedestrian area."

"And Hutch," I added, "was the taller, and the biggest threat, and I moved so fast he thought he'd shot me in the face. And, if he had a good, plausible, logical reason for killing Hutch, he wouldn't have asked Orville to stuff the body into the canal and stake it down."

"And," said Meyer, "were I Orville, I would be a little queasy about making a date with that fellow."

"Ready to go?"

"We should, I guess, before the mosquitoes remove the rest of the blood."

"And when anything comes from any direction, we flatten out in the brush on this side of the road."

"I think I will try to enjoy the walk, McGee."

"But your schedule is way the hell off."

So we walked. And were euphoric and silly in the jungly night. Being alive is like fine wine, when you have damned near drowned and nearly been shot in the face. Perhaps a change of angle of one degree at the muzzle would have put that slug through the bridge of my nose. So we swung along and told fatuous jokes and old lies and sometimes sang awhile.

TWO

AT THE FIRST LIGHT OF ONCOMING dawn, just when the trees were beginning to assume shape and identity, we came out at the intersection of Florida 112 and the Tamiami Trail. There was a big service station and garage across the main highway. The night lights were on. The sign over the office door said: MGR: AL STOREY.

Traffic was infrequent, and very fast. I was heartened to see a squat, muscular wrecker with big duals on the rear, and a derrick with a power hoist. It was going to take muscle to pluck Miss Agnes out of the canal. The more muscle, the less damage to her.

We looked the place over. Coke machine and a coin dispenser for candy bars and cheese crackers and such. I found a piece of wire and picked the lock on the men's room. We washed up. There was no other building within sight. Management had thoughtfully provided a round cement table and benches off to one side, with a furled beach umbrella stuck down through the hole in the middle of the table.

As half an orange sun appeared over the flat horizon, off in the direction of Miami, we sat at the table and ate our coin-slot breakfast and spread the contents of the

17

wallets on the cement top to dry. Licenses and money.
The mosquitoes had welted us abundantly, but I knew the
evidence would disappear quickly. There is a kind of
semiimmunity you acquire if you live long enough in
mosquito country. The itch is caused by the blood-thinner
they inject, so they can suck the mixed fluids up their
narrow snouts. But the redbug bites are something else.
No immunity there. We both had them from ankles to
groin. The itch of the chigger bite lasts so long that the
mythology says they lay eggs under the skin. Not so. It is
a very savage itch, and the only way to cut the weeks
down to a few days is to use any preparation containing a
nerve-deadening agent, along with a cortisone spray. The
sun warmed us and began to dry the money. More cars
and trucks began to barrel through with fading Doppler
whine. A flock of ground doves policed the area. I
scratched the chigger bites and thought of a big deep bed
with clean white sheets.

At twenty of seven an oncoming VW panel delivery
slowed and turned in and parked on the other side of the
building. Two men in it, both staring at us as they passed
out of sight. The money and papers were dry enough. We
gathered them up and started toward the front of the place
and met one of the men at the corner of the building. A
spry wiry fifty. Khakis, baseball cap, with AL embroidered
in red over the shirt pocket. I could hear the twanging and
banging as the other man was sliding the big overhead
doors up.

"You broke down someplace?" Al asked. It was com-
plimentary. We did not look as if we could afford to
operate a bicycle.

"We went into the canal last night, a ways up 112."

"Lots of them do," said Al. "Narrer road with a lot of
lumps in it. Lots of them don't get out of the car neither.
Let me get the place opened up, and when my other man
comes on we'll see about getting you out."

"Hope you don't mind," I said. "I slipped the lock on
your men's room so we could clean up."

He gave me a quick and narrow look and went quickly
to the door to the men's room and inspected the lock. He

found the right key in his pocket and tried it. "Long as you didn't bust nothing, okay. How'd you do it?"

"Piece of wire."

"That there's supposed to be a good lock."

"If it was, I couldn't get in. It looks good, but it's builders' junk. If you've got the same junk on your main doors, you better get them changed."

With a certain suspicion and reluctance he thanked me and hurried off to get his station set up. I wandered around. The place was well run. Tidy and clean, tools in the right places, paperwork apparently under control. The other fellow was big and young. It said TERRY on his pocket. Snug trousers and tapered shirt and big shoulders. Face that could have looked handsome in a rugged way, but the eyes were set too close together, and the chin receded just enough to keep the mouth ajar. So he merely looked tough, coarse, and dumb. They were beginning to get some gas trade and some diesel fuel business.

Then a Highway Patrol sedan stopped at the near island. Al went to take care of it, then called and waved me over. The trooper was older than average, and heavier than average, with a broad red face and very large dark sunglasses.

He asked me if I was the owner and then if I had my license and registration. Then he sighed and dug around for the proper form and we went inside the station and used Al's desk.

After copying the information off my license, he studied the registration. Miss Agnes's age apparently upset him. "A Rolls Royce what?"

"Well, a custom pickup. I mean somebody turned it into a pickup truck a long time back."

"Is it worth all the trouble and the expense to get it out of where it is, McGee?"

"She . . . uh . . . it has a certain sentimental value."

"Pass the inspection? Got the sticker on the windshield?"

"All in order, officer."

He sighed again. "Okay. Any other vehicle involved?"

"No."

"Where and when did it happen?"

"About twenty miles north of here on Route 112. A little after ten o'clock last night. I was heading south."

"How fast?"

"Sixty to sixty-five."

"In a crock that old?"

"She's very able, officer."

"You were driving and your friend there was with you. And you were going sixty-five and no other vehicles were involved and you put it into the canal?"

"Not exactly like that. A woman ran across the road directly in front of me. She came out of nowhere. I had to swerve to keep from hitting her."

"Sure you didn't?"

"Absolutely positive. I nearly lost it right there. I was all over the road trying to bring my car out of it. I finally started to make it. Then a rear tire blew and that did it. She went in fairly easy. It's in about ten feet of water, aiming back the way we came, resting on the left side. We got out of it. Then we came here and waited until Al showed up to open up."

"Point of departure and destination."

"We were coming from Lake Passkokee and going home to Lauderdale."

"Twenty miles north from here would put you in Cypress County. Here. This copy is yours. Al will probably call them on his radio when he's in range. If Sher'f Norm Hyzer has a car come out to look it over, this is your proof you turned in the accident report. And maybe your insurance will want to take a look at it, too."

He went out to his car. I saw him talk into the hand mike and knew he was checking in to make sure there was nothing out on the car or the driver. It is standard procedure and seldom forgotten, as nothing makes a cop look sillier than finding out later that the plausible stranger is wanted for a bank job.

He talked for a long time, then reached in and hung the mike up, shoved his hat back a little with one paw, and unholstered the Police Positive with the other. "Okay.

Both of you. Face down. Spread it out. Grab the back of your neck."

Quick, rough, thorough, and very cautious. Officer Nagle was a competent cop.

"What'd they do, Beef?" Al asked.

"I wouldn't hardly know. All I know is Norm wants 'em, and he'll be coming right along to get them."

"Isn't there something about rights?" I asked humbly.

"If I was the arresting officer, I'd read you what it says on the little card, McGee. But all I'm doing is detaining you, a professional favor for the sher'f of Cypress County. Move back there in the shade, and lean against the wall. Move a little further apart from each other, boys. That's fine."

"You're making a mistake," Meyer said.

He looked owlishly astonished. "Me? How can I be making a mistake doing what the man asks me to do, asks me nice? Any kind of mistake in this is all Norm Hyzer's, and I hear he doesn't make too many. Int that right, Al?"

"They seem to keep on electing him up there," Al said. From the tone I guessed he wasn't a Hyzer fan. He headed out to the island to take care of a dusty Buick with a noisy fan belt. The big young one named Terry stood and stared at us with vacuous, adenoidal intensity.

A blue Rambler came down Route 112, waited at the stop sign, then came across and parked beside the station. A broad brown man with a white grin got out. It said HENRY over the pocket of his coveralls. "Hey there, Beef. What's going on?"

"How come you can't hardly ever get here on time?" Al demanded.

"Now look, honest, I had a bad night, and I clean slept right through that alarm again, and . . ."

"And Hummer was promised the Olds at ten-thirty and you haven't even started on the brake job yet, so don't stand around asking dumb questions. I don't want Hummer so damn mad he starts yelling in my face again. He sprays spit."

Time passed. Traffic was picking up, but visibly and audibly slowing at the sight of the patrol car with the

distinctive blue roof lights. Meyer started to say something
to me, and Beef Nagle said politely that he'd rather we
didn't carry on any conversation.

At last I heard the thin distant scream of an
approaching siren. It came down 112, slowed a little at
the sign and plunged across, swung and left rubber on the
apron in a dramatic smoking stop. Green sedan with a red
flasher on the roof. Cypress County Sheriff's Department.
Sheriff Norman L. Hyzer. The man who climbed out
quickly from behind the wheel wore a khaki uniform that
said DEPUTY SHERIFF on the shoulder patch. Long lumpy
face, sallow complexion, blond-red hair, and glasses with
steel rims that did not give him the slightest look of
bookish introspection.

So the other one had to be Hyzer. Late forties. Tall and
slender and very erect. Black suit, shiny black shoes, crisp
white shirt, dark blue necktie, gold wedding ring, white
Stetson. He had dark hair and noble-hero face, expressionless. He kept the mouth pinched shut. The eyes were
very blue, and his examination of each of us was long,
intensive, unrevealing.

Next he examined the pocket-contents Nagle had taken
from us, and the accident report Nagle had filled out. The
occupations as listed on the Florida driver's licenses
seemed to intrigue him.

"Salvage consultant?" he said in a deep, soft voice,
barely audible over traffic sounds. "Economist?"

"Unlikely as it may seem at the moment," said Meyer
in his best guest-lecturer delivery. It didn't match the
bristled jowls, the mud-stained clothes and the sorry
shoes.

"You have the right to remain silent. You have the
right to legal counsel. If you cannot employ an attorney,
one will be provided for you. If you choose to answer
questions, anything you say may be used in evidence
against you. Do you understand, McGee? Do you understand, Meyer?"

"We understand," I said. "We'll answer anything you
want to ask. But it would be nice to know the charge."

"Suspicion of premeditated murder." His face showed

nothing. Nothing at all regional about his voice. Not your stock Florida sheriff by any means. A lot of ice-cold class. Made me wonder why he was content to be sheriff of Cypress County, a lot of swamp and palmetto and maybe, by straining hard, twenty thousand people. "Get into the cruiser." His deputy opened the rear door and stepped back.

"I'd like to make arrangements about getting my car pulled out of the canal, Sheriff."

"We'd arrange that in any case, McGee."

"Can I show this man where it is?"

"We know where it is."

Al said, with a mocking smile, "And no damn need of my asking for the business, is there, Sher'f?"

"I hardly think so, Mr. Storey."

"Who got killed?" big Terry asked.

Hyzer hesitated, then said, "Frank Baither."

"Overdue," said Al Storey.

We got in. Steel mesh between us and the two in front. Safety glass at the sides, with no cranks and no inside door handles. The deputy picked a hole in the traffic and scatted across, and barreled it on up to ninety. Hyzer sat erect, silent, and motionless. A few miles along the road an egret came out of the brush on the canal side, tried for altitude and didn't quite make it. It thudded against the high right corner of roof and windshield. I looked back and saw the white feathers falling to the roadbed like strange snow.

We were in a cage that smelled of green disinfectant and last week's vomit, and was going too fast. Meyer rode with his hands loosely clasped in his lap, eyes closed, half smile on his mouth, swaying and bouncing to the hard movements of the sedan.

Far ahead I saw vehicles and activity. The deputy waited a long time, then braked hard and pulled over. They both got out, banged the doors shut, and walked up to where a big blue-and-white wrecker was working. It was backed close to the edge of the canal. Traffic was blocked in both directions. On the side door of the wrecker was printed JOHNNY'S MAIN STREET SERVICE. The cable stretched down into black water, under tension as the big winch wound it up. There were some shouts and arm-waving. Then I saw the gleaming, stately, angular contours of the front of Miss Agnes appear.

"They're doing it just right," I told Meyer. "Stood her up on the back end and the angle brought the wheels right onto the bank."

"Hooray," he muttered.

"They've got the wheels cramped right, so they can bring her up and out in one swing."

"How marvelous."

"Usually you enjoy seeing something done well, Meyer."

"I do not like this, not any part of this."

Neither did I, and maybe not for the same reasons. The wrecker eased forward and brought Miss Agnes out swiftly, gently, and deftly. Made the turn away from us, and pulled over onto the shoulder. The few cars and trucks that had waited were waved on. Hyzer spent a long time checking over old Miss Agnes. The cruiser was getting up to baking temperature inside, sweat popping out and rolling down.

At last they came back and got in. I asked about damage. Nobody answered. On the way to Cypress City we swung out and passed Miss Agnes. She looked a little crumpled around the corners, and there were bright green strings of algae across her windshield and hood. I was happy to see that somebody had been sportsman enough to put the spare on. It would have hurt a little to see her clopping along on the rim.

We couldn't give answers until they came up with the questions. And then it would be apologies, smiles, handshakes.

Maybe.

THREE

IT WAS A LITTLE AFTER NOON WHEN A fat elderly deputy brought me a cold and greasy cheeseburger wrapped in waxed paper, and a cardboard container of tepid coffee with too much sugar and cream already in it.

"Why the delay?" I asked. "What's going on?"

"Beats me, friend," he said, and went out and locked the door behind him. It was a small room with a heavy table bolted to the floor, heavy benches bolted to the plaster walls, wire mesh over the ceiling light and over the single window. The window was on the second floor of the Moorish structure. It looked out across a narrow courtyard at another wing of the U-shaped building. The floor of the room was asphalt tile in a mottled tan and green. The walls were yellow tan. I had opened a shallow drawer in the heavy table and found it full of dead cigar stubs and burned matches. Distant sounds of traffic. Radio rock in the distance, on a cheap set. Bird sounds. The room was too warm. I improvised a pillow by rolling my shoes in my shirt, stretched out on the bench, and dozed off.

"Come on," said the deputy with the steel glasses. I stretched and yawned, rolled the stiffness out of my shoulders, worked my way into the shirt and shoes.

"You got a name?" I asked him.

"Billy. Billy Cable."

"From around here?"

"All my life. He's waiting on us. Come on."

He directed me ahead of him to different stairs than I had used coming up. "He said to take you the long way around."

The long way around included a short side trip into the county jail. Billy said this was a brand new part of it, new just three years ago. And these were the maximum security cells. Very bright overhead lights. About five by eight, with a bunk, a sink, a toilet. Meyer sat on the low bunk, hunched forward, head bowed, forearms braced on his knees. The thick, slow, half-clotted blood dripped from his mouth to the cement between his bare feet, into a small puddle as big around as a saucer.

I said his name. He looked up slowly, tilting his head to bring the one slit of one eye to bear. The crushed mouth said, "I still don't like any part of it, McGee."

As I turned on Billy he moved back swiftly, hand on the holster. "Easy now. Easy," he said.

"*Why*, goddammit!"

"You better ask him about that when you see him, McGee."

Hyzer's office was austere. Bare walls, bare desktop, blue carpeting. Efficient air conditioning made it very chilly. I was directed to a straight chair placed about six feet back from the edge of Hyzer's desk, which put me in almost the exact center of the room. A very large deputy sat on another straight chair placed against the wall just inside the door. He looked vaguely familiar to me, but I couldn't come up with the association. Big freckled arms folded. Belly sagging over the belt. Broad, soft, drowsy face.

When I was seated, Sheriff Norman Hyzer said, "This session is being recorded on magnetic tape. When it is transcribed some minor editing will be done to eliminate repetitions. If you have any question regarding the accuracy of the transcription, you will be permitted to listen to the pertinent portion of the recording to satisfy yourself."

"May I make a comment for the record?"

"Go right ahead."

"My friend Meyer is a reputable economist internationally known in his field. He is a gentle person, without malice or enemies, or police record of any kind. We planned to cooperate with you, Sheriff. Get it settled and be on our way. But now you have bought the whole package, Hyzer. I am going to personally nail you to the wall, if it takes five years. From now on I'm coming at you. I'm bringing it to you."

The big deputy sighed and belched. Hyzer opened his pocket notebook. "First interrogation of Travis McGee. Fourteen-forty hours. April 24. Pritchard monitoring tape. Sturnevan witnessing interrogation. Now then. From whom did you hear that Frank Baither had been, or was about to be, released from Raiford State Prison, and, to the best of your recollection, tell me the date on which you received this information?"

"The only previous time in my life I ever heard the name Frank Baither was when you said that name this morning in front of Al's service station, Hyzer."

"Was there a third man with you last night?"

"You're playing your game, Hyzer. The officer of the law. The professional. *If* you were a professional instead of a swamp county ham actor, you'd find out who we are, where we were yesterday, and where we were heading. You'd verify the girl running across the road. You'd make a couple of phone calls. Not you. No, sir. Don't confuse yourself with logic. Net result is you aren't going to play sheriff much longer."

"An unidentified woman ran across the road. We found the place where she crouched in the ditch. Bare footprints in the mud. A place where she braced herself, making an imprint of the knuckles of her right hand. We used the skid marks to locate the area. Sooner or later we'll locate her body."

"She's dead?"

"She almost got across, but you swerved and probably hit her."

"Now why did I do that, Sheriff?"

"Because she was with Baither and saw you and got away from you and you people had to hunt her down."

"With an old Rolls, for God's sake?"

"And you lost control when a tire blew."

"Hyzer, you are having dreams and visions and fantasies. I will tell you who to phone at Lake Passkokee. I will pay for the call. He is an old friend. We went to the wedding of his eldest daughter. He has a fish camp. We went bass fishing. There were rods in that car of mine. And three fresh-cleaned bass on ice."

"Deputy Billy Cable says they were fresh enough."

"Will you phone?"

"This is a small county, McGee. And I am in a small job at small pay. But I am not a fool. Four years ago you people, along with Frank Baither, planned that job down to the last small detail. And there was just as much at stake now as then. More, because this time you had to kill one you knew of, and one you didn't. First things first. When the time comes to dismantle your alibi, it will fall apart. You know it and I know it. Please stop making speeches. Answer my questions. Was there a third man with you last night?"

"Meyer and I were alone."

"Did Meyer finish him off with the ice pick or did you?"

"Hyzer, the car went into the ditch, and we got out of it by great good fortune, and we walked all the way down to the Tamiami Trail to that station where you found us."

"That is most unlikely, McGee. We had an anonymous call at one in the morning. A man, whispering to disguise his voice. He said Frank Baither phoned him every night at midnight, and if some night there was no call, and no one answered at the Baither place, he was to call the law. He went out there and found Baither still taped to that chair. From that time on I had cars on the road all night. You would have been stopped and questioned."

"There is very damned little traffic on that Route 112

after dark. And when we saw lights coming, we got out of sight."

"Now why would you do that?" He smiled for the first time. I think it was a smile. The corners of his mouth went up about a sixteenth of an inch.

So I told him about the nut in the old truck who'd tried to pot us from the truck window, and thought he'd gotten one of us, thought he'd scragged somebody named Hutch, then tried to dicker with the survivor, somebody named Orville. I said it happened about one hour and four miles south of where I had put Miss Agnes into the canal.

"Describe the truck."

"An old Ford pickup, rough, noisy, and beat. I think it was red. A junker. Not worth licensing."

He slowly turned the pages of his pocket notebook. "So, being the innocent law-abiding citizens you people claim to be, you made no attempt to report somebody trying to kill you, either at the time or this morning to either Officer Nagle or to me."

"Sheriff, neither of us saw the man. The plate was too dirty and the light too weak to read the number. You know your own county better than I do. There are probably a lot of fine citizens living back in the boonies off that road. And there are some very rough ones too, native-born swamp rats and poachers, and people that came a long way to find a place where they're not likely to be found. A long time ago I spent one weekend here in Cypress City, and after I saw how Saturday night was shaping up, I went back to the motel room and put my cash money in the Gideon and went back out with one ten-dollar bill and had what you could call a memorable evening. I don't really much care if your people kill each other, Hyzer. We were just making certain they didn't kill us and then feel apologetic because the dead bodies didn't turn out to be Hutch and Orville. There wasn't any phone booth handy after that clown drove off in his junk truck. I thought of a way I could attract official attention. We could have walked back four miles and I could have dived down and gotten my tow chain out of the tool compartment and heaved it up over the power lines. Then pretty soon we would have had the use of the CB radio in the Florida Power and Light truck that would show up. I thought of it, and I thought of making a neighborly call at the next house we came to. But I didn't like either of those ideas, Sheriff."

"McGee, you had bad luck, didn't you? When you lost that car in the canal, you went back to Frank Baither's place and tried to use his old Ford truck, but the battery was too far gone and you couldn't get it started. Then, while you were walking, you did some thinking. Somebody was going to spot that car sooner or later, and it could be traced to you, and that was a risk you couldn't accept. So you had to put something together that sounded good, and get Al Storey to hoist it out of the canal and tow it in."

"Hyzer, you are one dumb, blind, stubborn man."

"You have a good act, McGee. So does your partner. Aren't you wondering, a little, why you can't sell it to me?"

"More than a little."

"Then there must be a little more bad luck along with what you already know about. Bad luck or judgment. What could you have forgotten? Think about it."

I thought. "You must have something you like. I don't know what it could be. I will tell you one thing. Don't depend on it. Because whatever it is, it isn't going to prove what you think it proves, no matter how good it looks."

"You never saw or heard of Frank Baither in your life?"

"No."

"You were never inside his house?"

"Never."

"I am going to describe an exhibit to you. It will be a part of the file I am going to turn over to the State's attorney. It is an empty envelope addressed to you, at Bahia Mar, date-stamped a week ago, April 17. On the back of it, possibly in your hand, are some notes about highway numbers and street names. It had been folded twice, and had been immersed in water. Do you recognize it from the description?"

"I think so. Yes. I don't know where you're going with it, though. Jimmy Ames phoned me last Saturday and invited us to Betsy's wedding. He said that the road I'd normally take was closed, that a bridge was out. He gave me directions. I reached down into the wastebasket near the phone and took an envelope out and wrote down the directions. Get hold of him at Jimmy's Fish Camp. He'll verify it."

"When the call came in about the Baither murder, Deputy Cable phoned me at my home. I got dressed and drove to the Baither place. I supervised the investigation. After the county medical examiner had authorized the removal of the body, I posted Deputy Arnstead there to make certain nobody entered the premises before a more thorough daylight search could be made. I was on my way to participate in that search when the call came from Officer Nagle. After he described you and told me about where your car was, and said you had walked all the way to the Trail, I had no choice but to bring you in for questioning. I returned at eleven-fifteen to the Baither place and, with Deputy Arnstead, completed the search of the house and the area. The envelope was found on the floor of the room where Baither died."

So what do you do? The big soft sleepy deputy shifted in his chair, creaking it. One thing you do is stop thrashing and flapping. You back up a couple of steps, tuck the elbows in, get the jaw out of range.

"Question?" I asked.

"Can you change your mind about your rights? Yes. At any time."

"That wasn't what I was going to ask."

"What then?"

"I can tell you exactly what I did with that envelope, where, and when. But I don't know you, Hyzer. It's planted evidence. You had somebody dance Meyer around. I don't like the way you think. I don't like the way you do your job. If I don't want to answer any more questions, and if you have nothing to do with the plant, then you are going to be that much more convinced you've got the right people to make your case. But if I tell you about the envelope, and you are in on building the case against us any way you can, then you can listen to the truth and go plug the holes in your evidence. I don't even know if this *is* going onto tape and, if it is, whether you erase the ones you don't like. I'm boxed because I can't figure out what you are, so I don't know which way to go. You talk about some action four years ago, something we are supposed to have planned with this Baither. Check us out. There's no record of any convictions."

"Which means only that up until now you haven't made any serious mistakes, McGee."

"So *why*, Sheriff, would I go to all the trouble of faking up this wedding story and having the fishing gear and the bass in the car, just to come sneaking into your county after dark to knock off a recent graduate of Raiford? Where's the sense to it?"

"About nine hundred thousand dollars worth of sense, which you are quite aware of. And the chance you might have to go through a roadblock on your way out of the area with it. Misdirection, McGee. A car so conspicuous no fool would use it for this kind of purpose. Fresh bass packed in ice. It should have worked, McGee."

So another shaft of light in the murk. That much money is worth a lot of care and attention. And it could maybe buy a matched set of Hyzers.

"I think I'd better stop right now, Sheriff. I'd like to phone an attorney."

"A particular attorney?"

"Yes. In Miami. He'll accept a collect call."

"May I have his name?"

"Leonard Sibelius."

I looked for a change of expression. Nothing. He said, "You can make your call at nine o'clock tomorrow morning, McGee."

"Why not now? Isn't that a violation of my civil rights?"

"It would be if you'd been booked, and I'd turned your file over to the State's attorney for indictment by the grand jury. You chose to answer questions. You've been in custody for interrogation since eight-forty hours this morning."

"Tomorrow is Saturday, Sheriff."

"The twenty-fifth. King, have Priskitt put him in a single twelve or fourteen, and move somebody if he has to. I want no contact between McGee and Meyer."

I fitted the two parts of the big deputy's name together. King Sturnevan. I looked at him again and made sure. I'd seen him fight years ago at Miami Beach, at about two hundred then. Maybe sixty pounds heavier now. A spoiler, a mawler. Looked slow, but surprisingly hard to hit. Clever on the ropes and in the clinches, ripping those hooks up into the body, snuffing and grunting with the effort. Would have done better in the division except he had a tendency to cut, which put too many TKO's on his record. So the smart way they took him was to put the little twist of the wrist on the end of the jab, hoping to open up his brows before he bombed their innards to pulp.

"Sheriff, would you please tell this fat, sloppy, old pug not to try to do me the way he did Meyer? Lennie Sibelius can give you enough trouble without that, too."

"There were three witnesses to your partner's accident, McGee. He had taken his shower. He was stepping into the issue coveralls when he lost his balance and fell, striking his face on the wooden bench in the shower room."

"Then I guess if the same thing happened to me, it would look like a strange coincidence."

He didn't answer. He picked up the phone. Sturnevan beckoned to me and held the door open.

As we went along the corridor he said, "Hey, you knew me, huh? You seen me in there, ever?" His voice was soft, husky, high-pitched.

"Miami Beach, just once. Eight or nine years ago."

"That must have been close to the last. Who was I going with?"

"I can't remember the name. A great big Cuban boy."

"Sure! That was a ten-round main. Tigre something. Tigre means 'tiger,' and he had a big long last name, and I knocked him out in the ninth, right? You know what? That *was* the last one. Honest to Christ, that boy was, I mean, conditioned! Like an oak tree, the whole middle of him. He kept moving the wrong way and giving me perfect shots, and I couldn't even take the grin off his face. Then like twenty seconds into the ninth, he cut me. See this one? He popped it just right by dumb luck and opened it up, and I knew it was bad. All I could do, see, was keep turning to keep the ref from getting too good a look at it and hoping before he did, that boy would tangle his feet and move the wrong way again, so when he did I had to put the right hand right on the shelf. I knew it would bust and it did. But he stayed down. All the time I was in there, what I had was bad managers and bad hands. I had to go for the middle because my hands bust too easy. So you saw that one, hey! I was going to go again, all lined up with I forget who, and I bust the hand in the same place on the heavy bag, working out."

As we went down the stairs, I said, "But you didn't chop Meyer bad enough to hurt your hands?"

"He fell on the bench, like Mister Norm said."

"And his head bounced up and down on that bench like a big rubber ball. Must have been interesting to watch."

"What I can tell you is I didn't work him over. Mister Norm got on me about that, and I swore on my baby daughter's grave I never touched him and didn't see anybody else touch him. I told Mister Norm it didn't make sense after all the times I worked a little on some of the people without marking them, all of a sudden I forget how and start hitting a man in the head? Not me. Not the King. Right through here. Hey, Priskie? Fresh fish. Mister Norm says single twelve or fourteen."

"We can give you twelve, sir. A very nice room. I'm sure you'll be very happy with it. Anything you want, just ring." Priskitt was somewhere between fifty and ninety, spry, bald, and shrunken by the heat of time and fortune. He dug into a bin, selected a tagged bundle, put it in a wire gym basket. "All our guests wear costumes," he said. "Gets you in the spirit of the thing."

"Priskie, this here fellow saw my last fight, where I chilled the big Cuban kid and busted my hand. I told you about that one, right?"

"Not over forty times."

I said, "I don't want to spoil your comical routine, Priskitt, but how is Professor Meyer making it?"

"I got him some aspirin and some ice to suck on. I wouldn't say he feels great. But maybe not as bad as he did."

"I got to look in Nat's book and find out what the last name was on that Cuban kid," King said. "I'll get him showered. Come on, McGee. Tote that basket."

The cement shower room smelled of mildew, ammonia, and Lysol. There was a sliver of green soap and a drizzle of tepid water from a corroded shower head, and a thin gray towel.

What you need on the inside of any institution whatsoever are friends. "King, I'm a little ashamed of thinking you busted my friend up. I should have known you've got more class than that."

"Aw, what the hell. I mean I can see why."

"No, really. I saw you fight. You could have been one of the great ones. You know that? A few breaks here and there."

"Breaks, sure. They woulda helped. But I coulda stood better equipment. I cut too easy and my hands were brittle. But I could always move good, and I could take a punch off anybody."

"Where are you from originally?"

"New Jersey. Nutley. Fourteen years old, I was in the Golden Gloves. Fleet champion in the Navy, coming in light heavy. Had fourteen years pro, two in the amateurs. Ninety-one bouts. I win sixty-eight, lose seventeen, draw six. It's all in the record. McGee, what do you go? Maybe around two-o-eight?"

"Very close."

"The clothes on, I would have said one ninety, maybe less. You fooled me. You holding pretty good shape, fella. You ever do any fighting when you were a kid?"

"Nothing serious. Just horsing around."

"You can keep your own underwear. And put the coveralls and these here straw scuffs on and put your other stuff in the basket."

I did as directed. The twill coveralls had been washed threadbare, and they were soft as the finest lightweight wool.

"Come at me a little, McGee. I want to see if you know how to move. Good Christ, don't look at me like that! I'm not making up some kind of way to bust you up."

So I shrugged and went at him, doing my standard imitation of a big puppet badly manipulated from above, jounce and flap, keeping an assortment of elbows and shoulders and wrists in front of the places I don't like to have thumped, keeping a wide-focus stare aimed at his broad gut, because that is the only way you can see what the head and hands and feet are doing, all at the same time.

I don't know how many years older he was. He moved in a slow, skilled, light-footed prance, and the slabbed fat on his body jounced and shook like the pork fat on a circus bear. He held his big paws low and stayed pretty much in the same place. Had it been for real, I would have had as much chance against him as a little kid with a piece of lathe against a member of the Olympic fencing team. Pro is pro. I slapped empty space, sometimes a shoulder. Each effort of mine resulted in a quick little stinging whack of fingertips against jaw, cheekbone, rib cage. Then I decided to try to protect myself. But here is how it is with a pro: You duck under a high left jab, and you see the feet, body, shoulder, head, all moving into the logical right hook, and when you move to defend from that, you are suddenly open for two more quick jabs. You shift to handle that, and there is the right hook you were going to block earlier, so you rush him to get inside, and he isn't there because he has twisted, tipped you off balance, and stands braced and ready for you to bounce back off the wall. Explosive snort. Grin. Hands raised in signal of peace.

So I gratefully emerged from my ineffective shell and said, "You are real quick, King."

"Hell, I'm slowed down to nothing. Reflexes all shot. Seems quick to you because I know where you're going to be by the time I tap you. Listen to me huff and puff. McGee, you would have made it pretty good if you started soon enough. It would be hard to take a good shot at you. I'd have to bomb you downstairs until you couldn't get your arms up. Then drop you."

He led me to the single cell, telling me, on the way, of the time he had come the closest to top ranking, when Floyd Patterson had nailed him as they came out for the second, and he had faked rubber legs well enough to bring Patterson in, too eager and careless, and he had pivoted and stuffed his big hand and glove deep into Floyd's tough middle, just above the belt, turning him gray and sweaty and very tired. Chased him for seven rounds, while Floyd had slowly regained his strength and health despite all King Sturnevan could do in the way of wearing him down. And then Floyd stabbed and chopped and split his way to the technical knockout.

He dogged the door shut, big face still rueful with the memory of not being able to nail down the disabled Patterson. I said, "What's with this sheriff of yours, King?"

"How do you mean?"

"What kind of an act is it?"

He shifted the wire basket to his other arm. "It's no act. Mister Norm upholds the law, and the County Commission backs him a hundred percent. We got modern stuff here, McGee. We got a teletype tied into FLEX, and one of the first things he did was see if there was any package on you with the F.C.I.C. and then the N.C.I.C., and it puzzled him some, maybe, to come up empty on both of you."

"Real modern methods, King, spoiling Meyer's face."

"All you got is my word, but it isn't like that around here."

"Then why did Deputy Billy Cable bring me through here to admire Meyer before he took me to Hyzer?"

"Billy got gnawed down to the bare bone on that one.

He was off in the MP's for a while. Sometimes he forgets Mister Norm doesn't like those little tricks."

"Now how would you know Hyzer came down on Billy Cable?"

"You learn to read that man's face. It isn't easy, but you have to learn. I saw he was upset, and I could guess why. He'd already found out about Meyer, and he was upset about that, too, about it happening at all. By now he's got Billy all peeled raw."

"Who did it?"

"I didn't see a thing."

Priskitt came to the cell. "I thought this man had probly jumped you and made good his daring escape, champ. You want me to lock you in there with him so you can keep the dialogue going, or do you want to go back to work? As a special favor to Mister Norm."

"He called for me?"

"He surely did."

And with a single bulge-eyed look of anxiety, King Sturnevan went off, in a light-footed, fat-jouncing trot.

"The department seems to have a plentitude of deputies, Mr. Priskitt."

He looked at me happily. "Plentitude! One rarely hears the good words around here, Mr. McGee. I would say that Mister Norm has an adequacy of deputies. Not a superfluity. Whatever Mister Norm feels is necessary for the pursuit of his sworn responsibility, he asks for. And gets. We must chat later."

He hurried away and I stretched out. . . .

FOUR

IMMOVABLE BUNK AND A THIN HARD mattress pad. Cement floor with a center drain. Bright bulb countersunk behind heavy wire mesh in the cement ceiling. Iron sink with a single iron faucet and no drain pipe so that water from the sink would run down the pitch of the floor to the drain three feet away. Toilet with no lid or seat. No window. No way to see any other cell through the top half of the door which was of sturdy bars. The lower half was steel plate.

Stretch out on the back, forearm across the eyes. Shove the whole damned mess over into a corner cupboard and kick the door shut. Save it until later, because trying to think about it would only bring the anger back. Angry men do a bad job of thinking.

There had been a lot of waiting-time in my life. Sometimes it was cat-time, watching the mouse hole for all the endless dreary hours. Sometimes it had been mouse-time, waiting all the day through for the darkness and the time for running.

So you learn the special resources of both memory and imagination. You let the mind run through the old valleys, the back hills, and pastures of your long-ago years. You take an object. Roller skate. The kind from way back, that fastened to the shoes instead of coming with shoes attached. Look and feel and design of the skate key. With old worn shoes you turn the key too much and you start to buckle the sole of the shoe. Spin one wheel and listen to the ball-bearinged whir, and feel the gritty texture of the metal abraded by the sidewalks. Remember how slow and strange and awkward it felt to walk again, after all the long Saturday on skates, after going way to the other end of town. Remember the soreness where the strap bit into the top of your ankle. When it got too sore, you could stop and undo the strap and run it through the top laces of your shoe. Thick dark scab on the abraded knee. The sick-making smack of skull against sidewalk. Something about the other end of the skate key. . . . Of course! A hex wrench orifice that fit the nut on the bottom of the skate so you could expand it or contract it to fit the shoe. If you didn't tighten it enough, or if it worked loose, then the skate would stealthily lengthen, the clamps no longer fitting the edge of the shoe sole, and at some startling moment the next thrust would spin the skate around, and you either took one very nasty spill, or ended up coasting on the good skate, holding the other foot with dangling skate up in the air until you came to a place to sit down and get the key out and tighten everything again. Roller skate or sandbox or apple tree or cellar door. Playground swing or lumberyard or blackboard or kite string. Because that was when all the input was vivid. All of it is still there. So you find a little door back there, and like Alice, you walk through it into the magic country, where each bright flash of memory illuminates yet another.

It doesn't work that way for everybody. Once I worked a stakeout for two months with a quiet little man. We were talked out after two days. But he seemed totally patient, totally content. After a month I asked him what he thought about. He said he was a rubber bridge addict. So mentally he would deal himself a random hand, then out of the thirty-nine cards left, deal a random hand to the opponent at his left, then to the one at his right, and give what was left to his partner. Then he would go through the bidding, the play of the cards, and mark the result on the running scorepad in his head. He said that sometimes when he was a little fatigued, he might forget whether the jack of diamonds had been dealt at his left or his right. Then he would have everybody throw their hands in and he would deal again.

When the people we were covering finally made their move, there was a communication problem. We couldn't get through to the vehicle parked six blocks away. So the bridge player handled that problem, at a dead run. He got there in time and they closed that door before the quarry tried it. He sat in the back seat, they said, and gasped and laughed, then squeaked and died. I saw him for a couple of moments, and thought of all the bridge games that died inside his head when all the other things stopped.

"McGee?"

I looked up and got up and went over to the door. "Sheriff?"

"I researched that problem you raised, McGee. I do not want to take any chance of reversal of conviction on a very minor point. I think I am right. If tomorrow were a working day, I would take my chances. But running it over into a Saturday might be questionable. It's a little after four now, but you should be able to reach your Mr. Sibelius, I think."

The operator left the line open on my person-to-person collect call, and I could hear the girl at the other end being professionally indefinite about where and how Lennie could be located.

"Operator, is that Miss Carmichael."

"Trav? This is Annie, yes."

"Are you accepting the collect call, Miss?"

"Well ... I guess so. Yes. Travis? Why collect, for goodness' sake?"

"It seemed simpler, on account of I am here in the county jail in Cypress County on suspicion of killing people."

No gasps or cooing or joshing or stupid questions. She went to work. She got the phone number. She said that if we were in luck, she could catch Lennie between the apartment and the marina, on his telephone in his car. If he had already taken off, she wouldn't get him until he monitored the Miami marine broadcast at six o'clock. Then she broke it off.

I told the hero sheriff the call would come back quickly, or not until after six. He looked at his watch. "Wait here for ten minutes. Stand over there against the wall."

No readable inflection, no emotion in the delivery. So you stand against the wall, in your ratty straw slippers, the pant legs of the coveralls ending about five inches above where pants should end, the top buttons unbuttoned because it is too small across chest and shoulders, the sleeves ending midway between elbow and wrist. So you are a large grotesque unmannerly child, standing and watching an adult busy himself with adult things. Man in a dark business suit, crisp white shirt, dark tie, dark gloss of hair, opening folders, making small marginal notes.

The law, in its every dimension of the control of criminals, is geared to limited, stunted people. Regardless of what social, emotional, or economic factor stunted them, the end product is hate, suspicion, fear, violence, and despair. These are weaknesses, and the system is geared to exploit weaknesses. Mister Norm was a creature outside my experience. There were no labels I could put on him.

He answered the phone, held it out to me.

"Hello, Lennie," I said.

"From this phone booth, Trav, I can see the *Witchcraft*, all fueled and ready, and my guests carrying the food and booze aboard, and a pair of blond twins slathering oil on each other up on the fly bridge. It was nice to have known you, pal."

"Likewise. Take off, playboy. Cruise the ocean blue in your funny hat. Kiss the twins for me."

"So all right! Bad?"

"And cute. And for once in your brief meteoric career, you'd be representing total innocence."

"Now isn't that nice! And I can't get into a front page with it, because if I make you a star, you are going to have to find useful work or starve. Status right now?"

"Held for questioning. I waived my rights, and then all of a sudden a very bad question came along, and after thinking it over, I took it all back." My mind was racing, trying to figure out some way to clue him into checking out Sheriff Norman Hyzer, because, had I been sure of Hyzer's integrity—and sanity—I would have explained the envelope he had found.

"Innocence can answer any kind of question that comes up."

"If everybody is truly interested in the concept, Lennie."

"Chance of the law there looking for a setup?"

"It's possible."

"Annie said something about killing people."

"At least one, they claim. They haven't said why. Just hinted about some kind of a job long ago netting nine hundred thou."

"So the area swarms with strobes and notebooks and little tape recorders?"

"Not a one."

"So they can put a tight lid on and keep it on. Very rare these days, pal. I know they have a lumpy little patch of grass over there because I had to put down on it a year ago when my oil pressure started to look rotten and the mill started to heat on me. Look, I'll have Wes take this party out and anchor someplace down the bay. I'll make some phone calls here and there, and ... let me see. I want to hit that grass patch by daylight, so let's say that by six-thirty I'll be holding your hand."

"And Meyer's."

"I always told him evil companions would lead him astray."

Hyzer had me taken back down to my private room. I sat on the bunk and felt very very glad not only about knowing Leonard Sibelius, but about having done him a favor he was not likely to forget. Not a tall man, but notable, conspicuously skinny, with a great big head and a great big expressive and heavy-featured face, and a wild mop of rust-gold hair. A big flexible resonant voice that could range from mountaintop oratory to husky, personal, confidential whisper. Fantastic memory, vast vocabulary, capable of making speeches on any subject at any time. A con artist, a conniver, a charmer, a spellbinder, an eccentric. Italian clothes, fast cars and fast planes and fast boats. In spite of the emaciation, which made him look like a chronic invalid, he could work at top speed all day and play all night, week after week. Charging through life, leaving a trail of empty bottles and grateful blondes and thankful clients. Huge fees from those who could afford it, and when they couldn't afford it, there was always a market for the life story of any man defended by Lennie Sibelius, after the accused had signed over his rights to the fees and royalties therein. Total defense, in the courtroom, the newspapers, and on the television talk shows. Making it big and spending it big, and running all the way. And, somehow, laughing at himself. Ironic laughter. His black jest was that he had lost only one client. "It took that jury two days to bring back a guilty verdict. There were so many errors by the court, I knew it wouldn't stand up. The route was through the appellate court to the state supreme court to the federal district court to the Supreme Court. And I had just finished a beautiful brief to present to the district court when the silly son of a bitch hung himself in his cell, just two weeks before our book climbed onto the best seller list."

It felt fine to know he was on the way. This whole thing was making me very edgy. It is one of the penalties of playing one of the roles society wants you to play. No regular hours, no mortgage payments, life insurance, withholding, retirement benefits, savings program. "Okay, where were you, Charlie, at two o'clock on Tuesday afternoon, the tenth of April, seven years ago?"

"April? Tuesday? Unless I was sick, and that would be on the office records, I was right there at my desk in room fifteen-twenty on the fifteenth floor of the First Prudential Building. I work for Hutzler, Baskowich, and Troon. Mutual Funds. I'm an analyst. I've been with the firm eleven years now. Ask anybody."

So where was McGee on any April Tuesday you want to name? The best I could do would be a plausible guess.

Maybe I should keep a diary. Or have a time card and punch clock. Or is it a punch card and a time clock. Something that goes ding.

So you roam the fringes of the structured society, and it is just fine until they hold you up to the light. Then, somehow, in their eyes and yours, too, you begin to look like a cat burglar.

FIVE

AT FIVE-THIRTY JAILER PRISKITT came around and said I could take my chances on the American plan dinner, or sign a chit for a take-out meal from a restaurant down the street, said chit to be deducted from my captive funds when they were returned to me. He recommended the special deal. It turned out to be a piece of fried meat, boiled potatoes, overdone turnip greens, battery acid that smelled somewhat like coffee, and a soggy little wedge of apple pie. Four and a quarter, plus seventy-five cents for the trusty who had been sent to get it.

Lennie Sibelius did not appear at six-thirty, nor at seven, nor at seven-thirty, nor at eight. I began to wonder if he had tucked his Apache into a swamp.

At almost eight-thirty Priskitt came and got me and took me to a small locker room at the far end of the lower corridor. It smelled like stale laundry. Lennie was sitting on a battered metal table, custom shoes swinging. Lemon-yellow shirt and pale blue slacks.

"Your tailor isn't doing much for you, pal," he said.

"So let's leave and you find me a new one."

"We'll leave. Don't worry about it. But not right now."

I sat on a bench in front of the lockers. "When did you get in?" He said he'd been around for more than two hours, having some interesting conversations.

"Anything you want to repeat for the tape recorder?"

"My guess would be that this room is clean, Trav. I think he goes by the book. Lawyer and client relationship is confidential stuff. He might stick a shill into a cell with a suspect and bug the conversation to pick up a lead, but I think the rules mean something to him."

"He is something else entire, Lennie."

"He makes better sense when you know the whole pattern. Local boy. Hell of a high-school quarterback. Offers from all over the country. Picked one from Michigan. Did well, but not quick enough for the pros. Married a bright girl up there. Both of them became teachers. She taught speech. She worked on his accent, weeded it out. Both of them worked in the public school system in Rochester, New York. Hyzer's mother became ill, very ill, and Norman and his wife and baby daughter came down here. Hyzer's mother died. He was still here trying to get the house cleared out and put it up for sale when a couple of Miami kids in a stolen car knocked over one of those mini-markets on the edge of town in broad daylight, pistol-whipped the clerk, but suddenly had a cop cruiser riding up on them with the flasher going. They came through town at high speed and lost it on a turn and rode the sidewalk and smashed into a concrete power pole. It killed one of them and crippled the other. But they mashed Hyzer's bride and baby against the front of the post office thirty feet before they got to the pole. Killed them instantly. Hyzer buried them beside his mother and disappeared. Almost a year later he showed up here and announced for sheriff. No party affiliation. Independent. He won big. Sentimental favorite. Two years later he barely squeaked in, because he had done no glad-handing at all. Next time he won big because of his record. Lives for the job. Runs a taut ship. Keeps this county squeaky clean. No outside interests at all. If he is crazy, it is a productive compulsion. The rumor is that he has quietly built up files on every politician in the county, and they would rather not see anybody run against Hyzer. He takes correspondence courses. Law, criminology, ballistics, sociology, crime prevention, rehabilitation, penology."

"And I'm just another of those people who smash wives and babies against the post office wall?"

"Maybe. But buried deeply enough so you won't see any outward effect from it."

"Like Meyer did?"

"That part doesn't fit. It puzzles me. I am going to make it fit, and somebody is going to be sorrier than they can possibly imagine. But there's more we have to know before that is going to make any sense."

"How much did Hyzer tell you?"

"All the questions and all the answers up to the point where you stopped playing his game."

So I told him about the envelope with the directions I had scribbled on the back. I told him how I could remember clearly what I had done with it. Everything in our wallets had still been sodden by the time we reached Al Storey's gas station in the early morning. "I took everything out. Every time you have to go through your wallet you find junk you don't need. I made a pile of that junk on top of that tin table out in the morning sunlight. I know the envelope and instructions were there because I unfolded it to see what it was. And by then, if what Hyzer says is true, this Frank Baither was already dead. After the station opened up, I picked up Meyer's discards and mine and dropped them into a can by the side of the building, on top of some old newspapers, oil cans, and wiper blades."

"Meaning that somebody took it out and carried it twenty miles north and sneaked past the deputy guarding the Baither place, and planted it inside where it would be found. Meaning that Hyzer has to believe it happened just that way."

"It must have slipped out of my pocket while I was killing Frank Baither."

"Steady as she goes, pal. Now here is something that bothers Hyzer also, I think. You were bound for Lauderdale. You left Lake Passkokee. Did you plan any stops on the way?"

"No."

"Then why come down 112 to the Trail? That's doing it the hard way."

"We *did* it the hard way. I picked a little unmarked road that was supposed to take us right on over to the direct route. But with the roads torn up, everything looked different. After about three miles I knew I had the wrong road. So I kept going, hoping the damned thing would come out on the road we wanted. But it wandered all over hell and gone and finally came out onto 112 about fifteen miles north of the Cypress City cutoff. By then it was obviously shorter and quicker to come down 112 and take the Trail over to Route 27, then cut over to the Parkway on 820."

"And Hyzer keeps thinking about how you and Meyer match the description."

"What description, dammit?"

"Remember four years ago the way some people hit the money truck with all the racetrack cash aboard?"

"Just outside Miami? Vaguely. I've forgotten the gimmick."

"It was beautiful," Lennie said. "Absolutely beautiful. The three clowns who had truck duty stuck to the same routine every time they made the racetrack run. They would get there empty and park in back of a drive-in, and all three would go in, eat, kill some time until the big parking areas emptied and the people in the money room had time to weigh, band, sack, and tally the cash. Then they would go get it, and make a fifty-minute run back to the barn. It was after a very big handle that they were hit. They woke up on a little shell road way back in some undeveloped acreage. The locks had been drilled and the truck and radio disabled. They were too groggy to walk for help right away. They were separated and questioned. And examined. Same story. Each had become very very sleepy about fifteen minutes after they had loaded the money and left the track. Heavy dose of some form of barbiturate. Traces still left in the bloodstream. The driver had pulled over and stopped, thinking he would just take a nice little nap like the guard sitting there beside him, snoring. The police turned up a few people who had seen a bit brute of a wrecker put a hook on the armored truck, lift the front end, and trundle it off. They traced it back to the drive-in, a very small place with normally two people working during the daytime, a man in the kitchen and a girl working the counter. At night they'd have a second girl car-hopping. This was the pickup after the big Sunday afternoon race card, with the take including the Friday night and Saturday night meets. The men said the girl on the counter was new. A blonde. They had kidded around with her. By that time they had already had another report which dovetailed. A girl and three men had hit that drive-in a half hour before the money-truck people walked in. They had taped up the waitress and the chef and stashed them in a supply closet. The man had been too frightened and hysterical to pick up anything useful. The girl gave a full report of what she had noticed and remembered. One man was your size, Trav. One description fits Meyer. The third was average height, but very broad and thick in the shoulders and neck. She thought there might be a fourth man on watch outside the rear entrance, but she wasn't certain. She said the girl was young."

"You know a lot about it, Lennie."

"I had a client they were trying to set up for that truck job. And now, all of a sudden, better than three years later, I've got two more."

"This Frank Baither was in on it, then?"

"Sheriff Hyzer didn't exactly break down and tell me all his problems, pal. We established a relationship of mutual respect. There have been generations of Baithers in this county, some very solid and some very unpredictable, but all of them tough and quick, and a few of them tough, quick, and smart. Like Frank. Lived alone in the old family place along that route. He'd be gone for weeks or months. Tax bills and utility bills and so on went to the Cypress Bank and Trust. He kept money in a special account and the bills were paid out of it. No visible means of support. When he'd move back in, he'd usually have a houseguest. Some pretty dolly in tight pants, visiting for a while. Hyzer is concerned about Cypress County, not about what Frank Baither might be doing elsewhere. Then a funny thing happened. Smart Frank Baither, on a Saturday night, got stumbling drunk and held up a gas station right here in town. Went lurching off, spilling the cash out of the till. Got grabbed and put in a cell. Didn't make bail. Pleaded guilty, and got hit by the circuit court judge with five for armed robbery. Got transported off to Raiford. Did three and a half at Raiford before they let him out twelve days ago."

"So?"

"Item. The blood test on the stumbling drunk, taken under protest, showed that he could have had two small beers, maybe three. Item. Discreet investigation showed he had enough in his special account so that he could have made bail during the three months he had to wait here for trial, but he didn't. Item. For a man so involved with the outdoors, the swamps and the glades, Frank made a happy adjustment to this place and also to Raiford. Item. When Hyzer went out and checked Frank Baither's place after arrest, he found that Frank had done all those little chores a man living alone will do when he expects to be away for a long long time. Put up the shutters and drained the pipes, disconnected the pumps and greased them. Drained the aerator."

"Okay. He wanted to be tucked away."

"Hyzer reasoned that if somebody was out to kill Frank Baither, Baither would have ambushed them rather than hide in jail. Hyzer checked out the big scores made anywhere in the country just before Baither set himself up for a felony conviction. He kept coming back to the money truck in Miami. Baither was medium height with a bull neck and very broad thick shoulders. As a kid he had worked for his uncle who operated a little yard, making cement block, and he had carried enough tons of mix and tons of finished block to give him that muscular overdevelopment. Hyzer reasoned that Frank Baither had somehow tricked his partners, eased out with the track money, hid it well, then set himself up for free room and board for a long time, counting on the odds that the partners on the outside would not last long enough to be waiting when he got out. The hard-case operators have very few productive years, Trav. Then they are tucked away, underground or behind the walls. Frank had about two weeks between the money-truck job and landing in the Cypress County jail, assuming he was involved. Hyzer wanted more to go on. He arranged to get word from Raiford on Frank's activities in prison. By the end of the first year he learned that Frank had cultivated a few Latin Americans there. He was diligently studying Spanish. And it looked as if he would become reasonably fluent. The parts fitted together. Get out, pick up the money, and go. And live like a Greek shipowner for the rest of his life, with enough Spanish to learn who to bribe, and enough money to guarantee immunity."

"He told you a lot, Lennie."

"Some of it he told me, some of it he hinted at, and some of it is what I came up with to fill in the blanks. That sheriff went over every inch of the Baither place, and came up empty every time. Now here is another part. Somebody gave Frank a good rap on the head and taped him to a chair, and wound his head with tape, leaving a hole over one ear, and a hole over the mouth. Then they worked on him. They spoiled him. He had to know he was done, and so with nothing left to save except a little more agony, he talked. Then they shoved a rusty ice pick into his heart."

"Assumption?"

"A finality about it. End of interview. From the look of the rest of him, they would have kept going until he died of the special attentions."

"So Hyzer," I said wearily, "buys the idiot idea that we teamed with Frank Baither and took the money truck, and we kept track of him, knew when he got out of Raiford, and set up this complicated cover story, got to him, tortured him and killed him, left an incriminating envelope behind, lost my old car in the canal, and then. . . . For God's sake, Lennie! Can't you straighten him out? Where's the money?"

"Right where Frank Baither hid it. But now you and Meyer know where it is, and you can take your time picking it up."

He made me go over the incident we should have reported and didn't. Lots of questions. Estimates of elapsed time.

He paced in the constricted space, glowering. "The only way to defend a case is to build an alternate possibility up to the stature of reasonable doubt, McGee. There was a girl in the mud beside the canal. Let's say she was the young girl who played waitress. Let's say Frank Baither was prowling after her in the night. Hutch is the big one who fits your description. Orville fits Meyer's description. They came after Frank Baither last night. The girl got away. Baither got in his old truck and went cruising looking for Orville and Hutch. You went in the canal at ten o'clock. The shots were fired a little after eleven. He thought he hit Hutch in the head. He offered to make a deal with Orville. He drove back to his place, off guard because he thought he knew where Hutch and Orville were. He got back and they jumped him. Maybe they had a car hidden away nearby, and maybe the two of them and the girl are five hundred miles gone by now, laughing and singing, with the trunk packed with money. But that damned envelope, Trav. That is physical evidence. You are *absolutely* positive about what you did with it?"

"Beyond any doubt."

"Then the deputy he posted at the Baither place has to be lying when he told Hyzer nobody entered the place. Can you remember the deputy's name?"

"Arnstead, I think. But why would somebody . . ."

" 'Why' comes way down the list, client. It comes after 'how', 'when', 'where', and 'what'. 'How' is the big word."

He opened the door and whistled. Priskitt took me back

after Lennie Sibelius wished me a nice night's sleep, saying he didn't count on getting much himself.

As Priskitt caged me, I asked him about Meyer.

"Feeling much better. Fascinating man. It's guests like
you two who make this almost a civilized occupation,
McGee. Nighty night."

They had the cell lights on a rheostat. At ten o'clock
they faded from white glare to yellow glow.

You can't help wondering what it would feel like to be
in such a box for the next dozen years, and wonder if you
could handle it, and walk out of it still reasonably sane.

I remembered reading a sentence long ago, I know not
where or when, or who wrote it. It said, "The only thing
that prisons demonstrably cure is heterosexuality."

Back to the envelope. It had to be an unplanned act on
someone's part. An improvisation. A way to muddy the
water. Somebody made the decision after Sheriff Hyzer
and Deputy Cable had driven off with us. A customer or
an employee. Or the boss. Al Storey, or the big young
dull-looking one named Terry. Or the older one who had
arrived late in the blue Rambler. Henry . . . The one with
all the white teeth. Or somebody who came on duty later.
Al, Terry, and Henry had all heard Hyzer say that Frank
Baither had been killed. His attitude made it evident he
thought Meyer and I were involved.

I dug away at my chigger bites. Get me out, Lennie.
Get us out of here.

SIX

UP UNTIL ELEVEN O'CLOCK IT WAS A very dull morning. Then Priskitt arrived, humming happily, carrying a hanger with freshly cleaned and pressed slacks and shirt thereon. He had my toilet kit in the other hand.

He unlocked the cell door and said, "Priskitt at your service, sir. You will wish to shower? You are free to go right ahead, by yourself."

"Those clothes were . . ."

"In your suitcase which was in your car, and so was the toilet kit. Still damp, but not at all bad. Compliments of Cypress County, Mr. McGee. I'll be along with shoes and socks and underwear."

"Where is my friend?"

"Under the shower, one might expect."

But Meyer was out of the shower, standing at the sink, and carefully, tenderly, shaving the black stubble from his swollen and discolored face. He turned and said, "Don't make me laugh, please."

"How bad is it?"

"It will add up to a good dental bill. The thing that worries me is a persistent headache, dizziness, some double vision. And something seems to grate in my cheek.

Lennie is going to fly me back to Lauderdale and I'll go in for observation."

"Who did it?"

"A large fellow with big cheekbones and small dark eyes and very long sideburns. I wondered why he was putting a leather glove on. You'd mentioned a few useful things one could do under those circumstances. I tried them and they didn't work very well."

"Who was there at the time?"

"Deputy Cable. Objecting."

"Making any physical attempt to stop him?"

"Finally, yes. But at first I would say he was merely whining at the fellow, something about Mister Norm getting upset. He called the sideburned fellow Lew. I discovered the whole name later on. Deputy Lew Arnstead."

"Where was Sturnevan? The big sloppy one."

"He had stepped out. Lew didn't take long. It seemed long. Maybe fifteen or twenty seconds. By then I wasn't aware of whether Sturnevan came back or not, but I think he was one of the two men who helped me to the cell."

"Meyer?"

"Mmmm?"

"I'm sorry about this."

He turned and looked solemnly at me, puffy eyes staring out of the big yellow-blue-green-purple face. "Where is any man's immunity from the unexpected, McGee? I could deny myself the pleasure of your friendship, and decrease the chance of the unexpected. But there is a case on record of a woman in her own bed being struck on the thigh by a bounding chunk of red hot iron, a meteorite that came whistling in from God only knows what corner of the galaxy. I value that night hike, Travis. And the way the dawn looked, and the feeling of being alive after being shot at. I am a grown-up, making choices. And sufficiently grown up to live with the choices I make. My face hurts and my head aches, and I would like to kill that sideburned fellow with anything I could lift. I feel outraged, humiliated, and very very tired. But I'm glad I came along."

"You do go on."

"Do us both a favor and get out of that garment."

He was ready and I was almost ready when Sturnevan came to get us. He clucked and turned Meyer toward the light and gave him a close inspection. "And you weren't very pretty to start with, Professor."

"King," I said, "I might get a chance to strike up an acquaintance with Lew Arnstead when he's off duty."

"Which is now sort of one hundred percent of the time, I hear. You serious, McGee?"

"Serious enough to ask you how to do it."

"He's a strong boy. He likes all the odds his way. With somebody your size, he'd try to fix the odds fast, like a quick kick in the balls. What you do is, you make it look as if he can get away with it. He's right-handed. He'll kick with his right leg. Watch for the weight shift, sidestep the kick and get his ankle, and swing it on up. Then if you can hurt him fast enough and bad enough, he'll be all through."

"Thanks, King."

"Mister Norm is waiting on you fellows."

No guard just inside the door this time. Just Lennie Sibelius and Sheriff Hyzer, and some exhibits on the bare desk top.

Lennie slouched, smiling, in a wooden armchair. Hyzer sat at attention behind his desk. He asked us to sit. He said to Meyer, "I assure you that what happened to you is against the policy of this department."

"My client accepts that," Lennie said quickly.

"Arnstead was not officially on duty at the time of the ... incident," Hyzer said. "He had no business being here. His act was without official sanction or official knowledge. He has been dismissed with prejudice, booked for aggravated assault, and released on bond pending trial. Deputy Cable has been fined and reprimanded for permitting it to happen. Please accept my personal apology."

"I accept it," Meyer said.

"Mr. Sibelius has suggested that any dental or medical bills be sent here to my attention. They will be taken care of, if not by the county, then by me personally."

"Do I get one of those, too?" I asked.

Hyzer swiveled slowly and stared at me with those frozen eyes. "One what?"

"An apology?"

"He's making a joke, Sheriff," Lennie said.

"He is? I have very little sense of humor, Mr. McGee. Your rights . . . and your person . . . have been protected. I am releasing you from further questioning because Mr. Sibelius prevailed on me to more carefully investigate your . . . version . . . of what happened Thursday night." There were little hesitations, pauses in which he carefully composed his phrases, making the end product so stilted, so stuffy that it became, in one sense, an armor against the world.

He indicated a .38 automatic pistol, an old one, rust flecked, with the bluing worn away in places. "This handgun was found on the Baither property under a clump of palmetto about fifteen feet from where the pick-up truck was parked, and almost in line with the back porch. There were two rounds in the clip. There is a partial print on the side of the clip which matches Baither's left thumb print, and is in the place where a man would logically hold it while loading the weapon. We can assume it was Baither's weapon and was lost in the darkness when Baither was overpowered while walking from his truck to his house. There is no way to tell how many shots were fired, as we do not know how many were loaded into the clip. Examination proved it had been fired recently. A wax test on the right hand of the decedent indicates he had fired a gun not long before death."

He moved along to the next item, three empty brass cartridge cases neatly aligned. "One of these was found on the floor of the truck. The second one was found this morning on the shoulder of the highway three and two tenth miles south of the point where your car went into the canal. That area was searched carefully after certain marks and footprints were found in the soft earth beside the canal. This plaster cast of the best footprint matches the left shoe you were wearing, Mr. McGee, when you were taken into custody. This third case is a test round fired from this handgun. Though we have not arranged a ballistics examination with a comparative microscope, examination through a hand magnifying glass indicates the probability that the indentation made by the firing pin is distinctive enough to allow eventual proof that all three rounds were fired from the same pistol."

"This is very reassuring to my clients," Lennie said.

"Taken alone," Hyzer said, "these indications would not be enough to cause me to release these people. There could be too many alternative explanations. And the fact of the envelope seemed conclusive evidence that one of you or both of you were inside the Baither house. However, Mr. Sibelius suggested a method of ... making Arnstead change his report to me about his assignment to guard the Baither house."

"All Arnstead had to do," Lennie explained, "was leave one little hole in his story, one period of time when that envelope could have been planted. I could drive trucks through any hole like that. Norman, my friend Meyer is looking rocky, and with your permission I'd like to fly him over to Lauderdale. Trav, I'm assuming you'd like to get that old crock truck of yours dried out and running."

Hyzer said, "I would prefer to have Mr. McGee remain in Cypress County until I have completed my—"

"But, Norman, you have my personal guarantee, my personal word that I can produce them right here any time you say."

"I think it would be better if—"

Lennie smiled his best smile. "Hell, Norm, it's all give and take, after all. Famed economist brutally beaten and held, without charges, in Cypress County jail cell."

"I refuse to be—"

"Come *on*, Norm! I like the way you're thinking. I think you are the first lawman who's got a decent lead on that racetrack money. I don't blame you for keeping a tight lid on it because if word got out, somehow, people would be swarming all over you. I wouldn't want that to happen because I wouldn't want you to look foolish. I wouldn't want one of those hard-case types the *Miami Herald* would send over here asking you, for the record, if you were so sure Baither was in on the money-truck job, why you didn't have him under twenty-four-hour surveillance. They wouldn't understand your reasoning, and they might use some rude head such as: HICK SHERIFF BLOWS BIG CASE." He shrugged and, turning, managed to wink at me—a combination wink and frown.

I caught on and grabbed my cue. "Lennie, look. It isn't that important I get home. I'm perfectly willing to hang around if Sheriff Hyzer wants me to. But I haven't even got enough cash to take care of the car. If you could . . ."

"Any time at all, pal," Lennie said, and produced the platinum money clip with the emeralds, the one given him in gratitude by the Other Woman after he had secured an acquittal for the heir to a pulp mill and timberlands fortune who had shot and killed what he thought was a prowler, but who had turned out to be his insomniac wife.

Counting off money for me would not have been consistent with Lennie Sibelius's life style. He slipped the cash out of the clip, took off a couple of fifties for himself, put them back in the clip, and handed me the rest of it.

"I appreciate your cooperation, Mr. McGee," Hyzer said. "Let me know where you will be staying."

Meyer and I collected the rest of our gear. Laundry and dry cleaning courtesy of Cypress County. A form of apology. We put the small amount of luggage into the white Buick convertible Lennie had rented. I could see them off and bring it back into town from the airstrip, and either turn it in or keep it. I sat in the back. It was impossible to talk with the top down and with Lennie pretending he was being challenged for the lead in the Daytona 500. The strip was about five miles east of the city limits. He drove past the hangar and on out onto the hard pan and stopped next to his Apache, all chocked and tied down to eyebolts.

"You can get a very nice room at the White Ibis Motor Inn," Lennie said. "You go back through town—"

"I saw it when they were taking us in."

"But don't eat there. Eat right in town at Mrs. Teffer's Live Oak Lodge and Dining Room. Exceptional!"

"Now hold it a minute, Lennie. I picked up your cue.

But it would be very comforting to know what the hell is going on."

Meyer said, "Nine hundred thousand dollars is going on." His voice was slightly blurred by the mouth damage.

"So don't be in too big a hurry to leave," Lennie said.

"This is one of my stupid days," I told them. "Draw me some pictures."

"I like Norm's thinking. It all seems to fit together. And I think that sooner or later he's going to pick somebody up for it."

"Wouldn't they be long gone?"

Lennie smiled. "By Gad, it *is* one of your stupid days. If they were long gone, there would be very little point in going to the trouble of planting that envelope. One or more of the people involved have to be right here in the area, tied to it in such a way that the act of leaving would blow the whistle. When Norm grabs somebody, they are going to need the best legal talent they can find. And they should be able to afford me."

"I can have a sandwich sign made and walk back and forth in front of the jail?"

"The Association would frown on that. Hell, they even frown on my little decorations on the airplane and the cruiser."

He pointed and I stepped up and took a closer look. They were small decals, hardly bigger than a postage stamp. A stylized gallows in black on a white background with a black border, and with an X in red canceling out the gallows. The custom decals were on the cowling under the pilot's window. Almost three rows. Twenty-eight of them.

"All this trouble to plant a shill in the area?"

"Trav, pal, I had the idea you might stir around a little. A catalytic agent, bringing the brew to a nice simmer. Then Norm might be able to nail somebody sooner than otherwise."

"He is going to frown on meddling. I will be right back inside his hotel if I try that."

"If you're clumsy, sure. But I have a lot of confidence in your discretion, and if you do slip, I'll be right back to pry you out again. Sibelius never sleeps. Think of it this way. You've agreed to help me out on the pretrial investigation."

"I don't have a license. I don't want a license. I'm tired of Cypress County already."

"Why should you have a license? For what? You've gone on my staff payroll as a researcher."

I took the folded money out of my pants pocket and counted it. "Nine hundred and forty?"

"Let me know when you need more, pal." He clapped me on the shoulder. "Think of it this way. Without Sibelius, you'd still be inside. And so would Meyer. You called and I came over. Am I charging you? Would I charge a friend for a little bit of a favor? What do you think I am? Greedy or something? All you have to do is stir around, talk about Frank Baither, buy a drink here and there, and tell people the truth about me. Don't overdo it. Just tell them I'm the greatest criminal lawyer around. Is that so hard?"

"You are something else, Sibelius. By the way, how did you get Arnstead to change his story?"

Lennie shrugged. "He had to be lying. If he wasn't, you were. Last night I came across the interesting information that Lew Arnstead is the number one stud in Cypress County. It's more obsession than hobby. I straightened out the timetable. You were at the gas station when Storey opened up at twenty to seven. At about seven-thirty you and Meyer left with Hyzer and Cable. Because you stopped while your car was being pulled out, you didn't get to the jail until about eight-fifteen. Arnstead was turning out to have a very long shift. At eight-thirty he went into the Baither place and used the phone to call in and ask if he was going to be relieved. Hyzer told the communications clerk to tell Lew Arnstead to stay right there and that he would be at the Baither place about eleven o'clock, and after it was checked over, he could go off duty. Ask the logical questions, McGee."

"Let me see now. He was expecting Hyzer earlier. Then Hyzer changed his schedule by coming to take a look at us, and take us in. So he had something lined up, and he wanted to be relieved so he could take care of it. But he found out he had another two hours to wait, plus the time it would take for the daylight search. And he had the use of the phone. Sorry, honey, I can't make it, so why don't you come on over here?"

"Inside Baither's house?"

"I ... I wouldn't think so. Not with Hyzer due to prowl the place."

"How about a narrow old mattress on the slab floor of the pump house about thirty feet from the back porch?"

"Handy."

"So Hyzer took my suggestion and had Lew Arnstead brought in, and asked him to explain why he was in the pump house with a woman at nine o'clock Friday morning instead of keeping an eye on the house as ordered. Arnstead tried a lot of footwork but Hyzer pushed until he broke through. Arnstead got very virtuous about refusing to name the woman. He said he was with her about ten minutes, and he could see the entrance road from the pump house. She arrived and left by car. She was an old friend. So while you are churning around, see if you can come up with an I.D. on the lady, pal. She could have been sent in as a distraction while somebody planted the envelope. A cub scout could unlock that house with a kitchen match."

"While I'm churning around. Anything for a friend."

A redheaded boy in greasy khakis came out and brought the gas ticket for Lennie to sign, then untied the aircraft and pulled the chocks away. I handed Meyer's and Lennie's duffle up. Lennie cranked it up and trundled off to the end of the marl strip. He warmed it up there, and the boy and I stood and watched him make his run and pluck it off and climb over the cabbage palms and live oaks, heading east over the swamps and pasturelands. Good luck, Meyer. No bleeding inside the head, please. It is too valuable and kindly a head.

So I got into my white Buick with the black plastic leather upholstery and the stereo FM radio, and the power brakes, power windows, power steering, air, and super-something transmission, and took half again as long getting back to town as Lennie had taken coming out.

Smile, McGee. Show your teeth. Honk at the lassies, because here it is nearly one o'clock Saturday afternoon and you don't know where they keep the action. Not the kind you've had so far. The other kind.

SEVEN

THE WHITE IBIS MOTOR INN HAD A LITtle symbol on the signs and the registration card indicating it was one of the creatures of a subsection of one of the more ubiquitous conglomerates. So they could afford to operate it at a percentage of occupancy that would hustle an independent owner into bankruptcy.

Some precise fellow in some distant city had used the standard software program for site location, and fed into the program the regional data for population movement and growth, planned and probable highway construction, land cost, *ad-valorem* tax rates, pay scales, and the IBM 360 had said to build one on Alternate 112 west of Cypress City and operate it at a loss until the increased demand for the transient beds would put it into the black.

Teletype network for instant reservations, approved cards for instant credit, a woman at the desk with instant, trained, formal politeness, who assigned me to Unit 114 and made a little x on a map of the layout, and drew a little line to show me where to drive so that I would end up in front of the x, in the proper diagonal parking slot. She looked slightly distressed when I said I had no idea how long I would be staying. People should know, so they can keep the records neat.

I closed myself into the silence of Unit 114, unpacked, and took a better shower. Stretched out on the bed. Things to do, but no will to do them. A listlessness. A desire to disassociate, to be uninvolved. The fashion is to call it an identity crisis. I was not doing things very well lately. A juvenile, big-mouth performance for the sheriff, windy threats signifying nothing.

Somebody had made a very cute try to get the two of us involved in a private and violent nastiness, but Lennie's gifts of persuasion and the thoroughness of Norman Hyzer had collapsed the improvised structure.

All cages are frightening. And sometimes a little time spent in a small cage merely gives you the feeling that you have been let out into a bigger cage, the one you have built for yourself over the years. The delusion of total freedom of will is the worst cage of all. And it gets cold in there. As cold, perhaps, as inside Miss Agnes under ten feet of canal water, if Meyer hadn't clumsied me out of there. Or cold as the grave would be had Frank Baither hit me in the face with that first shot.

With enormous effort I forced myself to reach the phone book, look up the Sheriff's Department, and phone in my temporary address to the dispatcher. I got dressed and got into the white car and went looking for Johnny's Main Street Service. I found it down by the produce sheds and the truck depots.

There was diesel fuel, and a half dozen big stalls for truck repair work. There was a paint shop and a body shop, and a side lot piled with cars which had quite evidently slain their masters in a crunch of blood, tin, and glass. I saw the big blue-and-white tow truck. There was no shop work going on, the whole area somnolent in the perfect April afternoon. An old man sat in the small office, reading a true-crime magazine. A scrawny girl in jeans and a halter was slowly spreading paste wax on a metallic green MG.

Among a line of cars against a side fence Miss Agnes stood out like a dowager among teenagers. I got out of the Buick and walked over to her. A large young man about nineteen came angling across the hardpan from the shop area. Low-slung jeans and a torn and grease-blackened T-shirt. Thick black glossy hair that fell to his big shoulders.

"You Mr. McGee?" When I nodded, he said, "I'm Ron Hatch. My father is Johnny Hatch. He owns this place. He didn't want me to fool with that Rolls on account of on an impounded car, we're stuck with it. But I couldn't stand having it just sit. So he said it had to be on my own time. I just finished with it maybe an hour ago. I pulled the tank and the head, got it all kerosened out, blew the fuel lines, got the ignition system all dry, coil and all. The battery took a charge. That tire is done, and I guess you'll have to check around Miami to find a Dunlop that'll go on that rim."

"I'm grateful you didn't let it sit, Ron."

"Hell, it's a great old brute. All that hand-lapping and custom machining and fitting. The bushings are like perfect, Mr. McGee. But there's this problem." He had the big leathery banana-fingered hand of the born artisan. He pulled a complex fitting out of the pocket of the jeans. "See where this is broke off fresh? It maybe happened when you hit the bank, going down. It's the fitting out at the end of the steering arm, front left. I put a clamp on there for temporary, just enough to baby it out here to park, but you couldn't drive it. There's no machine shop I know of can make one on account of right in here, and here, they're not standard threads, so they wouldn't have the taps the right size, and it isn't something you can cast because it takes a lot of strain."

"I've got a mechanic friend in Palm Beach at a place where they stock Rolls parts from the year one."

"Maybe he'll have to have this to match it up right. Meanwhile ... maybe I could do some body and fender work."

"What do I owe you so far?"

He looked uncomfortable. "The way it works, garages have to bid for the county contract. So it's seventy-five dollars for towing, and ten dollars a day for it while it was impounded. With the tax that's a hundred and nine twenty. Once we got word this morning from the sheriff's office we could release the car to you, then the ten a day stopped."

"And if they'd kept me in there for ninety days?"

"Then . . . if people don't want to pay the storage, like if the car isn't worth it anyway, Dad wholesales them for what he can get. The word around was that you and your friend had surely killed Frank Baither and you got caught, and that's why my father said it didn't make any sense working on your car. But . . . I just couldn't stand seeing it sit the way it was, machinery like that. I mean I did it on my own and if you figure you don't want to pay anything over the towing and storage, that's okay."

I separated two bills from the packet Lennie had handed me. A fifty and a hundred. "Get me a receipted bill on the towing and storage, please. And put the rest against your hours and we'll settle up when you're done."

"Body work?"

"You wouldn't use a filler, would you?"

"You better be kidding." And I knew how he'd do it, banging the dings out with the rubber mallet, sanding, burnishing, smoothing, using a little lead sparingly where it couldn't be helped, sanding down a couple of coats of primer, then using a top-quality body paint, sanding between coats.

"Do you expect to be able to match that paint, Ron?"

"It's a terrible paint job anyway. I'd rather do the whole thing. What I'd like to do it is yellow in a lot of coats of a good gold flake lacquer with a lot of rubbing between coats."

"Sorry, but it has to stay blue. Sentimental reasons."

He shrugged. "That same shade?"

"Not exact."

He smiled for the first time. He looked relieved. "I can get it looking fine. Wait and see. I hope you get that fitting soon. I can't really fine tune it unless I can open it up some on the road. On the lift isn't the same."

The old man in the office came out and bawled, "Ronnie! Come get the phone!"

The boy took off, big lope, long strides. And the immediate image was superimposed on memory. The determined look of the girl, running in the night, the dark hair flying, bare knees lifting. An elusive similarity, like a family resemblance. No more than that, because the girl had been all girl, and this runner was totally male. I find I have one small hang-up regarding young males with masculine features and shoulderlength locks. When they have a mustache or beard or both to go with the hair, they make a fine romantic image, an echo of a distant gallantry, of the old names like Sumter, The Wilderness, Sherman's March, Custer. But when, like the Beatles and Ron Hatch, there is no beard or mustache, then I have to get past the mental roadblock of recalling too many Army nurses I have known.

I wondered if Mister Norm had gotten a line on the running girl. It would be too much of a miracle of coincidence for her not to be involved in some way. Involved, possibly, from the beginning. The very young girl playing waitress, in a blond wig, the weekend afternoon when they had mickeyed the money-truck men.

Or maybe she was a decoy, a diversion, setting Frank Baither up so that Orville and Hutch could get at him. Or Baither's woman, local or import, sweet young flesh after over forty months of doing without. The fairly safe guess was that she was woods-wise, and she thought, rightly or wrongly, that somebody was tracking her down in the night, and she used the rush and rumble of my car to cover the sound as she went crashing through the weeds and brush on the far side of the road. Misjudged the distance. Cut it too close. But why the hell not *behind* the car?

I was looking inside the car when Ron came back. It had been cleaned out thoroughly, mud, weeds, water, and everything else.

"Oh, I forgot. All your stuff, the fishing gear and tools

and so on, they're locked in a storage room here. I wrote a list of everything. Things disappear. Maybe some stuff is gone already, before I wrote it down. You want to check?"

"Later, I guess."

"Nobody thought you'd get out. That way it isn't so much like stealing."

"People around here think that when Sheriff Hyzer grabs somebody, he's always right? Is that it?"

His gaze was direct for a moment, and then drifted away. "They say he's a good sheriff. They say he's fair."

"Thanks again for going ahead with my car. I'll be around on Monday."

So I drove around and about, getting the feel of the town and the area, had a late lunch in a red plastic national franchise selling the Best Sandwiches Anytime Anywhere, and had a medium bad sandwich and very bad coffee, served in haste by a drab, muttering woman.

On the way in, I had picked up the local morning paper. Eight pages. *The Cypress Call & Journal.* The masthead said it was owned by Jasson Communications. They own a few dozen small-city papers in Florida and South Georgia. Guaranteed circulation of five thousand seven hundred and forty, by the last ABC figures. It had the minimum wire service on national and international, and very exhaustive coverage of service club and social club doings. Typical of the Jasson operation. Cut-rate syndicated columnists, ranging from medium right to far right. Lots of city and county legal notices. Detailed coverage of farm produce prices.

I found myself on the bottom right corner of page two.

HELD FOR QUESTIONING

Two Fort Lauderdale men were taken into custody Friday morning by the County Sheriff's Department for questioning in connection with the torture murder

of Frank Baither at his residence
on State Road 72 Thursday night
after it was learned that the vehicle in which they were riding
had gone into the drainage canal
sometime Thursday night not far
from the Baither house.

And that was it. Local yellow journalism. Sensational-
ism. Who, what, why, when, where, and how. Exquisite
detail.

So after my late and sorry lunch I went around to the
Call & Journal. It was printed on the ground floor of a
cement-block building on Princeton Street. The editorial
and business offices occupied the other two floors.

According to the masthead, the managing editor was
one Foster Goss. Enclosed in glass in the far corner of the
lazy newsroom. A couple of hefty women pecking vintage
typewriters. A crickety octogenarian on the copy desk. A
couple of slack young men murmuring into phones, heels
on the cheap tin desks. Offstage frantic clackety-whack of
the broad tape.

Foster Goss was a fat, fading redhead, with thick lenses, saffroned fingers, blue shirt with wet armpits. He
waved at a chair and said, "Minute," and hunched over
the yellow copy paper once again, making his marks with
soft black lead. He finished, reached, rapped sharply on
the glass with a big gold seal ring. A mini-girl got up and
came in and took the yellow sheets, gave me a hooded,
speculative glance, and strolled out. Foster Goss watched
her rear until the half-glass door swung shut, then creaked
back in his chair, picked one cigarette out of the shirt-
pocket pack, and lit it.

"Meyer or McGee?" he said.

"McGee. I want to complain about all the invasion of
privacy, all the intimate details about my life and times."

Half smile. "Sure you do."

"So I came around to give you an exclusive, all about
local police brutality and so forth."

"Gee whiz. Golly and wow."

"Mr. Goss, you give me the impression that some-where, sometime, you really *did* work on a newspaper."

His smile was gentle and reflective. "On some dandies, fella. I even had a Nieman long ago. But you know how it is. Drift out of the stormy seas into safe haven."

"Just for the hell of it, Mr. Goss, what would happen if you printed more than Mister Norm would like to have you print?"

"My goodness gracious, man, don't you realize that it has been the irresponsible press which has created com-munity prejudice against defendants in criminal actions? As there is absolutely no chance of anyone running suc-cessfully against Sheriff Hyzer, he doesn't have to release any information about how good he is. And very damned good he is indeed. So good that County Judge Stan Bow-ley has a sort of standing order about pretrial publicity. So the sheriff would read the paper and come over and pick me up and take me to Stan and he would give me a sad smile and say, 'Jesus Christ, Foster, you know better than that,' and he would fine me five hundred bucks for con-tempt."

"Which wouldn't stand up."

"I *know* that! So I go to the Jasson brothers and I say, look, I've got this crusade I've got to go on, and I know the paper is turning a nice dollar, and I know you nice gentlemen are stashing away Jasson Communications stock in my retirement account every year, but I've got to strike a blow for a free press. Then they want to know who I am striking the blow against, and I tell them it is the sheriff, and they ask me if he is corrupt and inefficient, and I say he might be the best sheriff in the state, who took a very very rough county and tamed it without using any extralegal methods."

"Then what if a hot team comes in here from Miami to do a big feature on this cozy little dictatorship, Mr. Goss?"

He smiled again. "No contempt charges. Maximum co-operation. Guided tours. Official charm. No story."

"But Meyer got badly beaten."

"By a deputy who was immediately fired and booked for assault."

"You keep track, even though you don't print much."

"Old habits. Ancient reflexes. Interested me to find that Lennie Sibelius came on the run when you whistled. That's why we're getting along so well. I wanted to find out what kind of cat you might be, Mr. McGee. Hence the open door, frank revelation policy."

"Learn anything?"

"Hired gladiators like Sibelius, Belli, Foreman, Bailey, and so on seldom waste their talents on low-pay representation unless there is some publicity angle that might be useful. None here. I'd guess it was a favor. Maybe you work for him. Investigator, building defense files, or checking out a jury panel. You handle yourself as if you could give good service along those lines."

"Have you ever thought of going back into journalism?"

"I think about it. And I think about my mortgage, and my seventeen-year-old daughter married to a supermarket bag boy, and I think about my twelve-year-old spastic son. I catch pretty fair bass twelve miles from my house."

"Do you think about Frank Baither?"

"I try not to. Mister Norm will let me know what I need to know."

Then we smiled at each other and I said my polite good-by. He was like King Sturnevan, long-retired from combat, but he still had the moves. No wind left, but he could give you a very bad time for the first two rounds.

I went out into the late April afternoon, into a spring scent of siesta. Head the Buick back toward the White Ibis, where I could make a phone call and find out how Meyer was making it.

EIGHT

I PARKED EXACTLY WHERE THE MO-
tel architect had decided the vehicle for Unit 114
should be. Inside the room the red phone light was blinking. I wrote down the numbers the desk-lady gave me.
The Lauderdale call was from a very very British female
on Lennie's staff, relaying the diagnosis on Meyer: a mild
concussion, hairline fracture of the cheekbone, and they
were keeping him overnight for routine observation.

The other one was a local number. I let it have ten
rings, just like it says to do in the phone book. Hung up.
Then I called the sheriff. He was there.

"Yes, Mr. McGee?"

"I don't want to do anything I'm not supposed to do. I
was thinking of driving down to Al Storey's station on the
Trail. Then I remembered it's outside the county."

"What would be the purpose?"

"I would sort of like to know how somebody set me
up."

"That's under investigation. We don't need help."

"Are you getting anywhere with it?"

"I'd rather not comment at this time."

"It's your best approach, isn't it?"

"I'd appreciate it if you'd stay inside my jurisdiction, Mr. McGee."

"So be it, Sheriff."

I glowered at the unspottable, unbreakable rug for a time, then looked up Arnstead in the phone book. No Lew, Lou, Louis, or Lewis. There were three of them. J. A., and Henry T. and Cora.

I tried J. A. "Lew around?"

"Not around *this* house, ever, mister." Bang.

So I tried Henry T. "Lew around?"

"Not very goddam likely, buddy." Bang.

Started to try Cora, then decided I might as well drive out to the address and see for myself. The book said 3880 Cattleman's Road. I found Cattleman's Road a half mile west of the White Ibis, heading north off of Alternate 112. Flat lands, and frame bungalows which were further and further apart as I drove north.

A big rural mailbox on the right-hand side with red stick-on letters spelling Arnstead. Sand driveway leading back to a pink cement-block house, a small place with a lot of unkempt Mexican flame vine climbing its walls. Cattle guard at the entrance to the drive. Outbuildings beyond the house, and some fenced pasture with a big pond. A dozen head of runty Angus grazed the green border of the pond. A small flock of Chinese Whites cruised the blue pond, and after I rumbled over the cattle guard and parked near the house and turned the engine off, I heard their goose-alarm, like a chorus of baritone kazoos. In an acre of marsh across the road, tree toads were beginning to tune up for evening. An inventive mockingbird swayed in the top of a punk tree, working some cardinal song into his repertoire.

A leathery little old woman was yanked out of the front door by a crossbreed dog the size of a bull calf, mottled black and brown, hair all ruffed up around his neck and standing erect down his spine. He made a rumbling in his throat, and showed me some very large white fangs. "Buttercup!" she yelled. "Hold! Hold!"

Buttercup stopped, all aquiver with anxiety to taste me. The old woman wore ancient blue jeans, a dark red pullover sweater, and blue canvas shoes. She clung with both hands to the hefty chain fastened to the studded dog collar. She was thin as one of the stick figures children draw.

"Hoped it was Lew," she said. "Or maybe Jase or Henry coming around finally to see I'm all right. But he's still growling. Who are you? They can't do my eyes till the cataracts get ripe, and I can tell you I'm sick and tired of waiting. Who are you?"

"My name is Travis McGee. I was looking for Lew."

"What for?"

"Just a little talk."

"You stand right still. I got to tell this here dog everything is all right. Buttercup! Okay! Okay! Hush your noise! Down!"

He sat. The rumbling stopped. Tongue lolled. But the amber eyes looked at me with an obvious skepticism.

"Now you come slow right toward him, Mr. McGee, right up to where he can snuff at you. Don't come sudden."

So I made the slow advance. He growled again and she scolded him. He sniffed at a pant leg. She told me to hold my hand out and he sniffed that. Then he stood again and the tail wagged. She said I could scratch behind his ears. He enjoyed it.

"Now he won't bother you. If you come in here and he was loose, he'd come at you running low and fast and quiet, but stand your ground and he'll get a snuff of you and he won't bother you none. I'd get edgy out here alone so much if I didn't have Buttercup."

"He must be a comfort to you. Do you know when Lew . . ."

"Before we get into that, would you kindly do me a favor. I been wondering if I should phone somebody to come help me. That black horse of Lew's has been bawling off and on since early morning, and I can't see enough to take care of whatever's bothering him. It's the near building, and he's in a stall that opens on the far side. Know anything about horses?"

"They're tall, have big teeth, give me a sweat rash, and they all hate me on sight."

"Well, what I think it is, Lew having so much on his mind, he could have forgot feed and water."

I walked out behind the house and found the stall, the top halves of the doors open and hooked back. There was a black horse in there, standing with his head hanging. His coat looked dull. The stall had not been cleaned out for too long. Flies buzzed in the heavy stench. Feed bin and water trough were empty. He snatched his head up and rolled wild eyes and tried to rear up, but his hooves slipped in the slime and he nearly went down. From the dried manure on his flanks, he had already been down a couple of times.

I went back to the house and told Mrs. Arnstead the situation and asked her if there was any reason he couldn't be let out.

"Lew was keeping him in the stall on account of he had a sore on his shoulder he had to put salve on, and it was too much trouble catching him. I guess you best let him out and hope he don't founder himself sucking the pond dry."

When I unlatched the bottom halves and swung the doors open and stepped well back to one side, he came out a lot more slowly than I expected. He walked frail, as if he didn't trust his legs, but slowly quickened his pace all the way across to the pond. He drank for a long time, stopped and drank again, then trudged away from the pond, visibly bigger in the belly, and went slowly down onto his knees and rolled over. I thought he had decided to die. But then he began rolling in the grass, squirming the filth off his black hide.

I looked around, saw rotten sprouting grain in an outdoor bin, saw trash and neglect.

Mrs. Arnstead sat in a cane chair on the shallow screened porch. She invited me in. I sat and Buttercup came over and shoved his big head against my knee, awaiting the scratching.

There was a golden light of dusk, a smell of flowers.

"I just don't know anymore," she said. "Shouldn't heap

my burdens on a stranger. Lew is my youngest, the last one left to home. Did just fine in the Army and all. Came back and got took on as a deputy sheriff. Worked this place here and kept it up good, and he was going with the Willoughbee girl. Now being a mother doesn't mean I can't see things the way they are. Jason was my first and Henry was my second, and then it was sixteen long years before I had Lew. Lord God, Jason is forty-three now, married twenty-four years, and their first was a girl, and she married off at sixteen, so I've got a great-grandson near six years old. I know that Lew was always on the mean side. But he always worked hard and worked good, and cared for the stock. It's the last six months he turned into somebody else, somebody I don't hardly know. Broke off with Clara Willoughbee, took up again with a lot of cheap, bright-smelling, loud-voice women. Got meaner. Got so ugly with his brothers, they don't want to ever see him again. Neglects this place and me to go run with trash like them Perrises. Now he's done something, I don't know what, to get himelf fired off his job, and he might even have to go to jail. I just don't know what's going to happen. This place is free and clear and it's in my name, but the little bit of money that comes in won't cover food, electric, taxes, and all that. Jase and Henry, they'd help out, but not with me staying out here this way. They got this idea I live six months with one and six with the other, like some kind of tourist woman all the rest of my days. What was it my boy did to get Mister Norm so upset he fired him? Do you know?"

"Yes. It isn't very pretty."

"It's like I've run out of pretty lately."

"A very pleasant and gentle and friendly man was picked up for questioning. He knew nothing about the matter under investigation. Your son gave him a very savage beating for no apparent reason. The man is in the hospital in Fort Lauderdale."

She shook her head slowly. In that light, at that angle, I suddenly saw what she had looked like as a young girl. She had been very lovely.

"That's not Lew," she said. "Not at all. He was always

some mean, but not that kind of mean. It isn't drinking, because since my eyes have been going bad my nose has got sharp as a hound's. It's something gone bad in his head. Acts funny. Sometimes not a word to me. Set at the table and eat half his supper and shove his chair back and go out and bang the door and drive off into the nighttime. And sometimes he'll get to talking. Lord God, he talks to me a mile a minute, words all tumbling to get out, and he keeps laughing and walking around and about, getting me to laughing, too."

"When was he here last, Mrs. Arnstead?"

"Let me think back. Not since noontime on Thursday. I keep fearing he went off for good. It was yesterday toward evening somebody told me on the phone about him getting fired off his job. I was wishing I could see good enough to ... well, to look through his stuff and see if I could find something that'd tell me where he'd be. Hate to ask my other sons to come here. What did you say you wanted to talk to him about?"

"I guess I wanted to make sure he was Lew Arnstead, and then I was going to give him the best beating I could manage. That man in the hospital is the best friend I have ever had."

She stared in my direction with those old frosted blue eyes, then laughed well. A husky caw of total amusement. She caught her breath and said, "Mr. McGee, I *like* you. You don't give me sweet lies and gentle talk. And you wouldn't be a man if you didn't come looking for him. But you got to be a lot of man to take my Lew. When I see your shape against the light, you looked sizable enough. But size isn't enough. You got to have some mean, too."

"Probably enough."

"Well, you want to find him and I want to know where he is, so you could maybe come to his room with me and tell me what you can find."

Work clothes and fancy clothes and uniforms. Barbells and hair oil and a gun rack with two rifles, two shotguns, a carbine, all well cared for. Police manuals and ranch journals and comic books. Desk with a file drawer. Farm accounts. Tax papers. She sat on the bed, head tilted, listening to me scuffle through drawers and file folders. Tried the pockets of the clothing in the closet. Found a note in the side pocket of a pair of slacks, wadded small. Penciled in a corner torn off a sheet of yellow paper, a childish, girlish, illiterate backhand. "Lover, he taken off Wesday after work drivin to Tampa seen his moma. I will unhook the same screen windo and please be care you donit bunk into nothing waken the baby. I got the hots so awful I go dizy and sick thinken on it."

No signature.

"What'd you find?" the old woman asked.

"Just a love note from a woman. No signature. She wants to know why he hasn't come to see her."

"No help to us with no name on it. Keep looking."

I kept looking. There wasn't enough. The man had to have keepsakes of some kind. So he hid them. Probably not with great care. Just enough to keep them out of sight. Easy to get at. But after a dozen bad guesses I was beginning to think that either he had used a lot of care, or threw everything away. Finally I found the hidey-hole. I had previously discovered that the drawer on the bedside stand was a fake. Just a drawer pull and a drawer-shaped rectangle grooved in the wood. But when I reached under, I found there was enough thickness for a good-sized drawer. I took the lamp and alarm clock off the table. The top had concealed hinges.

Plenty of room for dirty books, and for some vividly clinical love notes from female friends. Room for a few envelopes of Polaroid prints. Room for three chunky bottles of capsules. About one hundred per bottle. One was a third empty. All the same. Green and white, and inside the one I pulled open were hundreds of tiny spheres, half of them green and half of them white.

"What did you find now?" she asked.

"The stuff that changed your boy."

"You mean like some kind of drugs? My Lew wouldn't take drugs. Not ever."

"He's got about two hundred and seventy Dexamyl

spansules hidden away in here. They're a mix of dex-
edrine and phenobarb. One of them keeps your motor
racing for eight hours. It's what the kids call 'speed.' Super
stayawakes. Take two or three for a real good buzz. You
can hallucinate on an overdose."

"Speed?" she said. "They said that on the radio way
last October. That was the name of some of the stuff they
took out of the lockers at the high school. Mister Norm
and my Lew and Billy Cable went in with a warrant and
went through all the lockers. And that was ... about
when he started changing."

"At least we know that if he wasn't coming back, he
would have taken this along."

"Thank the Lord for that, at least. Anything else in
there?"

"A lot of letters."

"From those women of his I expect."

"That's right."

"Well, don't you be shy about reading them. But you
don't need to read them to me. Just see if you can find out
where he might be."

No need to tell her I was looking for some clue as to
who he had entertained in the shed when he was supposed
to be guarding the Baither place.

Few of them were dated. But I came across one with a
mid-March date that was more literate and less torrid than
the others, and interested me mightily.

Dear Lew,
I ran into Frannie in the Suprex yesterday and she was
trying to stick the needle in, like always, and she told me
she saw you twice with Lilo. Now you can tell me it's none
of my business because the thing we had going is over and
done, and you know why we had to quit for good. But this
is like old times sake, because for a while before it got
sour, I really and truly loved you, and I guess you know
that. I have never really forgiven you for beating me up for
no reason and I guess I never will, but I couldn't stand for
you to get in some kind of stupid trouble. LEAVE LILO

ALONE!!!! She is bad news for one and all. I know all about her because for a while she and a girl I know well were friends. The reason she went with her mother after the divorce was on account of her father knew he couldn't handle her. He had custody of both kids, but he let Lilo go. Her mother and her stepfather couldn't control her either, and not many people know this, but when she was seventeen, like a year after she dropped high school, she was fooling around with Frank Baither, and he's old enough to be her father, and they say he's getting out soon, and if he wants her back, you better not be in the way. Now I'll tell you something else I happen to know, and I hope it turns your stomach. I'm not making it up because I haven't got the kind of sick mind that can make up something ugly. It happened on a Sunday afternoon last December. Roddy Barramore broke down on Route 112 down by where Shell Ridge Road turns off. A water hose busted, and he decided the best thing to do was walk into Shell Ridge Road to the Perris place, figuring Mr. Perris would have some hose and clamps or at least some tape. It was a warm Sunday and when he got near the house he could hear through the screen in the open windows that Mr. Perris had the football pro game on turned up loud. So he thought instead of ringing the door, he'd go holler in the window, and he had his mouth open to holler and then he saw Lilo and Mr. Perris on the couch, making out like mad, all their clothes in a pile on the floor. Roddy scrunched down quick before they seen him, and walked back and first he told Rhoda there was nobody home, and she said he was quiet for a while and then he told her what really happened. What do you think of a girl who'll make out with her stepfather knowing her own mother is there helpless in the bedroom maybe fifteen feet away, unable to speak or move much since she had the stroke over two years ago which some say was the judgment of God, but I say we aren't to judge because we don't really know what reasons she had for breaking up her own marriage the way she did. Rhoda told me about it. It made me want to throw up. I hope it does the same for you. I don't

*care that you aren't seeing me anymore, really. I wish the
best for you always, Lew, but you won't have anything
but heartache and bad trouble if you run around with Lilo.*
                                    Always your friend,
                                            Betsy

I went through the Polaroid prints. Amateur nude
studies. Thirty-two different poses. Many different girls. A
lean blonde with an insipid leer and huge meaty breasts
figured in ten of them, prone, supine, standing, reaching,
kneeling. Five were of a woman with a superb body, a
body good enough to overcome the incompetence of the
photographer. In each she kept the lens from seeing her
face.

Then there were thirteen different females, which I
suppose could be thought of as trophy shots, all head-on,
naked, some taken by flash, some by available light, some
indoors, some outdoors. Estimated ages, eighteen to thirty-
two. A variety of expression, from timorous uncertain
smile to dazed glaze of sexuality, from broad grin to
startled glance of herself surprised, to theatrical scowl.
The sameness of the pose removed all erotic possibility.
They became record shots, and could have been taken in
the anteroom of the gas chamber after a short ride in a
cattle car.

It was the remaining four shots which gave me a prick-
ling sensation on the backs of hands and neck. Solid,
shapely, dark-haired, suntanned chunk of girl. Evenly and
deeply tanned everywhere, except for the surprisingly
white bikini-band, low slung around the functional swell-
ing of the sturdy hips. One of those pretty, engaging,
amusing little toughy faces. An easy-laugher. A face for
fun and joy, games and excursions. Not at all complicated
unless you looked more closely, carefully. Then you could
see something out of focus. A contradiction. There was a
harsh sensuality in that face which was at odds with the
merry expression. There was a clamp-jawed resolve con-
tradicting that look of amiable readiness for fun and
games.

I had seen that face, for a micro-instant, several busy

seconds before Miss Agnes squashed into the canal. I felt
sure of it. And this chance for a more careful examination
confirmed the fleeting feeling that my young volunteer
mechanic, Ron Hatch, had to be related to her by blood.
Though his face was long instead of round, doleful rather
than merry, the curves of the mouth, the set of the eyes,
the breadth and slant of forehead were much alike.

"Must be a lot of letters," the old woman said.

I put everything back except the most explicit picture
of the dark-haired girl, closed the lid, put the lamp and
clock back in position.

"Nothing that helps much. But I want to ask some
questions, if you don't mind, Mrs. Arnstead."

"Don't mind a bit. Talked too much already, so I might
just as soon keep right on. That's what happens when
you're old and alone. Talk the ear off anybody that wants
to stop by and listen. But let's go back to the porch. Lew
could come roaring in, and he'd get mean about a stranger
being in his room."

The sun was down and the porch faced the western
sky, faced a band of red so intense it looked as if all the
far cities of the world were burning. It will probably look
much like that when they do burn.

"Mrs. Arnstead, I remember you said something about
your son running around with trash like the Perrises. Is
there a Perris girl?"

"There's Lillian, but she's not rightly a Perris. I did
hear she's tooken the name, but whether legal in a court, I
don't know. Her real name is Hatch. Her daddy is John
Hatch, and he has a lot of friends and business interests
around Cypress City. He's the kind that's real shrewd
about a deal and sort of stupid about women. Anyway he
married one that turned out to be trashy for sure. Wanda.
He brought her back here from Miami. Must be : . . let
me see now . . . oh, many years ago. The first baby was
Lillian, and then there was Ronnie, then there was one
that died. I'd say there was trouble all along between John
Hatch and Wanda. Maybe he worked so hard he left her
too much time on her hands, and she was built for trouble. They fought terrible, and the way they tell it, Johnny

Hatch finally had enough, and so he set out to get grounds to get rid of that woman. About seven years ago, it happened. He had a good mechanic working at his garage name of Henry Perris, and he had the idea Henry was getting to Wanda every chance that came along. So he brought in a fellow and he got the goods on them for sure, tape recordings and pictures and all. She had no chance of child custody or alimony or anything. Soon as the divorce was final, Henry surprised everybody by marrying her. Lillian was fourteen or fifteen then, and wild as any swamp critter, and when she made up her mind she'd rather be with her mother, John Hatch had the good sense not to fight it. They say Ron is a nice boy. John married again a couple years ago and there's a couple babies now. Let me see. Where was I? Wanda and Henry moved into a place way south of town, down there on the edge of the swamps. She took on a lot of weight they say, and I guess she had the high blood, because she was always high-colored. She had a little stroke about three years ago I guess it was, and then she had a big one and she's been in the bed ever since, helpless as a baby. There's some other Perrises down there, trashy folk, fighting and stealing, running in a pack with the other trash. Lillian is as bad as the worst. Lilo they call her. And my Lew has been messin' with those trashy people."

"You're sure of that?"

"She was calling here, giving me orders, telling me to tell my son Lilo called. I told him to tell her not to call him here. He got ugly about it." She sighed. "He turned from my youngest into a stranger. I guess it was those pills, not really him at all."

"Where does Henry Perris work?"

"He sure doesn't work for Johnny Hatch. He could work anyplace he wants to go, on account of being so good of a mechanic, they say. I heard he works someplace south."

"In a station on the Trail?"

"Could be. I don't rightly know."

"What kind of a car does Lew have?"

"He had a real nice car up till three months back, and

then he smashed it all up so bad it was a wonder he wasn't killed. There was something wrong about the insurance, so what he's driving now is the old jeep that was here on the place, fixed up some. It was dirty yellow and he got it painted black, he told me. I've been wondering something."

"Yes?"

"I'm a silly old woman but I'm not foolish. Seems like you have the thought in your mind my Lew might be in some kind of trouble more than from just beating up your best friend."

"He might be. I don't know."

"Then . . . if he is, I hope you find out and I hope you tell Mister Norm. If he is, I want him put away someplace because he's getting so wild he might kill somebody, then he wouldn't have any life left at all. Better he loses a piece of his life and gets over what those pills done to him than lose the whole thing. Unless maybe . . . already he killed somebody?" The dread in her voice was touching and unmistakable.

"Are you thinking about Frank Baither?"

"It was on the radio."

"I think he was on duty when that happened."

"Thank the Lord."

She asked me to phone her if I heard anything about Lew. I told her to let me know if he came home. She said she could use the phone by counting the holes in the dial. I gave her the White Ibis number. I started to repeat it and she said not to bother, that her memory seemed to be getting better instead of worse as time went by. But she sure did miss the television. It was just shapes and light that didn't mean anything. She wished the cataracts would hurry and get ripe enough.

As I drove back toward town I was thinking about that ancient and honorable bit of homely psychology, that myth of the ripeness of cataracts. The lens capsule can be removed as soon as it begins to get cloudy. But postoperative vision with corrective lenses is a poor resource at best, compared with normal sight. So the ripeness they speak of is the psychological ripeness of the patient, a time of diminishing vision which lasts long enough, and gets bad enough, so that the postoperative vision is, by comparison, a wonder and a delight. The patient is happy because the basis of comparison has changed.

There are some extraordinarily cruel men in the primitive rural areas of India who travel from village to village curing cataracts for a few rupees. Their surgical tool is a long, very slender, very sharp and hard thorn. They insert it from the side, behind the lens, and puncture the lens capsule. The cloudy fluid leaks into the eye itself and is replaced, or diluted, by the clear fluid within the eye. Sight is restored. It is a miracle. In sixty to ninety days the patient becomes totally and permanently blind, but by then the magician is a dozen villages away, busy with new miracles. Perhaps they do not think of themselves as cruel men. In a country where the big city syndicates purchase children, and carefully maim and disfigure them in vividly memorable ways, and distribute them by truck throughout the city each morning to sit on busy sidewalks with begging bowls, and collect them at dusk, as impersonally as one might empty coin machines, cruelty itself is a philosophical abstraction.

The April night was turning cool, so after I stopped back at the White Ibis and picked up an old blue sailcloth sportcoat, laundered and pressed as a courtesy of the Cypress County taxpayers, I went to a place I had spotted when driving around the town. The Adventurer. A lot of blue neon, tinted glass, an acre of asphalt packed with local cars. Frigid air conditioning, exhaust fans hustling the smoke out, ceiling prisms beaming down narrow areas of glare on the Saturday night faces. Long bar packed deep, and people sitting at small tables, leaning toward each other to shout intimacies over the shattering din of a hundred other people shouting to be heard over the sound of a trio on a high shelf in the corner, three dead-faced whiskery young men boosting by about five hundred watts the sound of an electric guitar, electric bass, and a fellow who stood whapping at a tall snare drum and singing sounds which may or may not have been words into the microphone. The obligatory birdcage girl had her own high shelf. She was meaty and energetic, snapping her hair across her closed eyes, tromping out the big beat with a simple repetitive pattern of bump and grind, belly dance and Tahitian flutter. She was not strictly topless because she had a narrow band of fabric around the busy bouncing boobs. There was a spotlight on her that changed from pink to black to blue to black, and in the black light only her teeth and the two narrow bands of fabric, and her high silver shoes glowed with an eerie luminescence.

As I waited to move in close enough to the bar to get my order in, I looked the crowd over. High school kids and ranch hands and packing-house workers. Single swingers and young marrieds. Bank clerks and secretaries and young realtors. Carpenters and plumbers, electricians and hard-wall plasterers, along with young dentists and soldiers and sailors home on leave and hospital technicians and nurses and bag boys and store clerks, and a handful of the customary predators, middle-aged men in youthful clothing, watching, appraising, singling out potential prey of either sex, planning their careful, reassuring campaigns. It was half beer and half hard. The beer was draft, in chilled heavy glass mugs that hold half what they appear to hold. Waitresses hustled the tables, serving either roast beef sandwiches or bowls of shrimp boiled in beer. So the fun place was a nice money machine, because when the waitress slapped the check on the table you either paid and left, or ordered more. I got hold of a cold mug and got back thirty cents change from my dollar and too much head on the dark beer.

I moved out of the crush and sipped the beer and looked for the controls. When you have a big noisy center-ring act that mixes lions, tigers, bears, sheep, rabbits, weasels, and cobras, you need the men with the whips and kitchen chairs and shiny pistols, or you start losing too many animals, and end up with an empty ring and a legal paper nailed to the door.

A disturbance started at a far corner of the long bar, and two quiet men appeared out of nowhere and moved in before it had a chance to spread. A good pair, swift and professional, and they picked the right one without hesitation. When they took him by me I saw that his mouth was wrenched apart by pain and his eyes were frightened, his face pallid and sweaty. The two men were smiling, joking with him. A painful come-along of some kind, manual or mechanical, is better for business than a half dozen old-fashioned bouncers. They had hit so quickly, I knew that the place had to be under observation. So by picking the best spot from which one could watch the whole room, I finally picked out the watch station. A mirrored insert was set high over the bar. From there a man could sit at his ease and watch all of the bar, all of the tables, the small dance floor, the cash registers, the entrance, and the doors to the rest rooms. The two men came back in and took up their position to the right of the main entrance. One of them pressed the switch of an intercom box and spoke into it. I could guess the probable message. "He quieted down nice, Charlie. He's driving home, and he won't be back tonight."

So I stood there, in that absolute and lonely privacy that exists only in the middle of a crush of strangers and a deafening din of festive voices and festive rock, staring at the hefty fleshy pumping of the tireless blonde, and wondering why I should feel that too many important parts were missing from my equation.

I had been luckier than I deserved, first in finding that lonely, troubled, talkative old woman, secondly in having her relate to me quickly and trustingly, and thirdly in getting my good look at the private hidden life of Lew Arnstead.

A lot of pieces fit beautifully together, but in some way the fit was too good to be true.

I wished Meyer was standing beside me, so I could try it on him. "Frank Baither planned the money-truck job. He used Hutch, Orville, Henry Perris, and Lilo, Perris's stepdaughter. We saw Henry, Meyer. He was the broad brown guy with the white teeth who arrived late for work at Al Storey's station that morning. Driving . . . a blue Rambler. So Henry was in on the Baither killing. It was Lilo Perris (or Hatch) who ran across our bows. Henry

set up a little smoke screen. It was too cute because maybe
he was too nervous. Grab that envelope and somehow get
it to Lilo. Then she went to the Baither place and faked
Lew Arnstead into giving her a chance to plant it in
Baither's house. Arnstead is on speed and it has turned
him erratic and dangerous. All Mister Norm has to do is
trace the envelope, from Henry to Lilo to the Baither
house, and bring them in and open them up—Henry and
Lew and Lilo. In a hurry, before Lew and Lilo run for it
with the money off the truck."

And suddenly I knew Meyer's reaction. I could almost
hear his voice. "If our Sheriff Norman Hyzer knows as
much about this county as I think he knows, then he
certainly knows that Frank Baither's little girl friend, before the money-truck operation, was Lilo Perris. He
knows a young girl was involved. He might suspect that
Henry Perris was in on it, too, and he would check back
and find out where Henry was that weekend. He seemed
absolutely convinced we were involved. As if he *had* to
believe we were. Why?"

"A blind spot, maybe. Maybe he's too close to it to see
it. Maybe he's involved in some way. The pieces fit so
well, Meyer."

"Do they always?"

"Hardly ever."

"So why do you keep asking these dumb questions?"

Meyer disappeared when big King Sturnevan appeared
in front of me, Coke bottle dwarfed by his big malformed
fist.

NINE

"McGEE, YOU DIDN'T COME ACROSS OUR buddy Lew yet, huh?"

"How do you know?"

"I'd put my money on you, like I said, but he'd mark you some. You wouldn't be able to help that. I been asking around. Nobody's seen that sucker."

King's civilian garb was a big red sport shirt with white palm trees on it, and a tent-sized pair of wrinkled khaki slacks. He had a small straw hat with a narrow brim perched on the back of his head, and a row of cigars in the sport-shirt pocket.

We had to roar at each other to be heard, and I didn't want to roar what I wanted to say to him. So he willingly followed me out into the abrupt silence of the night, and we went and sat in the top-down Buick.

"Would you say that like six months ago Arnstead started to go bad?"

"Maybe that long ago. I wasn't paying attention."

"Before that, he was okay?"

"He was pretty good. He was maybe as good as Billy Cable, and Cable is one hell of a cop, and you can believe it. But ... I don't know. The broads, I guess. A few months back he beat up one of his broads. She filed a

complaint and then pulled it. There was something maybe
I should have reported. I was in my own car. Six, seven
weeks ago. He come the other way, alone in our number
four cruiser, on 112 and he had it wound right up to the
top. We use Fords with heavy duty suspension and the
Cobra 428 mill with a three-point-five-0 rear end, so you
got an honest hunner twenny-five, and he come by with
that needle laying right on the pin. Hell, I turned around
and went in, thinking maybe somebody had hit the bank.
Nothing going on. I ast him, what the hell, Lew. You
could kill yourself on that kind of road. He told me to
shove it. Take fighters now. There have been some greats
who went right down the chute when the wrong kind of
broad started pecking away at them."

"Ever think he might be on anything, King?"

He took his time, glowered at a long cigar ash, tapped
it over the side onto the parking lot asphalt. "Now that
you bring it up, pally."

"Suppose I say he is? Definitely."

"Then I say two things. I say you shouldn't ought to be
poking around enough to find out, because it will make
Mister Norm a little on the soreass side. And I say the
more I think, the more it fits. Speed, maybe? You take
fighters, there isn't maybe one these days doesn't go into a
main bout without being stepped up with superpill. It's no
good, pal. They go like hell and they don't get tired and
they get a little more quick, but they can get hurt bad and
not know it and get up and get killed. You spend more
than you got, and you sack out for two, three days to get
back up to normal. Staying on it is something else. Come
to think of it, he hasn't been sleeping much lately, and
he's dropped weight. What would get him on it?"

"Like the preacher says. Evil companions."

"Pally, we all got a few of those. All it means is you
better not try to find Lew. You better stay the hell away
from him."

"And it means his judgment has gone bad. That's why
he pounded on Meyer. He could have killed him."

"I stepped out at the wrong time."

"Why didn't Billy Cable stop him?"

"Because Billy and him haven't been getting along so good, and when you see a man bitching himself, why stop him? Anyway, Billy finally did stop him or Lew would have killed your friend. Then when it was your turn with Mister Norm, Billy took the chance of giving you a look at your friend so Mister Norm would get the picture on Lew loud and clear and soon. Poor bastard."

"King, the woman who signed the complaint and withdrew it against Arnstead, was her first name Betsy?"

"Jesus Q. Christ! You're supposed to be a stranger in town, McGee. Betsy Kapp. Mrs. Betsy Kapp. She's a divorced lady, works hostess in the dining room down at the Live Oak Lodge. Mrs. Teffer's place. Best food in the county."

Nice to have King confirm Lennie Sibelius's appraisal of the local cuisine. I went back inside with King, and twenty minutes later drove into the middle of the city. It was a little after nine when I walked into the dining room. There was a family celebration at a long table near the far wall, champagne and toasts by middle-aged males to a fresh-faced girl and her blushing husband-to-be. Two quiet couples at small tables, with coffee and dessert by candlelight. Three burly businessmen drawing plot plans on the tablecloth.

As the hostess approached me, menus in the crook of her arm, I knew she had to be Betsy Kapp. She was the lean-bodied blonde who had starred in ten of Lew's Polaroid shots, the one with the attempt at a sexy leer which didn't quite come off. She wore a dark blue shift with a little starched white collar, and that mixed look of query and disapproval which told me that it was a little late for dinner.

Before she could turn me away, I said, "My attorney, Mr. Sibelius, said that I'd be a fool to eat anywhere else, Mrs. Kapp."

"Oh?" she said. And then "Oh." She turned and looked at the foyer clock. "Well, it *is* a little late, but if you ... didn't want anything too terribly elaborate ..."

"Sirloin, baked potato, tossed salad with oil and vinegar, and coffee?"

"I think that would . . . Sit wherever you want, while I . . ."

She took off for the kitchen in a slightly knock-kneed jog and I picked a table by the wall as far from the other four parties as I could get. She came back smiling. "They hadn't turned the broiler off, thank goodness. But no baked. Home fries?"

"Fine."

"And the steak?"

"Medium rare."

"I can get you a cocktail from the bar."

"Plymouth gin, if they have it, on the rocks, straight, with a twist. A double. Booth's, if they don't."

She gave the order, came back with my drink, then went to the register and took care of the departing family party and then the businessmen. I watched her move around. She looked a little younger and prettier than in the amateur nude studies, probably because there was a lively animation in her face and because she moved quickly and stood well. Had I not seen the pictures, I would have wondered if the imposing thrust of bosom might not be a pneumatic artifice, a fabricated symbol of the culture's obsession with mammary bounty. But I knew they were real, imposingly, awesomely real.

When she brought my salad she said, "I have to be the waitress, too. Another drink?"

She brought the dinner. It was a splendid piece of meat indeed. When I was half finished, the last of the two couples paid and left, and I had the dining room to myself.

Betsy Kapp said, "Would you like your coffee now?"

I waved at the empty chair across from me. "With two cups?"

She hesitated. "Why not? Thank you. I've been on my feet since eleven-thirty this morning."

She brought the coffee and sat across from me, leaned to the candle flame to light her cigarette. "It was a real pleasure serving Mr. Sibelius. He's a very charming man."

And, I thought, he tips very big and tips everybody in sight. I held my hand out. "Travis McGee," I said. She shook hands, pulled her long-fingered hand away quickly.

"I heard that you . . . you were in some trouble."

"*Am* in some trouble. Had the very bad luck to be in the wrong place at the wrong time. But I think it's getting straightened out. I never heard of Mr. Frank Baither until we were picked up for killing him. I guess if the sheriff still thought so, I'd be back inside."

Somebody rattled the foyer door, then apparently gave up and went away.

"I keep wondering about something," she said.

"What is it?"

"Mr. Sibelius didn't know my name. I'm sure of that. But you did."

I shrugged. "Some people were standing outside talking. I asked if it was too late to eat here, and they said to come in and ask Betsy Kapp. So when you came at me with the menus, it seemed logical to call you Mrs. Kapp. Maybe that was a mistake. Maybe I made a mistake. Miss Kapp?"

She grimaced. "No. It's Mrs. But I'm not working at it."

"Is this your hometown, Betsy?"

"No. I'm from Winter Haven, originally. But they sent me here to stay with my aunt when I was twelve. She died when I was seventeen and I went back home, but things were terrible there and so I came back here and married the boy I was going with. Then he was killed in a terrible automobile accident, and after I got the insurance settlement I went to Miami and then Atlanta, but I didn't like it in either place. Then I came back here and married a fellow named Greg Kapp, and we fought like some kind of animals until I couldn't stand it anymore and divorced him. I don't know where he went and I don't care. So here I am, and pretty soon it will be four years I've been working here. I get sort of restless, but you know how it is. It's hard to break loose. I sort of like the work, and you get treated pretty good here. Why should I be telling you my whole life story?"

"Because I'm interested. Good reason?"

"I guess you are. God knows why you should be. Are you married, Travis McGee?"

"No. Never have been."

"You must have some kind of work that keeps you outdoors and all. You look like you're in great shape."

"Salvage work, out of Fort Lauderdale."

"Like on a ship?"

"No. I'm an independent contractor. I take whatever comes along. I live alone on a houseboat at a marina."

"Gee, that must be a great way to live. Well, I live alone too, but not on any houseboat. It's a little cottage that my aunt had, that she left me. The bank had it and rented it until I was twenty-one. Greg was after me all the time to sell it. I'm glad now I didn't. I moved in after the divorce, when the lease ran out on the people I had renting it."

"I guess you know Cypress City pretty well then."

"Well enough."

"I'd like to be able to ask somebody about it, about the people. Sheriff Hyzer and Frank Baither and so on. But you've probably got things to do."

"Because it's Saturday night? Hah! The only thing I've got to do is total the tape and count the money and give Frank, the bartender, the cash and checks."

"So I can wait."

"It doesn't take me long, really." Her smile, as she stood up, was the distillation of several hundred motion pictures, refined in the loneliness of the bathroom mirror, born of a hunger for romance, for magic, for tremulous, yearning love. This was the meet-cute episode, immortalized by all the Doris Days, unexpected treasure for a thirty-summers blonde with something childish-girlish about her mouth, something that would never tighten into maturity. It would always yearn, always hope, always pretend—and it would always be used.

She took one of Lennie's twenties and brought me my change and went back to the register. It made a delicate little problem. To tip or not to tip. A tip would put a strain on the relationship she was trying, with concealed nervousness, to establish. So I went over to her and put a five on the counter by the register and said, "Save this for the waitress who was in such a rush to leave, Betsy."

She giggled. "Like turning the other cheek, huh? Helen is a good waitress, but she's always in a terrible rush to get home to her kids. I'll see she gets it, and I'll see you get one of her tables next time."

We walked out together. I asked her suggestion as to where we could go for a drink. She said that first she ought to take her car home. I followed her. She had one of those little pale tan Volkswagens with the fenders slightly chewed up, some trim missing, some rust streaks. I followed her. She drove headlong, yanking it around the corners. She was silhouetted erect in the oncoming lights. We sped through old residential areas where the people sat in their dimly lighted rooms, watching all the frantic imitations of festivity on the small home screens, watching the hosts and the hostesses who were old, dear, and familiar friends. Long ago their parents had old familiar friends named Alexander Botts and Scattergood Baines and Tugboat Annie. But reading was a lot harder. You had to make up the pictures in your head. Easier to sit and watch the pictures somebody else planned. And it had a comforting sameness, using up that portion of your head which would start fretting and worrying if it wasn't kept busy.

"Your mission, Mr. Phelps, if you care to accept it, is to discredit the half brother of the dictator of Kataynzia, recover the nine billion in gold, and give it to the leader of the free democratic underground, and disarm the ICBMs now being installed in the Stammerhorn Mountains. If you or any of your I.M. Force are killed or captured . . ."

"Wait one cotton-pickin' minute! Accept it! Accept a dumb-dumb mission like that? Are you some kind of ding-a-ling? We'd never get out of that rotten little country alive."

"Mr. Phelps!"

"Barney won't try it. Paris won't try it. And *I* won't try it. Go get somebody else. Go get Cinnamon, even. Come back next week, boss, with something that makes sense."

And the screens go dark, from the oil-bound coasts of Maine to the oily shores of Southern California. Chief

Ironsides retires to a chicken farm. Marshall Dillon shoots himself in the leg, trying to outdraw the hard case from Tombstone. The hatchet bounces back off the tree and cuts down tall Dan'l Boone. The American living room becomes silent. The people look at each other, puzzled, coming out of the sweet, long, hazy years of automated imagination.

Where'd all the heroes go, Andy?

Maybe, honey, they went where all the others went, a long time ago. Way off someplace. Tarzan and Sir Galahad and Robin Hood. Ben Casey and Cap'n Ahab and The Shadow and Peter Rabbit. Went off and joined them.

But what are we going to do, Andy? What are we going to do?

Maybe . . . talk some. Think about things.

Talk about *what?* Think about *what?* I'm scared, Andy.

But there's no problem, really, because after the screens go dark and silent, all the tapes of the watchers self-destruct in five seconds.

Little mental games often compromise my attention. She braked so hard and unexpectedly I nearly climbed the back slope of the bug. She swung left into a narrow drive between tall thick hedges. I followed, and she drove into a small carport, cut the lights, got out, grinned, and squinted back into my headlight glare, turned on a carport light and pulled the edge of her hand across her throat. So I turned off my lights and engine and got out. April bugs were shrilling in the hedges, under a murky half moon.

"A lot of the meat is broiled," she said. "They have those exhaust fans and all, but I'm in and out of there enough so when I get home I smell like meat grease. It gets in my hair and my clothes. It won't take me long to get rid of it, Travis. Come and look at my little nest."

It was to be admired, even though she had enough furniture and lamps and department store art objects for a cottage twice the size. One careless move, and I felt as if I would welt my leg on a table and spill $19.95 worth of pseudo-Mexican ceramics. I had to admire the cat, which was easier. A big male neuter, part alley and part Persian, patterned in gray and black, a wise, tolerant, secure cat who mentioned, politely enough, that he would like to hear the sound of the electric can opener. She opened a can of something that looked horrid, dumped it onto a paper saucer and put it in his corner. He approached it slowly, making electric motor sounds, then hunched into the serious ceremony of eating.

"He can say his name," she said. "Raoul. Raoul?"

The cat looked up at her, chop-licking, and said, "Raoul," and bent again to his gluey feast.

"Come see his yard," she said. "Raoul's personal piece of outdoors."

We went through another door off the kitchen into a fenced grassy rectangle about twenty feet by thirty. She clicked on the outdoor floods as we went out. They were amber-colored. The grape-stake fence was about eight feet high, affording total privacy. There were flagstones, planting areas, vines against the grape stake, a little recycling electric fountain in the middle, which she turned on. There was some redwood furniture and a sun cot.

I had the feeling I had been there before, and then I recognized areas of it which had formed the background for the Polaroid poses.

"Raoul and I both love this place," she said. "Neighborhood dogs roam in packs, and he knows they can't get at him. And I can stretch out in the sun absolutely stark and just bake myself into a stupor. It's sort of pointless, really, because I can't ever get a decent tan. My skin resists it. I go pink and then it turns sort of yellow-sallow and then back to white. But I just love the feel of the sun."

I made admiring sounds and she led me back in and back into the living room. "Sit in that chair, dear," she said. "When you put your legs up, it's fabulously comfortable, really. Do you like Brazilian music? I have this thing about the samba. See, I've got it all on these cassettes."

"I like it."

"Good!" As she picked out a couple of cassettes, she

said, "A gentleman friend got me a wonderful discount on this stereo cassette player. He makes his own tapes off records and off the air and then he makes duplicates and leaves them with me when he comes through town. Travis, while you're waiting for me, would you like a drink? I've got practically anything. Gin, vodka, rum, Scotch, and so on. I don't drink gin, actually. So I don't know anything about it. There's almost a full bottle somebody left of something called Bengal gin. Is that any good?"

"It's excellent."

"I thought it might be pretty good. I've been meaning to ask Frank, the bartender, but I keep forgetting. I could fix you a drink like you had at the Lodge. Me, I like to come home and make myself a tall tall Scotch and water with lots of ice, and then take a long hot hot sudsy bath and take a sip of the icy drink every little while. It tastes fantastically marvelous then. I'm going to have the drink, dear, but don't worry about waiting for me to take a long bath. I'll make it a quick shower. Can I fix you what you . . ."

"That would be just fine, Betsy."

So she started the cassette and adjusted the volume. She came smiling back with a gin and ice for me in a giant crystal glass tinted green, with grapes and grapevines etched into it, placed it on a cork coaster on the table beside the tilt chair. The cork coaster had small bright fish painted on it. The paper napkin was pink, imprinted with BETSY in red diagonally across a scalloped corner. Beside the drink she put a little blue pottery rowboat full of salted mixed nuts.

"There!" she said above the music of Mr. Bonfa, and went off to get rid of the occupational odor of burning meat, leaving me in my fabulously comfortable chair, next to a drink that would tranquilize a musk ox, semirecumbent in a static forest of bric-a-brac, listening to Maria Toledo breathe Portuguese love words at me in reasonably good stereo.

A compulsive strangler would have damned few tactical problems. She had taken my word that Lennie Sibelius was my attorney. She took my word that my semiarrest was due to bad luck rather than guilt. She went on instinct, and trusted the stranger. But a strangler can look like me. Or thee. The guest could tiptoe in and clamp the sick hand on the soapy throat, and in the moments left to her she could remember an entirely different sequence of motion pictures. Death itself would not be real because it would look like Alfred Hitchcock.

In fifteen minutes she reappeared in the doorway. "*Look* at me!" she wailed. "Will you just *look* at me!"

She wore a floor-length terry robe dyed in a big bold psychedelic pattern of red, orange, pink, and lemon. She held it closed, one hand at her throat, the other at her waist. Her hair was sopping wet, pasted flat to the delicate shape of the skull.

"I am *so* dang stupid about mechanical things," she complained.

"What happened?"

"I got out of the shower and bent over and turned it so the water comes out of the faucets, and then I was going to close the drain for a minute, to sort of rinse the tub, and I hit the shower thing, dammit. I didn't want to get my hair wet. It's very dense and very fine and it takes like forever to dry. I'm terribly sorry, dear. But I can't go out like this, really. Would you mind terribly? We could talk here, couldn't we? And there really aren't that many nice places to go at this time of night. What time is it? My goodness, it's after eleven-thirty already! I had no idea."

"I was going to suggest a rain check. Maybe that isn't the right expression."

"Is your drink all right? Goodness, you've hardly touched the surface. Are you sure you don't mind if we just stay in? At least it isn't going to give me any big decisions about what to wear. Back in a jiffy, dear."

She went away. The music stopped. I went over and flipped the cassette and cut the volume back by half, and threaded my way back to the leathery refuge.

She was not, I decided, devious enough to shove her hair under the water and go into an act. Nor, having been asked out, could she step out of her own obligatory role and say it would be cozier if we stayed in. Doubtless it had happened just as she described it. But the mistake, though deliberate, was on a subconscious and inaccessible level. It was all part and parcel of the meet-cute. The entry in the locked diary—and it would be inconceivable for her not to keep one—would say, "Actually, probably nothing at all would ever have happened between us if I hadn't been so stupid and soaked my hair that way. Then again, maybe it would have happened anyway, but not so soon, not on the very first night I met him. There was something inevitable about Travis and me, and I guess somehow I sensed it from the very first minute."

She came out in about a jiffy and a half. She had wound a coral-colored towel around her wet hair and tucked it in place. Instead of the mini-brief, leggedy outfit I anticipated, she wore an ivory white corduroy jump suit, with a kitchy arrangement of wide gold zippers and small gold padlocks on the four pockets, a gold chain around the waist, and a concealed zipper from larynx to crotch. After she had moved through the room a couple of times, straightening and patting, I found myself reacting to the outfit, and decided that, given her figure, it was more provocative than had she worn what I expected.

She took my drink away and "freshened" it, and made herself another tall pale Scotch. She sat on a blue nubbly couch a yard from my leather lair, pulled her long legs up, and said, "I guess I'm a terrible party pooper, Travis, but I'm just as happy not to go out. I guess my little nest is really why I don't leave this town. When I'm here, I'm not really in Cypress City. I could be anywhere, I guess. Because if I were anyplace else, I'd build another nest like this one, with all my own things around me. I'm kind of ... of ... an inward sort of person. I don't *really* pay a lot of attention to what goes on ... out there. So I don't know if I can tell you the sort of things you want to know, actually."

I started her off by telling her I thought Sheriff Norman Hyzer a strange one. So she told me his tragic life story, and how everybody understands why he is so withdrawn and cold and precise. But a fair man, really. Very fair. And they say he is real up-to-date with all the gadgets and advances in police work. He lives for his work, and they say he's got it now so that the job pays so little money, really, that nobody else tries to get elected. He puts all the money into the department, into pay for the deputies, and patrol cars and radios and all that.

"Well, I know some Baithers, because there are a lot of them around the south county, dear. There was one rotten Baither boy in junior high with me. He got killed in Vietnam years ago. His name was Forney Baither. I don't know what relation he was to Frank Baither. But they were the same kind, I guess. Forney got a choice of going to state prison or enlisting. I'd say that a dead Baither isn't much of a loss to anybody, and I guess nearly everybody would agree with that."

I could feel a little Bengal buzz. She wasn't going to give me anything useful unless I found the right door and blew the hinges off. I looked at her blurred image through green glass.

"Penny for your thoughts?" she said.

"I guess I was thinking about the Great Sheriff, the tragic figure, the miracle of efficiency and public service. Why would he keep an animal on his payroll?"

"What do you mean?"

"A brutal, sadistic, degenerate stud animal like Lew Arnstead?"

She put her fingers to her throat. Her mouth worked and her eyes went wide. "Lew? But he's just . . ."

"Just the kindly officer of the law who put my gentle friend of many years in the hospital for no reason at all, and would have killed him with his hands if Billy Cable hadn't stopped him."

"That doesn't sound like . . ."

"He's suspended and facing charges, and I hope Hyzer makes sure he's sent away for a long long time. I'd like to get to him first, for about one full minute."

"But he isn't . . ."

"Isn't such a rotten kid after all? Come on, Betsy! I've been checking him out . . . while I was looking for him. He's been running up a big score in the Cypress County female population. Romping them and roughing them up, and entertaining his buddies with his bare-ass Polaroid souvenirs."

Her eyes went wide-blind, looking at me and through me as she added it up, her long throat working as she swallowed again and again. The cassette had come to the end. There was no automatic turnoff. There was a small humming, grinding sound as the tape drive kept working. This was her sweet nest, all bric-a-brac and make-believe. A talented lady once defined poetry as a make-believe garden containing a real toad. So I had put the toad in Betsy's garden.

She made a lost, hollow, plaintive cry, sprang to her feet, and ran for shelter. Miraculously, in her pell-mell dash for her bathroom, she did not smash a thing. The door banged. I heard distant kitten-sounds. I got up and ejected the tape and put a new one on.

You are a dandy fellow, T. McGee. All the lonely, wasted, wistful ones of the world have some set of illusions which sustains them, which builds a warm shelter in the wasteland of the heart. It does them no good to see themselves as they really are, once you kick the shelter down. This one was easy bed-game for any traveling man who wanted to indulge her fantasies by playing the role of sentimental romanticism, with a little spice of soap opera drama.

So, while you are digging up whatever might be useful out of the little ruin you have created, at least have the grace to try to put the make-believe garden back in order. If you get the chance.

First step. Go to bathroom door. Knock. "Betsy? Betsy, dear? Are you all right?"

Blurred and miserable answer. Something about being out in a minute. Fix a drink.

Fixed two. They looked the same as before. But hers was real and mine was tap water.

She came out at last, walking sad, shoulders slumping and face puffy, saying something about being sorry, terribly sorry.

Moved over to the couch. Sat beside her. Took her

hand. She tried to pull it away, then let it rest in mine. Her eyes met mine, then slid away.

"Betsy, may I make some very personal remarks?" Shrugged, and nodded. "I think you are a fine, generous, warm-hearted woman. People are going to take advantage of those qualities sometimes. But you shouldn't feel bad, really. When . . . a human being never takes any emotional risks, then she never gets hurt. But she isn't really alive, either, is she?"

"I . . . don't know. I wish I was dead."

"When I opened my big mouth, honey, I had no idea that you could have been involved with Lew Arnstead."

"I wouldn't have been. But he . . . but he was in trouble and he felt so lost and miserable."

"Why don't you tell me about it? That might help."

"I don't want to."

"I think it would be the best thing to do."

"Well . . . the background of it . . . and it took him a long time to trust me enough to tell me . . . he'd always had girls, before he went in the service and while he was away and after he came back. And he fell in love with Clara Willoughbee. Really in love. And I told him the trouble was probably some kind of guilt about all the other girls, and feeling unworthy or something. But after they had plans to get married and everything, he couldn't do it with her. He'd want her terribly, and then it would just get . . . he couldn't do anything."

She became more animated and dramatic as she got into the story. He and the Willoughbee girl had broken up. He had tried going back to prior girl friends, but he was still impotent. And one night, off duty, he had gotten drunk at the Lodge, too drunk to drive. She drove him around in the cold night air in her little car. He had cried and cried and said he was going to kill himself. He passed out and he was too heavy for her to manage, so she had to leave him in her carport asleep in her car. In the morning he was gone. He came back to find out what he had told her. Then he would stop by, just to talk to her. Finally he told her what was wrong. That was in October of last year.

"I have ... a kind of condition," she said. "It's a sluggish thyroid gland, and that gives me low blood pressure, and makes me feel kind of listless and depressed. I used to have to take thyroid extract, but it made me too jittery sometimes, and made my hands ice cold and sweaty. So a couple of years ago Doctor Grinner gave me a renewable prescription for something called an energizer. I take one every morning of my life. I noticed that sometimes if I get mixed up and take a second one on account of forgetting I took the first one, it makes me feel ... well, terribly sexy. I might as well say it right out. Anyway ... I told Lew how they made me feel, and he came over one Sunday afternoon and I gave him two of them, and about an hour later he thought he could. And so .... You understand I was helping him. He was so terribly depressed. Well, it worked. He was so happy and laughing and all. And so grateful to me. And we kept making love after that, and fell in love with each other."

"He kept taking your pills?"

"Oh no. He didn't have to, not after the very first time. It was all in his mind, actually. You know. Guilt and fear."

"Then you broke up? Why?"

Her eyes narrowed. "We were having a little bit of a quarrel. It wasn't serious at all. Then he slapped me, *much* too hard. And then he kept right on slapping and hitting me until he knocked me unconscious. I woke up right over there on that little white rug, and he was gone. I was all cut inside my mouth and my face was terrible. The next morning I was sore in a hundred places, and I could hardly get out of bed. I was off work for four days. I reported him, then withdrew the complaint. I told them I fell off a ladder, hanging a picture. And I had to wear dark glasses for a week until my black eyes didn't show anymore."

"How did he act when he was beating you up?"

"He didn't seem mad at me or anything. I was screaming and begging and trying to get away from him, but he didn't hear me, sort of. He looked ... calm. Sometimes I have bad dreams about it."

"And you've never seen him again?"

"On the street and in the dining room. But not like before. Not that way. I *wouldn't!* He could come begging and I wouldn't ever let him touch me. I wrote him never to come here."

"Are you in his Polaroid collection?"

"Of *course* not!" Too emphatic. Quick sidelong glance to see if I believed her.

"He could have tricked you somehow."

"Well . . . one Sunday afternoon, we had a lot of bloody Marys and we got kind of wild and silly and he had that camera and got it out of his car. They use it for accident investigations, and I sort of remember him taking pictures of me out in the back, in Raoul's yard. But I tore them up." She was frowningly thoughtful. "At least I *think* I tore them all up. He took lots and lots. I certainly wouldn't willingly let Lew or anybody walk away with . . . pictures of me like that in his pocket, would I?"

"Of *course* not!"

She looked grateful for my indignant emphasis. She took her tall drink down several inches. She smiled sadly. "Why anybody should want nude pictures of me is something else again. I'm built kind of weird, practically enormous up here and skinny everywhere else, like I'm thirty-nine-twenty-four-thirty-two. Well, now you know what kind of an idiot I can be, dear."

"I think you ran into a crazy, Betsy." There was no point in telling her that she had, by curing Arnstead's temporary impotence with a strong stimulant, put him well on the road to hooking himself or, more accurately, habituating himself. He matched the classic pattern of the amphetamine user. Mercurial moods, hilarity and depression, little sleep, weight loss, enhanced sexuality, inability to consistently carry out responsibilities, recklessness, increasing tendency toward violence and brutality.

"Lew didn't *seem* like a crazy person."

"The world would be a safer place if you could pick them out at first glance, Betsy."

"Like he could be . . . put away?"

"The odds are better that he'll kill someobdy, and get put away for that."

"You've been looking for him?"

"Yes. I talked to his mother. He hasn't been home since Thursday noon. Got any ideas?"

"I suppose he could be with some woman someplace."

"Who has he been running with lately? Got any idea?"

She turned and held my hand with both of hers. "Oh God, Travis, he could be out there in the night right now! We don't know what could be going on in his mind. He might even blame me for all his trouble. He could be ... waiting for you to go. Please don't leave me. Please!"

Mousetrapped. A device just as real-unreal as the soaked hair episode. Contrived, yet not contrived. Sincere, yet insincere on some level of mind and emotion she had no access to. We were trapped in her garden of make-believe. I told her she would be all right, that there was no cause to worry, but tears stood in her tragic eyes, and she said I could not leave her.

TEN

WHEN I AWAKENED THE FIRST TIME ON Sunday morning, I was able to give myself a long period of ironic amusement by reviewing the long chain of coincidence, episode, mousetraps, or delusions which had levered me into Betsy's bed at about two-fifteen in the morning. She had Doris-Dayed our coupling far out of the range of any casual accessibility. She had woven such a fabric of myth that I could have torn myself loose only by tearing away her illusions about herself. Sometimes there is an obligation to play the role that is forced upon you. She had indulged in a considerable drama. Tears and protestations. Retreats which made the reactive approaches obligatory.

She wrapped us in her compensatory aromas of fate, tragic romance, inevitable loneliness of human beings. She wept real tears for a variety of reasons. She made us both special people in a world of clods, because otherwise she would have been merely a dining room hostess who had brought the tall stranger back home for what the British sometimes call a bit of slap and tickle. I had, in short, so won her reluctant heart that she could not help herself. And we had to live forever with our sense of guilt and human weakness. It happened, of course, because it was written in the stars that it had to happen.

And, all dramatics aside, when it had begun, when it was an unmistakable reality superimposed on all the devices of any daytime serial, blanking out those devices in sensual energies, she was a steady, hearty workman, strong and limber and so readable that she was easily predicted and easily paced, so obviously relishing it, that I was fatuously gratified by the implied compliment, the implied flattery. So for me, too, it was charade, but I was far more conscious of it as charade than was she. Role playing, under an inevitable canopy over the double bed, by the small night light of a dressing table lamp with a rose-colored shade. The he-she game amid yellow sheets with blue flowers printed on them, after a welter of stuffed animals had been exiled to a white wicker divan with cantaloupe cushions which matched the overhead gauze.

Morning irony, flat on my back, feeling the roundness of her forehead against the corner of my shoulder, her deep, regular, warm exhalations against my arm. Could feel the thin slack weight of her left arm across my lower chest, sleeping pressure of a round knee against the outside of left thigh. Turned my head slowly and looked slanting downward, saw disorderly mop of the fine blond hair hiding the face. Could see tip of one ear, half of the open mouth, edge of a pink tongue, two lower teeth. Fanciful sheet down to her waist. The arm across me cut off the vision of one half of the great round whiteness of the left breast. Small veins blue against the white. Slow, perceptible lift and fall as she breathed.

She sighed audibly and the breathing changed. Then there was a little sound in her throat as she caught and held her breath. Left arm moved, and the hair was thumbed back. Blue-gray eyes looked solemnly up at me as the face turned pink.

"Darling, darling, darling," she whispered, then lunged and hugged herself into my throat, arms winding tight. "Don't look at me. I must look like a witch."

"You look lovely." The lines are effortless, because the role has been played a thousand times in daytime soap.

"I don't know what you must think of me," she whispers. "I'm not like this at all. I don't know what got into me."

An effort to stop the crude and obvious answer. But easy to read the words of the shopworn script. "We just couldn't help ourselves, honey."

"I love you so," she sighs.

Turn the page. Read the next line. "And I love you, too." How reprehensible is it? To love something is, in some simple sense, to be unwilling to hurt it needlessly. And it was not said to induce the lady to spread her satin thighs, because it had been said the first time after the deed was done, to make her fantasy more real to her.

Stroke the slow length of the white back, down to the uptilt of the buttocks. Slowly, slowly, following the instructions in the script, the part in brackets. Until her breath shallows and quickens, her body softens, opens, and she makes a small gritty groaning sound, brings her mouth up to mine, and the engine in her hips begins a small, almost imperceptible pulsation.

When I awakened the second time on that Sunday morning, it was when she stood beside the bed and gave me a quick little pat on the shoulder. Hair tied back with yellow yarn. Little white sunsuit. Eye makeup and lipstick most carefully applied.

"Darling, you can have the bath now. I laid out some things for you. Be careful of the shower. The knob for hot turns the wrong way."

Tiny bathroom. Narrow shower stall. Kept whacking my elbows against the tile. Big bar of sweet pink soap. Big soft tiger towel in black and yellow stripes. Tufted yellow bath mat. Mingled pungent odors of perfumes, salves, lotions, sprays, and of natural girl. Yellow curtains across steamed window. Yellow terry cover on the cover to the toilet seat. Glimpsed my tanned, hairy, scarred body in the full-length mirror. Great, knuckly, fibrous hulk, offensively masculine in all this soapy-sweet daintiness. New toothbrush. Mint toothpaste. Scraped beard off using bar soap and a miniature white-and-gold safety razor with a toy blade. Stopped and looked self in the eye in the mirror over the lavatory. Said severely, "Just what the *hell* are you doing here, McGee?"

Don't get churlish with me, fella. I got caught up in one of the games Betsy Kapp plays. This one was called the bigger-than-both-of-us game. All right. Sure. I could have walked out at any time. Big man. Sorry, honey, I like brighter, funnier, better-looking women. Sorry. You don't match up. Don't call us; we'll call you. Leave your name and address with the receptionist.

"McGee, don't try to kid me and don't try to kid yourself. I'm not interested in your rationalizations. It was handy and you jumped it. Right?"

If you want to be crude. But what you are leaving out is that I had every expectation that she would be a very tiresome item in the sack. Once I was committed, I was going to go manfully ahead with it. I expected a lot of elfin fluttering, and maybe a little bit of clumsy earnest effort, right out of the happy-marriage textbook, and some dialogue out of every bad play I can remember.

"But? But?"

All *right!* So call it an unexpected pleasure.

"McGee, you kill me. You really do. You go around

suffering so much. All this bedroom therapy you dole out must put a hell of a strain on you. How come, boy, you always seem to find broken birds with all these hidden talents? Just lucky?"

I couldn't answer him. I told him to go away. I got dressed and went looking for her. She had breakfast all ready on the redwood table in a shady corner of Raoul's private garden. Iced juice, a tureen of scrambled eggs, buttered toast stacked under a white napkin, crisp bacon, and a giant pot of steaming black coffee.

She was pleasured to watch a large man eat like a timber wolf. Ah, she was saucy. She was flirty and fancy, chortly and giggly, cooing up and down a two-octave range. She was busting with joy and jollity and high spirits, slanting her eyes at me, blushing now and again, guffawing at the mildest quip, hovering over my needs and my comforts. I was aware of an old and familiar phenomenon. I was no longer able to see her objectively, see her on any comparative basis, rate her on any kind of scale regarding face and figure. The act of complete knowing turns the lass into a familiarity, and she had become Betsy, a person entirely herself. I could see detail that I had not seen before, the extreme slenderness of her long-fingered hands, and the plumpness of the pads at the base of her fingers, a discolored eye tooth—dead perhaps. Two small pock marks on her left cheek, the little squint-lines of the mildly myopic, a puckered line of scar tissue on the side of her throat, less than an inch long. Detail that I could not evaluate as good or bad, tasteful or distasteful, could only observe as being part of this Betsy woman. She pranced and posed, patted and beamed, sighed and chuckled, and I was the great old fatuous toad-king in her garden of celebration, served and feted and extravagantly admired. It was all part of the script, obligatory sauciness of the Doris-Dayism the bright morning after the reluctant-eager surrender of the Most Precious Possession.

I found that she had to work alternate Sundays, and this was her Sunday off. Without any direct dialogue about what we would do with the day, she had begun indirectly to establish the shape of it, some sun-time in the garden, and a marvelous nap, and later on some bloody Marys and the marvelous steaks she had been hoarding in the freezer for a special occasion, along with some wine a friend had given her, and he said it was a marvelous wine, Château something or other, but she didn't really know very much about wine. There were these outdoor speakers a friend had given her and they were still in the shipping carton in the carport, and maybe I could help put them up out here because some of her favorite tapes would sound marvelous in the garden, and there was speaker wire and everything, but she didn't know what gizmo plugged into where. And we wouldn't think or talk about ugly things all day, not even once.

So I said that it seemed like good planning, but I would like to go back to the White Ibis and check for any messages and change into fresh clothes. So she said that made sense, and she leaned into me at the doorway for a kiss so long and intense it dizzied her into a little sagging lurch to one side.

I went out and stared at the empty driveway and thought for a moment somebody had stolen the white Buick, then remembered her asking me, after it had become evident I would stay the night, if I would go out and drive it back and over to the side of the carport. That way the neighbors couldn't see it, and it couldn't be seen from the street. No point in letting idle tongues wag, she had said.

So I walked toward the carport. I glanced up at blue sky and saw a large black Florida buzzard sitting in dusty, silent patience on top of a power pole at the rear of the lot line. Symbol of a Sunday funeral of some small creature. I glanced back at the house as I neared the car and saw the buzzard's brother standing on the ridge line of the cottage, at the rear corner.

And the next step brought me into view of what had engaged their hungry interest.

I had left the top down. He had been tumbled casually into the shallow rear seat of the convertible. One foot on the floor, the other caught on the seat, bending the knee at a sharp angle. A large tough muscular young man with

black hair, high hard cheekbones. Long sideburns.
Meyer had said that Lew Arnstead had small dark eyes.
These were small dark eyes, one open wider than the
other. He wore a stained ranch jacket and dirty white
jeans. His head was cocked at an angle, exposing the
crushed temple area, above and forward of his right ear.
It was smashed inward in a pattern that looked as if it
could have been done with a length of pipe about an inch
in diameter. There was a little blood, and a dozen shiny
flies were pacing the area.

In all such moments you do absolutely nothing. You
stand and concentrate on breathing deeply and fast. Hy-
perventilation improves the thinking. You start looking at
your options.

"Sheriff, I just spent the night here with Mrs. Betsy
Kapp and when I went out to get in my car a couple of
minutes ago, I found a dead man in there who might be
your ex-deputy. Come over any time. I'll be right here."

So the old lady knows you came looking for her son.
King Sturnevan gave you a little course in how to whip
Arnstead when you caught up with him. Arnstead broke
the face of your old and true friend. Hmmm. Betsy Kapp
would be questioned. Her relationship with Lew was
probably known. "Mr. McGee was with me. He couldn't
possibly have killed that rotten crazy person who beat me
up."

Somebody had gone to a lot of trouble to leave me this
little token. Somebody had taken some risk. Reasonable to
assume they had added a few other little touches to sew
me more tightly into the bag. Such as a weapon. The piece
of pipe under the front seat, or in the glove compartment
or in the nearby shrubbery.

I don't call Hyzer, then. I have to take the calculated
risk of not calling Hyzer, which might make things a lot
worse later on. Maybe Hyzer is already on his way, with
Billy Cable at the wheel.

Option. I put the top up and drive away and put him
somewhere. They could know it already, and be staked
out waiting for me to drive out with the package. That

would be a very unhappy scene indeed. The ultimate version of egg-on-the-face.

Or ... go back in and say I'd changed my mind, and there was no point in going to the motel. Play Betsy's game for a day and another night, and hope they would come and knock on the door, and then convince them with the totality of our horrid surprise.

Or ... bring Betsy into it right now. Look at this little inconvenience, sweetie. Gibbering hysteria, with a lot of flapping and squalling and running around in small circles.

Fact: I *had* gone out sometime between one-thirty and two and moved the car. Fact: I had stayed, in part, because Betsy had been terrified by the thought of Arnstead skulking about in the night. Fact: I had sought out Betsy because of the letter hidden in Lew's room, and in the course of events Mister Norm would gather up that letter as evidence. And King would remember he had identified Betsy for me.

Supposition: Had I not been roped into the Baither killing and released with a certain obvious reluctance by Mister Norm, I might be able to carry this situation off and make useful explanations. But it was a little bit too much to expect Mister Norm to swallow.

Uneasy suspicion: Dropping the package on me was just a potentially handy byproduct of the primary necessity to turn off the mouth and the memory of a link between Frank Baither and his executioners.

Forlorn option: Hide the package right here, and fast.

I did not like any of my options.

"Trav?" Betsy said, walking toward me. "Trav, honey, I didn't hear you drive out and I wondered ..."

"Go back in the house!"

"Darling, you're practically *barking* at me! I only—"

I moved to stop her, but she had taken that one step that brought her close enough to the convertible to see the dead face, the dried and dusty eyes.

She swayed, eyes going out of focus. She made a gagging sound. I got to her then, caught her by the upper arms. Her color was ghastly. Her teeth chattered, and there were goosebumps on her long pale arms and legs. She looked at him again, and I turned her away and led her over into the sunshine. She turned into my arms. I held her. She hiccuped, sighed, then pushed herself out of my arms and stared up into my face, frowning.

"I'm all right now. But *why?* My God, how did he get *here?*"

"It is Arnstead?"

She tilted her head. "Of course! Didn't you ever see him before?"

"No."

She tried to smile, a valiant effort. "For one second I thought that maybe he *was* around here in the night like I thought, and when you went out to move your car. . . . Forgive me, darling. You couldn't have come back into my house, into my bed, and . . . it couldn't have been the way it was for us. But what a filthy thing to do to us, to put his body here."

"Somebody had to know I was here."

She walked around me and went into the carport and came out with a ragged bedsheet which had been used as a drop cloth. She marched to the car, snapped the sheet open, floated it down over the body.

"Why don't you put the top up? You shouldn't have left it down anyway, dear. It's all soppy with dew inside."

I reached in and pushed the toggle. The top ground up out of the well and swung forward and whacked down. The buzzards winged away.

It was comforting to be unable to see him. I said, "You are coming on very staunch, woman."

She looked mildly surprised. "I feel like screaming my head off. But that wouldn't do much good, would it? Should we phone now?"

"Let's see if there's enough coffee left for two cups, and have a little talk and see whether we should phone."

She listened, with all the girlish games turned off. I had to start back at the beginning and cover everything that had happened. Not quite everything. I left out her letter and the pictures of her. I went through my options.

When it had all been said, she frowned at me and said,

"But suppose Sheriff Hyzer did jump to the wrong conclusion, and he put you back in jail. Wouldn't that be a lot safer than trying to ... do something that might not turn out so good? I mean you would certainly be cleared, because, after all, you are not some kind of a criminal, and you have friends and you are in business."

"Add one more murder, Betsy, and the *Cypress City Call & Journal* is going to have to stop covering it like a zoning violation. And there will be Miami papers and television coming in here. And it would not matter one damn if I got cleared and released later. I can't afford that kind of coverage, that much exposure."

"Why not? Are you ... are you wanted for something else?"

"No. And I am in the salvage business, but not like you think. Personal salvage. Suppose some cutie clips an innocent pigeon for a very big score, and the pigeon exhausts all the possible legal ways of getting it back. Somebody might steer him to me, and if I think there's a fair chance, I'll gamble my time and expenses against a deal whereby I keep half of any recovery I make. Last resort salvage specialist. A small and useful reputation for recovery. And the methods used aren't particularly legal. If Hyzer checks me out carefully, he's going to come up with a life style he's going to label unsavory. I am a lot more conspicuous and memorable than I would like to be. It's a handicap in my line of work. If they ever make me on the front pages, with picture and with colorful account of how I make a living, that is the end of the living, honey. I would never get a chance to get in close enough to make a recovery, and I would have the law keeping a beady eye on me from that point on. So no thanks."

"But you could find some other way to make money, couldn't you?"

"Wouldn't that be just a different kind of prison?"

She stared into space, then nodded. "I guess having the kind of life you want is worth taking a big chance for."

"But now you're taking part of the risk. It isn't fair to ask you to do that. The smart thing for you to do is make the phone call."

"Pooh. If I was any good at doing smart things, I'd have started a long time back. Darling, that houseboat you live on, does it have engines and everything, or does it just sit there?"

"It cruises. Very very slowly, but very very comfortably."

"They're shutting down the Lodge in June and remodeling the whole main part, the kitchen and dining room and bar. If a person takes a risk, a person ought to make a profit, don't you think?"

"Okay, honey. The month of June is yours aboard *The Busted Flush.*"

"I'll do the cooking and laundry and all that."

No phone call. And considering the various areas of unknown risk, she came up with the best idea. So she changed to a blouse and skirt and went tooling out in her Volks, with a rather shaky wave and a set smile. And I used the time in a careful search for any extra bonus which might have been left with the special gift. I saved the worst until last. He had stiffened up, and it was difficult to go through his pockets. The sun had moved and it heated the inside of the car. The dead deputy was beginning to smell.

Western wallet, cowhide with the hair still on, and L.A. burn-branded into it. Thirty-eight dollars. Scruffy cards of identity and credit. Cracked Kodacolor shot of his black horse. Two snapshots of commercial origin and vivid clinical obscenity.

Plastic vial containing eight of the bicolored spansules. Dull pocket knife full of lint and tobacco crumbs. Squashed pack containing three Viceroy cigarettes. Zippo lighter. Several keys on a worn chain. Twenty-six cents in change.

The jackpot was in the top right-hand breast pocket of the worn ranch jacket. Half a sheet of blue stationery, carelessly torn off. Hasty scrawl. "Lew if you ever come to my place again I swear to almighty God I've got a gun and I'll kill you dead on sight." Signed with a big B in ballpoint so firmly the downstroke had gouged a little hole in the paper.

Everything back as before, except for the note. No weapon in the car or shrubbery. Body covered with the drop cloth. I was careful how I had handled anything that would take a print.

I had seen Betsy's handwriting before, on the same blue paper, but in a much longer letter, with the words more carefully formed.

What the hell was keeping the woman?

I went in. Raoul wound around my ankles, making little ingratiating mews. I wondered if the lady did indeed have a gun. There is a pattern to hiding places, and you always save time by starting with the places most frequently used. Suitcases and hat boxes. Then covered bowls and cooking pots in the kitchen cabinets. Next you try the bedroom drawers. So it took perhaps twelve minutes to find the gun. Bottom drawer on the left side of her dressing table. In the front of the drawer was a plastic bag with a drawstring, containing the diaphragm in its pink plastic case, along with the accessory tube. The gun was in the back, under a batch of bright scarves, each carefully folded. It, too, was in a plastic drawstring bag, the bag wrapped in a fragrant silk scarf. No obscure little small-caliber ladygun this, no European purse-pistol with mickeymouse action and engraved floral pattern. A deadly, fourteen-ounce Colt .38 Special, trade name "Agent," drop-forged aluminum frame, full checkered walnut stocks, Colt bluing, equipped with hammer shroud. Six rounds in the cylinder, and a full box of ammo in the plastic bag, with just the six rounds missing therefrom. Almost mint condition. A very hard and heavy close-range punch for a lady to own. If you had an earnest and honest desire to kill somebody, this item would simplify the task and shorten the process.

I put it back exactly as before.

Five minutes later I heard the lawn mower engine of the VW come chattering along the driveway and into the carport. She came hurrying into the house and into my arms, clung for a little while then gave me a tired upslanted smile, quick peck on the corner of the mouth. She wandered over and dropped onto the couch, kicked her sandals off, leaned her head back, forearm across her eyes.

"Gone a long time, Betsy."

"Well . . . I wanted to find out anything worth finding out. For what it's worth, there is absolutely no one watching this place. I went around and around and came up on it from all the directions there are. Nothing."

"That's comforting."

"I went to the White Ibis and went to the desk and asked for you. They tried the phone and said you weren't in. I located the box for 114, and I couldn't see any message slips in it."

"You shouldn't have gone there."

"It was the quickest way to find out if anybody was trying to find you, dear. And if they were, and if I came there looking for you, the last place they'd look would be here. What are we going to do?"

"I found this on him," I said, and handed her the note.

She read it and it brought her bolt upright, astonishment on her face. "But I wrote this last year! Why would he be carrying it around? It isn't even all here."

"What was on the top half?"

"Let me think. The date, I guess. And something about how bad he'd hurt me, about how my face looked."

"You wrote it right after he beat you?"

"The second day. I was too sick to write anything the first day."

"Did you think he might come back here?"

She leaned back again. "I don't know. You see . . . I wanted him to come back. That was the sick part. I wanted him to come back, no matter what. I was afraid that . . . if he did come back, I'd go to bed with him if that's what he wanted. I hated him for beating me, but the wanting was stronger than the hate. So I don't know whether I was trying to keep him away from me until I could stop wanting him, or whether I was trying to . . . to challenge him so he would come back."

"Do you even have a gun?"

"Sure. Stay right there. I'll get it." She brought it into the living room, took it out of the plastic bag and handed it to me. "It scares me to look at it. Lew gave it to me. He took it away from somebody and didn't turn it in like he was supposed to. He bought the ammunition for it and loaded it for me and showed me how it works. But I never fired it. Is it a good gun?"

"Very reliable up to thirty feet or so."

"He said if I ever had to use it, not to try to aim. Just point it like pointing my finger and keep pulling the trigger. I don't think I could fire a gun right at anybody, no matter what."

I gave it back to her and she stowed it away. She sat as before and said, "It was just half the note in his pocket so that if somebody found it on his body they'd think he came here."

"Somebody put the note in a handy pocket after he was dead. They brought the body here. They saw the Buick and dumped him into it. They thought you would be alone."

"Then they changed their mind. What do you think they were going to do, if I'd been alone?"

"To set it up to look as if you killed him, there's the little problem of a weapon, something you could reasonably kill him with."

"I . . . I didn't look at him very long. I saw that terrible mushed-in place. What shape would it have to be?"

I demonstrated with my hands. "A piece of pipe about this long and about this big around would do it. You could do that much damage with one full swing."

She shuddered. "I couldn't do anything like that."

"Let's think this out. He's too heavy for you to carry. So the encounter had to happen outside the house. You wouldn't have come out into the night, so it had to look as if it happened earlier. You come home and drive into the carport and get out of the car and go to that side door, right?"

"Yes. It's a delay switch on the carport light. It gives me time to get inside before it goes out."

"So he could have been waiting for you in the carport, or in the bushes near the door. Handy places to drop the body. Now then, in one place or the other, there has to be something that you could pick up and swing."

She sat with elbows on knees, chin on fists, lips pursed.
"I can't think of a dang thing around here that . . . Oh!"

"Oh what?"

"Maybe it could be the handle for the doohickey for the
corner of the house. The estimate was two hundred dollars
to put in a new pillar. The old one sort of started sinking
into the ground for some reason and Mr. Kaufman down
the street said why didn't I mail-order that thing from
Sears for under nine dollars and it would work just as
well, and just leave it there."

"You've lost me. You better show me."

We went out, and she sat on her heels by the rear
corner of the house and pointed out the construction jack
that was bracing it up. It was the type that uses a pipe
handle.

The handle, about thirty inches long, was on the ground
under the house, beside the jack. I saw that it was too rusty
to take a print. I reached under and picked it up and
pulled it out. The far end was clotted with dark-dried
blood, some short black hairs, some bits of tissue.

She spun, ran three steps, bent over and threw up.
When she was finished she trotted into the house, keeping
her face turned away from me. I put the jack handle in
the Buick, on the floor in back.

I was sitting on the couch when she finally came out of
the bathroom. She was wan and subdued. She apologized.

"We have to keep going with it, Betsy. Okay, so they
leave him near the corner of the house. You find him in
the morning and phone the law. Hyzer is a thorough man.
You certainly wouldn't have looked through Arnstead's
pockets and found that old note."

"Never!"

"So they reconstruct. Certainly some people know
about the affair you had with him."

"Too many."

"You can't explain the note away, and you can't prove
it wasn't written yesterday or Friday, or prove he hadn't
come here recently. Hyzer gets a warrant. Your story
about how you happen to have that gun is a little frail,

without Lew around to back it up. So he was waiting when you came back from work alone last night."

"Thank God I didn't!"

"You had a quarrel. You edged over to the corner of the house. The delay light went out. You felt around and found that handle and lifted it and hit him in the skull and knocked him down. You didn't know you'd killed him. You went into the house. When you found the body this morning, you tried to lie your way out of it, bluff your way out of the jam."

"But nobody would really believe that I could ever . . ."

"There's something missing. How did he get here?"

So she went on a casual stroll in the quiet neighborhood. The jeep was four doors away, parked behind the overgrown masses of Cuban laurel in the side yard of a boarded-up house. The guard chain across the drive had been unhooked and rehooked. So I had to go into the dead pocket again, holding my breath, and finger the keys out. She took another stroll and came back and said that one of them fit the ignition, and she had left the keys right there.

The jeep was proof he had arrived alone to visit a woman who had threatened to kill him if he ever came around again. He did. And she did.

"Now what, Travis? Now what do we do? Wait until dark and then take—"

"Dark is too long to wait. Somebody can get impatient. And nervous."

So we had to take the gamble. Plan it first and then take it. A sickening gamble, because moving the body was prime meat for any prosecuting attorney. No jury would ever understand why we did it.

ELEVEN

I DROVE HER VW OUT OF THE DRIVE-
way and parked on the far side of the street. The big
banyans made dark shade. A fat lady in red pants knelt
three front yards away, troweling her weeds. A household
gas truck on special Sunday delivery went by and turned
at the next corner. By then she had time to move the
Buick to the mouth of her narrow sheltered driveway, so I
beeped the horn twice as prearranged, meaning that there
was no pedestrian or vehicular traffic.

I drove east, and looked in the rear-view mirror and
saw her come out and turn west. She had won the argu-
ment about the cars. She reminded me that I had told her
I was conspicuous, all by myself. And in the white convertible I was doubly memorable, and too many people
had seen me in it. Certainly, a lot more people knew her
by sight, but not in the big floppy broad-brimmed hat she
took from the back of her closet, or in the huge mirrored
sunglasses she had bought long ago and seldom worn. In
the very ordinary-looking VW and with the tweed cap
which her second husband had left behind and never
came after, I was not likely to be either recognized or
remembered. I had asked her three times if she was sure
she could handle the constant awareness of the body

directly behind her, and she finally said she planned not to think about it.

The place she had described to me was perfect. She had drawn a map, and I had repeated the directions after her until I knew just how to find it. As she was taking the more direct route, she would be there first. Neither of us would make the last turn unless the highway was empty in both directions.

Out Alternate 112 to where it joined 112 proper. North about four miles, and then turn left and go west on County Line Road. You can tell the turn by the deserted gas station on the corner. Grass is growing up through the cracks in the cement near where the pumps were. It was there, as promised, and I made the turn.

Go about five miles, maybe more, and there is a gradual curve to the left. After the road straightens out again, you'll see a place on the left where there was a house. Now there's just a chimney and foundation.

There was no traffic in either direction when I got there, so I turned into the overgrown drive and around behind the house site and then, as she had described, I drove on sand tracks through palmetto and scrub pine, past a marsh, and saw, ahead of me, the pond she had described, and caught a glimpse of the white car beyond the saw grass at the far end of the pond.

She was fifty feet from the car, sitting on the trunk of a fallen pine, looking at the pond.

"Any trouble at all?" I asked her.

"None. You?"

"Nothing. You better show me the place first."

She seemed slack and dispirited. "Sure," she said, getting to her feet. "It's over here."

The place was a hundred feet further. It was an old sinkhole. All this land was once the bottom of the sea. Marl and fossils and limestone. Fresh water runs down through the limestone in great underground rivers. Sometimes the underground chambers will collapse after dry cycles, and the land will sink. This was an old sinkhole, the fractures concealed by coarse brush and sizable trees.

She took me to the place she had described, a marl

slope, a sun-pale sculpturing of eroded limestone, a brushy pit five feet deep with a dark irregular hole at the bottom of it, at one end of the pit. The hole was about a yard across. I went down into the pit and knelt and looked down into the hole. There was a smell of coolness and dampness. I picked up a piece of limestone bigger than my fist and dropped it into the hole. I heard it hit the side, and in a second or two heard a smaller sound as it hit again. Then there was an almost inaudible thud a long time later.

"Donny timed it with a stopwatch once."

"Donny?"

"My husband. The young one that got killed. He used a stopwatch and figured out that per second per second thing. I remembered the figure he told me. Three hundred and six feet. He figured in the time for the sound to come back up. He was a real nut about math. Is it . . . a good place for what you want?"

"Do many people come here?"

"Nobody, as far as I know. I started going with Donny when we were both sixteen. We wanted a place where we could get away from people. We'd come out here on our bikes and bring picnics. Donny found this hole one time. I came here a lot after he died, before I got married again. I never brought Greg here, or anybody else. I still come here when . . . when I feel down. It's so quiet. I don't think about anything. I just walk around and listen to the quiet, and sit and listen. And I feel better then."

"Why don't you go for a walk right now, Betsy. I'll take care of it."

"Can't I help somehow?"

"No. No thanks."

I had to put the top down on the convertible to get him out. I couldn't move the car any closer. I wrapped the old sheet around him and stood him against the rear fender, on his crooked legs. I squatted and let him tip forward onto my shoulder, and as I stood up with him, the pressure forced gas through his voice box, a ragged croak that chilled me. Though he folded slightly, there was enough rigor to make him feel like a clumsy log.

The weight made me take short jolting steps, and the effort and the heat of the early afternoon brought out the sweat. It seemed a very long way to the pit. I dropped him on the edge, stood on the end of the sheet and rolled him into the small pit. In the unlikely event he was found, a police lab could make a spectroscopic analysis of the paint on the old sheet and compare it to the paint used somewhere in Betsy's cottage, and prove it identical.

I went into the pit, straddled him, picked him up by the waist and slid him headfirst into the hole. Listened. Heard the remote, softened thud. Same impact as going off the roof of a thirty-storied building, if the young husband's math had been accurate.

"I'll never be able to come back here again," she said. I looked up and saw her standing up on the rim of the small pit, outlined against blue sky and small white clouds. The big brim of the hat shaded her face, and the big mirrors of the sunglasses were like the eyes of some giant insect.

"You shouldn't have watched."

"It wouldn't be fair not to, somehow. Like not sharing bad things along with the good parts."

We went back to the cars and the pond. I gathered twigs and dry grass and small dead branches and built a small hot fire. I burned the sheet and the map she had drawn and the fragment of the old letter to Arnstead. I took the jack handle out of the Buick, scrubbed it in the wet muck at the edge of the pond, then held the end that had been stained in the fire for a while. I put it in the VW, and told her to remember to put it back under the house, just as before.

"Can we stay here for a few minutes, Trav? Can you stay with me for a little while?"

"If you want. I have to clean that back seat off anyway."

"I forgot. I'll do it."

I protested, but she insisted. She got the bottle of strong cleaner she had brought along, and the stiff brush and the roll of paper towels. She scrubbed the few small stains away, scrubbed all of the back seat area and the rug on the floor, making a mingled smell of ammonia and kerosene. There were enough embers left to catch the paper towels ablaze. She put the hat and glasses in the VW and roamed back to the log and sat looking at the pond. I sat near her, in front of the log, leaning back against it. A kingfisher hovered, wings blurred like an oversized hummingbird, then dropped and splashed and lifted away with a small silver fish in his bill.

"There's breem in the pond. Donny used to catch them. Travis, it's like we killed Lew."

"I know." And I did know exactly how she felt. Plan and execution. Terror and disposal of the body and a slack, sick relief.

"We fixed it so whoever killed him won't ever get caught."

"Maybe not for him. They'll be nailed for killing Baither."

"Does it have to be the same people? Or same person?"

"The odds favor it."

She was quiet for a long time. I tilted my head back and looked up at her, saw for an instant a look of a private anguish which changed at once to a small forced smile.

"Betsy, I think he had gone too far down whatever road he . . ."

"Not Lew. I . . . was remembering Donny. I was working waitress when they told me. He was driving back from the construction job he was working on that summer when he got killed. We were saving money. He was going to go to Florida State. They hadn't wanted him to get married so young, and we ran up to Georgia. We had ten months married, only. I dropped the whole tray of dishes. They had to give me a shot finally. I went sort of crazy, I guess."

"It can happen."

"We were such dumb crazy kids, coming out here all the way on the bikes, fooling around and getting each other all worked up, saying we wouldn't really do it, and getting closer all the time. There's a song or saying or something. 'She lost It at the Astor.' I lost it over there on a blanket under that pine tree, on the bed of soft needles, hanging onto him and crying, not because it hurt but on account of feeling sweet and sad and strange. Getting all over mosquito bites. There was a woodpecker way up the tree over us, and I watched him hopping around and turning his head this way and that way and then rapping and knocking that tree. Going home I felt so weak and sick and dizzy I nearly fell off that dumb blue bike. Then I turned seventeen and my aunt died and I had to go up home, but I wanted Donny so bad I thought I could die of it. And I came back and we got married."

Her eyes filled, and then she gave herself a little shake, tossed her hair, smiled brilliantly and said, "Well, I guess we shouldn't be taking the chance of being seen out here, huh?"

We walked toward the cars. She was being someone else, and it took me a few minutes to identify the role. Another one of the games Betsy played. Heroine in a movie of intrigue, suspicion, sudden death. Brave and pert in the face of danger. Ready to help with the schemes and plans.

"I guess we have to worry about that black jeep now, Travis."

"Not by daylight. It isn't a clear and present danger, the way it was before."

"You want me to go right home in my own car."

"I saw some stores open in that shopping center."

"Woodsgate."

"Stop there and do some shopping. Have you got money with you?" She had. She looked puzzled.

I said, "Mrs. Kapp, you left your house at noon or a little before on that Sunday. Please tell the court where you went."

"Oh. Sure. I see. And I should look around for somebody I know and make sure I say hello and say something they'll remember, and be . . . kind of happy and normal and all."

"Exactly. And I'll go back to the motel."

"Travis, darling. Please don't leave me alone in the house too long. I'll be okay for a while, but I think I'll start imagining I hear things. Somebody brought Lew there and killed him there while we were in bed. Somebody knew what they were going to kill him with. It has to be crazy people who hate me for some reason."

I took hold of her hands. "Listen. Nobody hates you. It's a part of a pattern. Somebody is hooked on misdirection. They're blowing smoke, laying false trails. They had that note Lew got from you. So they could quietly take a look around your place while you were working, to see the best way to set it up. I don't think he was killed there. It would be too clumsy and difficult. I think they took that jack handle away, killed him with it and brought the body and the weapon back. Then they saw my car there. Knew it was the car I was driving. Knew I was mixed up in the whole thing, and I think they were a little nervous about my being with you."

"Why?"

"Because of things you might be able to tell me that would make the pattern clearer?"

"What things?"

"We don't know yet. Maybe you've already told me, but it didn't mean anything to either of us. At least not yet."

"But . . . why didn't they just find someplace to put the body where it wouldn't be found? Like we did."

"All I can do is make a guess. I think that if Arnstead disappeared suddenly and for good, the pattern might look a little more distinct to Sheriff Hyzer, and he might go after somebody a hell of a lot more logically suspect than you."

Her eyebrows went up. "Then what we've done will make that happen!"

"It might help, if my guessing is any good lately. And some person or persons unknown are going to wonder just what the hell happened."

"And come around and try to find out? I don't want to go back there alone. Please!"

She needed time. There would be a series of delayed

reactions, little tremors on the psychic seismograph. Reality was an uncomfortable intruder in her garden of make-believe, and she needed time to transmute death-stink, rigor mortis, and the dusty eyes of the one-time beloved into the product of the special-effects man in a suspense cinema. So I told her to do her shopping and then come to the motel, to drive around to the side, park by the Buick and come to Unit 114. Her relief was evident.

She drove out first. There was a place you could stop and see the road in both directions. From time to time I had heard the distant drone of infrequent traffic. I heard her accelerate, heard the rackety little engine fade into the afternoon silence.

Kingfisher came back. The small fire was dead. I kicked the larger charred pieces into the pond, kicked sand over the ashes. I broke a pine branch off and retraced my steps to the sinkhole and the pit, brushing out those footprints so deep they were obviously those of a man carrying a heavy burden. I checked the edge of the hole and found some tan threads from his jacket caught on the limestone. I balled the threads and dropped them into darkness.

They used you, Lew, baby. And if Lennie Sibelius hadn't persisted, hadn't tricked you into revealing the way that envelope of mine could have been planted in the Baither house when you were otherwise occupied in the shed, you might still be one of Hyzer's faithful. But once you'd been opened up, it was only a question of time until Hyzer would get under your guard and find out the name of the woman who decoyed you. And a man hooked on uppers is too erratic. The original idea of planting that envelope was too fancy, Lew, baby. A spur-of-the-moment idea that made more problems than it solved. It turned you into a problem, and now I've turned you into another kind of problem for somebody. For Henry Perris, perhaps. And Lilo, and Hutch and Orville, maybe. Patterns emerging.

So you've got a nice deep black hole for the long long sleep, down there with your hairy wallet and your dirty pictures, and your fond photo of your neglected horse.

I stopped beside my rented car and decided that there was a reasonable possibility I might get picked up again. So I went through the pockets, just in case. Found what I had forgotten, the Polaroid print of my night-running girl, Lillian Hatch alias Lilo Perris. All that merry sensuality and that tough little jaw. Hair askew, and the hard little mouth recently bed-softened. A flash shot. She stood facing the camera, weight on the right leg, left knee bent, right fist on the right hip, muscular belly sucked in. Hard high conical breasts, the nipples fully erect. Spreading curly black pubic thatch, glossy and vital in the wink of the camera light, with the big pale weight of pudenda faintly visible through the whiskery thicket. I examined the background of the interior shot. It did not reveal much, as it was too shadowed. I could make out a corner of a bed, the edge of a table with a thin line of smoke rising from an ashtray improvised from a Planters Peanuts can. An object on the wall behind her which I couldn't identify. It was partially obscured by her head. A round thing with radiating spikes, like a child's drawing of the sun.

I did not want to destroy the picture, and I felt uncomfortable keeping it on me. I finally put the convertible top up and knelt on the rear seat and partially unzipped the rear window. There was a deep enough fold in the dacron canvas to slip the photograph in and zip it back up.

I drove out to the mouth of the sandy curving tracks and after making certain County Line Road was empty, I gunned it out and headed for Cypress City. There are a lot of places I never want to go back to.

TWELVE

I PARKED IN MY MOTEL SLOT AND went into the room. The phone light was blinking. I went out the other door and up the interior walkway past the pool and the small careful rock gardens to the rear entrance to the lobby.

There were two slips in my box. One was the message Betsy had left. The other said to phone Deputy Sheriff Cable. I took the slips back to the room. Some fat children were wallowing and whooping in the pool. Every year there seems to be more fat children, and they seem to be noisier.

I phoned the sheriff's office. Cable wasn't in. The dispatcher said he'd relay my message to Cable and he would probably get in touch with me. I said to tell him McGee was at the motel.

I saw the cruiser arrive a few minutes later, so I went to the door and said howdy to him as he got out of the car.

"Care to come in, Billy?"

"Don't mind if I do."

I had turned the color set on. A golf match had appeared. The players had green faces. Billy Cable went over and fixed the color, turned the sound down.

"Put the little round ball in the little round hole and

they give you forty thousand dollars. Jee-*zuss!* Got me into the wrong line of work, I guess."

He sat on the bed and leaned back, propping himself on his elbows. A very competent, tough, unreadable, watchful face. He had sunlenses clipped onto his steel-rimmed spectacles, and he reached and tilted them up.

"To what do I owe the honor and all the routine, Billy?"

"Mister Norm got edgy about you when he found out this morning you didn't sleep here. He wondered if maybe he made some kind of bad mistake about you, McGee."

"You better ease his mind."

"I already did, on my way over here. I wasn't as nervous as he was, though."

"That's nice."

"I did some backtrailing, and I found out from King you were looking for somebody named Betsy that had been close to Lew, and he told you probably Betsy Kapp. So Frank, the bartender, told me you ate at the Lodge and you and Betsy took off in your cars at the same time. Well then I went to her place but there was nobody there at all. But I went around and looked in the kitchen window and there were two of everything drying on the sideboard. Cups, saucers, and so on. Very cozy. I hear those tits are genuine. Hardly seems possible."

"You do good police work, Billy, but we can skip the editorial comment. Okay?"

"All right, you had to come up with that name someplace in order to ask King. And Mister Norm has had me looking all over for that damn fool Lew Arnstead. When I went out there his momma said he hadn't been home for three days and nights, and when I asked her if anybody had been looking for him she said that it was none of my damned business. So I asked if a big fellow named McGee had been looking for him, and she told me that if I knew already, why was I wasting my breath asking. You know, I like that old lady."

"So do I."

"Aside from Betsy, how many other names did you come up with? There'd be a pretty long list."

"I could tell you it's none of your damned business. But let's be friends. Clara Willoughbee. That's all. Maybe his mother didn't keep a running score."

"Clara is a nice girl. About to get herself married. To a rich kid from Fort Myers."

"I didn't look her up. Betsy came after Clara."

"But that was over quite awhile back, toward the end of last year, I think."

"I thought she might steer me to somebody more up to date."

"Why would you want that?"

"He's not an officer of the law at the moment. I thought I might locate him and see how much workout I could give him."

"King thinks maybe you could take him."

"I thought it might be worth a try. Incidentally, thanks for pulling him off Meyer."

"I should have moved faster. That last one came up from the floor. That's the one that did the big damage. One more like that and he could have killed the man."

"What was his point?"

Billy Cable sat up and took a half cigar out of the shirt pocket of his uniform and lit it, spat out a wet crumb of tobacco. "At that time it looked to us like you and Meyer gave it to Frank Baither. Frank was a rotten fellow, but nobody should have to die that hard. Both me and Lew saw the body. Lew knew Meyer hadn't given Mister Norm a thing to go on. Sometimes, in this business, you get to where you want to hit somebody."

"Do you obey the urge, Billy?"

"Me? Hell, no. But Lew is something else. Especially lately. Like his gears were slipping."

"Okay, why did you give me the guided tour before you took me to Hyzer?"

"Why not? The damage had been done. I didn't approve of it, and I knew Hyzer'd be scalded. But you use whatever's handy. Anything that might make you think twice, and sit up straight and say yes, sir to the sher'f couldn't hurt anything. But it didn't work that way."

"Because we didn't have anything to do with Baither."

"It's begun to look that way."

"When can I leave this garden spot?"

"That'd be up to Mister Norm. One thing I want to know. Did you find Lew?"

"Not yet."

"I suppose that if Betsy phoned around and finally found him last night and asked him to come over, he might have come over to her place. That would give you a crack at him."

"Good idea. I didn't think to ask her. What made you think of it?"

"A crank call came in about eleven-thirty this morning. I just now put two and two together. No name given. Said he lives on Haydon Street. That's the street behind Seminole, where Betsy lives. Said that about three in the morning there was a big fuss, men yelling and cursing and a woman screaming, and if we couldn't keep order in a nice neighborhood, maybe the people ought to elect a sheriff who could."

"A little Saturday night festivity. Sorry, but I wasn't at that particular party."

"Any idea where Betsy is?"

"I'm expecting her to drop by pretty soon. I think she went shopping."

He got up slowly, stretched, flicked ashes on the motel rug. "So now I got to chase my ass all over the countryside today locating crazy Lew. Glad you didn't cut out, McGee."

I went to the doorway with him and let him get about three strides toward his sedan and said, "Billy, I don't know if it would clue you on where to look for him, but his mother told me she didn't think he'd have gotten in trouble if he hadn't started hanging around with trashy people named Perris."

He had turned and he looked at me for too long a time. Too many thoughts tumbling around in his head. His expression revealed nothing. Then, too casually, he said, "Might as well check that one out, too. Thanks."

Betsy Kapp arrived ten minutes later, with a big brown paper bag hugged against her. She was pallid and edgy, and eager to get inside and get the door closed.

"I saw the police car, darling, and I went right on by. I went by twice. Who was it? What did they want?"

I gave her the full story, including my final line, and told her how silent Billy Cable became. "Does the name mean anything to you, Betsy? Perris?"

"Somebody told me he was running around with Lilo Perris. She lives down in the south county. She's young, and she's pretty, I guess, in a cheap obvious way. But she's been in trouble with the law over and over. She's loud and mean and hard as nails."

"Sounds like a rare jewel. Sounds like somebody who would know something about how Lew got killed."

"I don't think so, really. She hasn't been in that kind of trouble. Mostly fighting and disturbing the peace and public obscenity. She's just wild and tough, and she doesn't give a damn what she does or who she does it with."

"Not the kind an officer of the law should run with."

"Heavens, no! But she wouldn't be exactly exclusive property. He'd be more like a dog in a pack trotting after a bitch. Men say she's so sexy. I just can't see it. Maybe he's been down in the south county, back there in one of those shacky places along Shell Ridge Road, down there with the poachers and moonshiners. Travis, what did that phone call mean?"

"If you and I were in the county jail at the time, trying to tell them we didn't know where Lew's body came from, how would it sound?"

"Terrible!"

"And what if an autopsy established the time of death at about three in the morning?"

"We've been lucky, haven't we?"

"So far."

"Are you starving too, dear? Look! Good rye bread and lettuce and Black Diamond cheese and sardines and baloney and cold beer. Do you want me to make your sandwich, or do you want to?"

I told her to go ahead. She used the white formica countertop next to the almost inaudible golf match. I had taken the first bite of my sandwich, not waiting for her to make her own, when Billy Cable knocked at the door.

I let him in. She gave him a bright smile of welcome. "Hi, Billy. Make you a sandwich?"

"Just now ate, Betsy. Thanks. Guess I might go for one of these kosher dills though." He bit it, nodded approval, and while chomping away at it, "Saw a car that looked like yours, and McGee said you were going to come by, so I stopped to make sure."

"Make sure of what?"

He sat on the bed. "My life is a lot easier if I can do what I know Mister Norm is going to ask me if I did already. So he is going to ask me if I asked you if maybe you give McGee here a line on how to find Lew."

"I wouldn't have the faintest idea how to find Lew Arnstead, and I can't imagine ever wanting to."

"But Mister McGee here seemed anxious to find him?"

"Well ... sort of. And I can understand that, can't you? After all, that man Lew hurt was a very good friend of Travis's. Wouldn't you look for somebody who beat up a friend of yours? Of course, maybe you don't have any friend in particular, Billy."

I saw the momentary narrowing of his eyes. And then he smiled blandly. "Then McGee was only half anxious to locate Lew?"

"That's about it."

"Speaking of my having a friend, Betsy, you've got a real talent for friendship, believe you me."

She turned and leaned her hips on the countertop and bit into her sardine sandwich. "Why, thank you, Billy!"

"I think old Homer ought to write you up in that new brochure he's doing for the Chamber of Commerce."

"How do you mean?"

"I don't rightly know. Maybe like sort of a natural resource of Cypress County. It isn't every little city back here in the swamp country that's got a nice dining room with good food and a hostess with the biggest set of knockers south of Waycross."

Her lips tightened and she held her sandwich out of the way and looked down at herself. "Now Billy. They's not so much of a much." Her accent was turning swampy. "Must be forty, fifty women around these parts wear a D-cup, too. Looks like a lot to you on account of the rest of me is on the skimpy side."

"Well, I guess there's enough men around here and there who'd testify they're real enough, Betsy."

This was a strong sexual antagonism coming out into the open. She colored, then smiled. "Oh, Billy Cable, I know you're only funnin' me, but when you try to kid around, honey, it comes out like dirty talk. You just don't have the touch. I *know* you don't mean anything wrong."

"It's nice the way you throw everything into your work, Miz Kapp. Obligin'."

She made a plausible attempt at merry laughter, and looked over at me and said, "Darlin', ol' Billy here could testify how real they are. Must have been a year and a half ago—"

"Watch it!" Billy said sharply.

"Now you started this, Billy, and Mr. McGee might be amused. I thought some sex maniac had got me. Like to scared me to death. I was walking from the Lodge over to my car on a dark night and got grabbed from behind. A girl friend told me one time the thing to do is go all limp and fall down, never try to fight. Well, I sat down on the parking lot and he let go, and I got a look at him, and what do you know, there was ol' Billy weaving and smiling down at me, just couldn't stop hisself from reaching around me and grabbing away like he was trying to honk those old-timey automobile horns. A girl could get a cancer that way. Well, sir, I was so scared and mad I hopped up and swang my pocketbook and knocked poor Billy's glasses right off and they busted. And that made *him* so mad, he took a swing like to slap my head loose, but I ducked back and Billy fell down. Then what was it you were going to do to me, Billy?"

"Knock it off, Betsy."

"Something about I should take him home with me or I

was going to get arrested for every kind of thing he could think of. What did I say, Billy?"

"Shut up, Betsy. I forget."

"I said I'd rather spend five years in a prison laundry than five minutes in bed with you. Billy?"

He looked at her and did not answer. She took two steps toward him, thrust her jaw toward him and said in a low voice, "And it's still exactly the same way, Deputy. There's nothing you could ever do or say that'd make me change my mind."

He stared at her and then at me. Expressionless mask-like face, but the eyes behind the lenses held a cold reptilian venom. He spun and left, slamming the room door, slamming the cruiser door, shrieking rubber halfway to the front exit onto the highway.

She ran to me and I held her in my arms. She was trembling and panting. Aftermath of another of the games Betsy played. But this game was obligatory. And, in its own way, valiant. Nothing but a cap pistol and a cheap whip between her and the tiger.

"I . . . I'm sorry it had to be in front of you, Travis."

"I understand."

"Do you? I can't ever let him get away with any part of it, anywhere, no matter what. If I ever do . . . then he'll take me, and I don't think I could stand it. It wouldn't be . . . nice."

That was the inevitable stipulation. Nice.

"Go eat your sandwich, woman."

She walked over and took it from the countertop and said, "He's going to hate you now because you heard it all."

"So I'm about to faint with pure terror."

She hoisted herself up and sat on the countertop, thin legs swinging, holding the sandwich in both hands, munching.

"What a crazy day," she said. "What a weird kind of day."

"Just wondering something. How did Billy Cable take it when you and Lew Arnstead got together?"

"Not so good. I told Lew about how Billy kept circling

me. He thought it was funny. I told him he better not make any smart remarks to Billy about the whole thing. Billy is chief deputy, and there are ways he could make things bad for Lew. They had it out, finally. Lew whipped him, but he didn't tell me any details."

Thick sandwiches and cold beer. She yawned deeply, her face softening, and her eyes suddenly heavy, an abrupt change like that of a sleepy child. She slumped onto the bed and slipped her shoes off and yawned again. "Honest, I've got to have a nap."

"You have permission."

She pulled the pillow out from under the spread and lay back. "We can go home later. I wish I could think. What you said about my knowing something and not knowing what I know. There *is* something, but I can't find it in my head."

"Try again when you wake up."

"Dear?"

"What?"

"Don't try to make love to me, huh? I haven't got anything with me. And . . . I might be too willing. That's sort of nasty, isn't it? After . . . what we had to do."

"It happens that way. The body wants to celebrate being alive when somebody else is dead. Anyway I'm going to leave you alone here for a while, Betsy."

Sleepy eyes opened wide. "No!"

"I'll hang the DO-NOT-DISTURB signs on both doors, and I'll lock you in. You'll be fine. I ought to be back by five-thirty or six."

"Where do you have to go?"

"Just an errand. Nothing crucial."

"Okay, so be careful, lover," she murmured. She was on her side, fists under her chin, knees pulled up. In moments she was making a small buzzing sound, with slow deep lift and fall of the narrow, overburdened rib cage. I closed the draperies to darken the room, and floated a blanket over her.

The phone made half a ring before I caught it. It did not disturb her.

It was Meyer. "I am free," he said. "Marked fit for duty. I am an object of awe and curiosity. My once-handsome face looks like a psychedelic beach ball. There are two gentle maidens here aboard my humble vessel, taking turns holding my hand and applying cold compresses and fixing me little taste treats. They say to say howdy. Shall I return?"

"Stay where you are. Enjoy."

"And how are things on the frontier?"

"Confusing. A fine young man had the taste to give Miss Agnes a lot of tender loving care, but I have to get a part for her out of Palm Beach before she can move."

"Would the man let you move?"

"No point in asking him until I get the part installed."

"What are you doing for excitement?"

"Mighty interesting golf match on television today."

"McGee, do not make childish attempts to mislead me. My brain was not damaged. When we left, you were down. You wanted no part of that brouhaha over there. Your voice dragged. Now there is a lift, a hint of a pleasurable urgency. You have become involved."

"Now that you mention it, I guess I have."

"Have you been able to pay my respects to Deputy Arnstead?"

"Not yet. He seems to be absent. Or shy. But I still have hopes."

"If the car was roadable, and Sheriff Hyzer said you could leave, would you?"

"Probably not."

"Have you come across an opportunity for some small salvage contract, perhaps?"

"One might turn up. Meyer, I'm glad you're okay."

"I share your gladness."

After the conversation ended, I looked at the screen. A very somber young man in orange garments was hunched over a putt. A knot of muscle bulged at the corner of his jaw. He stabbed at it, and the ball went by the hole on the high side and stopped inches away. The young man looked at the heavens with an expression of agonized desolation, of classic despair. I punched the set off while he was still on camera. I hung the signs, locked her in, and left.

THIRTEEN

BUTTERCUP CAME AT ME, RUNNING low and rumbling in anticipation of the clamp of his teeth in the flesh of the stranger. I squatted and held my hand out and said, "Easy, Buttercup. Easy, boy."

He braked to a stop, leaned, and took a delicate sniff, compared it with the memory banks, and looked dejected. Cora Arnstead came out onto the porch and said, "Who is it now? You home, Lew?"

"Sorry. It's Travis McGee again, Mrs. Arnstead."

"You got anything to tell me about my boy?"

"Sorry. I wish I could tell you something."

"That Billy Cable was here today looking for him, too. They fired my boy. No reason why I should fall all over myself helping them. If they want him, they can find him."

"How is the stock making out? Anything I can do?"

"That's nice of you to offer. But I've got the Silverstaff boy from up the road taking care. He was here most of the morning getting caught up. Come on the porch and set."

A haze had moved across the sun. She leaned back in the cane chair and widened her nostrils. "Smell that stink, do you?"

"Afraid not."

"Acidy smell. We get it now most times the breeze comes out of the northwest. Phosphate plants up that way. Wind from the south, and you get the county incinerator smell. Nobody gives a damn, Mr. McGee. They talk about it, but they don't really care enough to do anything. So one day people are going to grab their throats and fall down dead all over the state of Floryda, and I hope I'm safe dead and gone before it happens. What do you want with me?"

"Sheriff Hyzer is trying to locate Lew. Now if he doesn't find him pretty soon, he might come out here or send somebody out here to go through his room, looking for a clue."

"And?"

"He'll find that hiding place just the way I did. I didn't exactly give you an inventory of what's in there."

"Figured you didn't. Filthy stuff?"

"Some standard under-the-counter dirt, and some pretty vivid love notes from some of his women. And a collection of Polaroid pictures he took of a batch of his girl friends, all naked. They could cause some trouble in the wrong hands."

"Like if Billy Cable got ahold of them?"

"That's right, Mrs. Arnstead."

"You said he had a lot of those speed pills in there. Would there be maybe enough so he could get into trouble on that account, too?"

"More than enough. They come under the narcotics legislation."

She glowered into space for a long ten seconds. "I don't hold with lying, Mr. McGee. I wouldn't want anybody to come here and find that place of his and find it empty and ask me if I'd let anybody into that room to take stuff away. And if they asked me if I emptied it out and asked me what was in there, I'd have to tell what I took out. No, sir, I can't let you go in my boy's room and take away

his personal private stuff and get rid of it any way you see
fit. I can't give you permission. Maybe you'd be so kind,
Mr. McGee, as to go on in the house and back to the
kitchen and get me a glass of water. Best let it run a long
time for coolness."

While the water was running, I emptied the cache.
Pictures and letters inside one of the books. Books and
pamphlets tucked into the front of my shirt. Pills in the
trouser pocket.

I took her the glass of water. She sipped and thanked
me.

"You come back and visit with me sometime, hear?
Sorry I couldn't give you the right to tote off Lew's
things."

"I understand."

"Somehow I have this feeling my youngest isn't going to
come back, not ever. I don't know why. An old woman's
notion. He was a good little boy. He really was. He always
liked to play by himself. Not much for running with the
pack. It was the Army changed him. He wasn't the same
after that."

It was uncomfortable booty to carry around. If Hyzer
had me picked up for some idiot reason, the list of charges
would be fascinating. In the milky fading light of late
afternoon I drove north, further out Cattleman's Road
into an area of bigger ranches and grove lands. It had
been a sentimental mission. After seeing the scene between
Billy and Betsy, there was no mistaking the use he would
make of Lew's artwork, or the amount of leverage possession would give him. There was the second objective of
sparing the old lady any additional pain. The final chick
was dead. Whether she ever learned that or not, never
seeing him again was enough of a hurt.

I came up on an unpaved road, braked and turned
right, and found an adequate place a mile from the highway, a small grove of live oaks heavily fringed with
Spanish moss, and a place to drive in where fencing had
rotted way. I gouged a deep hole in the soft dirt with a

stick, dumped the pills in, covered them, and stomped the earth flat.

His meager and unusual little library would not be easy to burn. I crackled my shoulder muscles rolling a log over, scooped a shallow hole and laid the books therein and rolled the log back into the earth-groove it had made when it fell.

I sat on it with the correspondence and the picture gallery. I remembered my previous impression of the many pictures of Betsy Kapp. Lean, anemic blonde with an insipid leer and comedy breasts. So the leer became a troubled and uncertain smile, and the breasts were oddly wistful, vulnerable. I decided that in some eerie way it was like those ubiquitous photographs of small boys holding up big fish they have caught. Too much camera direction makes them look uncertain. They ache to look like heroes and do not know how to manage it. And the long-dead fish has become a dead weight of reality, and there is no way to hold him to make him look alive.

I used one to light the next until all the shots of Betsy were charred. All ten of them. Then the five of the woman who had been so careful to hide her face. Then the extra three of the night-runner who had to be Lilo. I saved the thirteen trophy shots, the head-on singles. I went through the correspondence and burned it all—except Betsy's long letter of warning about Lilo.

All the photographs and the letter fit nicely into the same pocket in the double thickness of canvas by the rear window. I spread them out so that there was no bulge when I zipped it shut. The thought of how Billy Cable might use the pictures of Betsy gave me the idea of possible leverage, for quite different objectives. I had studied the faces. Lilo and the Unknown Thirteen. The odds were that most or all were in Cypress County on this final Sunday in April. Clerking, waitressing, dating, tending babies, fixing dinner, ironing shirts, dancing, watching television. Lew's little garden of ladies. There might be a certain amount of gratitude involved were a lady to get her trophy shot back, and be scratched off

Lew's local scorecard. So keep looking at the ladies, McGee. A fellow blundering around in the murk needs the loan of any thirty-nine-cent flashlight available.

The last thread of daylight was about gone as I turned into the parking area of the White Ibis. The little tan VW was gone, and my throat turned sour, and my neck-nape and hands prickled with that million-year-old reflex which tries to lift the coarse animal hair, to make the animal look bigger, more awesome, more difficult to chew. It was sick premonition. Too many old memories of mistake and remorse.

Unlocked the door, flicked the switch, saw the blanket shoved aside, the depression in the bedspread, the shape of the length of her in heavy sleep, the dented pillow.

Her note on the motel paper was on the carpeting, with an ashtray paperweight, in a conspicuous spot.

Lover darling,

I woke up and got thinking about that you-know-what in my car, and getting nervous about it and then not feeding poor Raoul and leaving him alone so long what I decided was put that thing back where it was like you said and feed Raoul and then go find out about that thing I couldn't remember before, which maybe hasn't got a thing to do with anything. And I decided while it is still light I can take a quick sneaky look and see if the jeep is still there in that yard behind the bushes but I hope it is gone and we don't have to think about it at all only about us alone together in my little house with all the world shut out, so what you can do is change your clothes like you never got a chance to and bring your shaving things and all and if you get there before I get back the extra key to the side door is where you go into the carport and reach around in back of the first can of paint on the top shelf the one to your left when you walk in but if my car is in there then you can just knock and if you are lucky I may even decide to let you in and feed you and all that.

Love ya!
Yr Betsy.

Very sweet and innocent and diligent, and very stupid, leaving a note with too many things in it to interest, for example, Billy Cable, if he should have taken a turn by the place, seen both cars gone, and decided to take a look. Motels have master keys, and local law has a conspicuous talent for collecting copies of same, because it is a lot less fuss than court orders and warrants and negotiations with management.

So I confettied it and flushed it down, took my fast shower and changed, whipped out of there with toilet kit and sweaty hands, and drove to her place on Seminole Street, making one wrong turn before I found it, because the only other time I had driven to it had been at night, following her.

When I turned into the narrow, high-hedged drive, I felt a sense of relief at seeing lights on inside the cottage, but the feeling clicked off when my lights swung to the empty carport. I put the white Buick at the side of the carport, this time with the top up, in the same spot as it had been when someone had tumbled the big ugly souvenir into it.

I stood in the night, listening, and felt my nostrils widen. Another atavistic reflex, snuff the air for the drifting taint of the stalking carnivore, long after the noses have lost their sensitivity and cunning. Heart bumping under the stimulus of adrenalin, readying the muscles, blood, brain, for that explosive effort necessary for survival in a jungle of predators.

But it was just a side yard of a very small residential plot in a peaceful neighborhood of a small southern city. A neighborhood of postal clerks, retired military, food store managers, bank tellers, watching the fare that came into their living rooms over the cable, checking the *TV Guide* during the rerun season to see if there was a "Bonanza" they had missed, or a "Mission Impossible."

The blood slowed, and I found the carport light switch, found the key in the place she'd described, and had time to get to the house corner and get a glimpse of the handle laying next to the supporting jack before the delay switch clicked the light off. In the darkness I squatted and reached under the house, felt and hefted the pipe handle to make certain. And in the darkness I went out to the sidewalk and kept to the shadows, went to the yard she had described, ducked under the chain and saw the dark, insectile angularity of the jeep parked there, nuzzling into the untended plantings.

I went back and let myself in. One lamp lighted in the living room, lacy shade on a brass post that impaled a shiny black merry-go-round horse. I trod a narrow route between fragilities and knick-knacks to the kitchen where the fluorescent light over the stove was on. Some crumbs of cat food in the dish in Raoul's corner. I bent and touched one. It was moist instead of being dried to the dish, so she had fed Raoul.

Next I went to her bedroom, found the wall switch. The blouse and skirt she had been wearing were on the foot of the bed. Raoul, curled upon the skirt, lifted his head and looked at me with the benign satisfaction of the full stomach and the comfortable place to sleep. There were water droplets on the inside of her shower curtain and the tiled walls. There was the scent of sweet soap and perfume and deodorant and hair spray, a damp towel spread on the rack, one misted corner at the top of the full-length mirror on the inside of the door.

I sat on the bed and rubbed Raoul's sleepy head and got his gritty, audible engine going. A puzzlement that she should be so full of nervous alarm, so anxious not to be alone, and then go out alone to find out God knows what. I finally realized that it had to be another one of the games that Betsy could play. A new script patterned on the late late movies, suspense, perhaps, with elegant quips and handsome sets, and she was maybe Myrna Loy tracing down one of those fragments of female intuition which would clear up the case which had William Powell baffled. And that, of course, made it all perfectly safe, because if somebody started to really hurt anybody, the Great Director would yell "Cut!" and we would go back to our dressing rooms and wait for the next call.

Eight o'clock. Nine o'clock. Ten o'clock, and that was all I could manage to endure. Locked up and left there and drove down to the complex of county buildings and services and went into the Sheriff's Department. A pair of strangers behind the high desk, cool, disinterested young men in fitted uniforms, busy with forms and routines, busy with the paperwork of booking Sunday drunks, brawlers, DWI's, a couple of fourteen-year-old burglars. The communications clerk finally sent word that I might find the sheriff over at the Emergency Room at City Memorial, and one of the busy young men told me how to find it.

I parked in the hospital lot and walked back to Emergency. Some bloody, broken, moaning teen-agers were being offloaded from a white ambulance with blue dome lights, and wheeled through the double doors into a corridor glare of fluorescence so strong and white it made the blood look black.

I saw a county cruiser parked over at the side, interior lights on, a shadowed figure behind the wheel. So I walked over to ask him if Hyzer was inside the building. But from ten feet I saw that it was Hyzer himself. He looked up from his clipboard and said, "Good evening, Mr. McGee."

"Sheriff. They told me I might catch you over here."

"What can I do for you?"

"I'd like to have a chance to talk to you. Maybe ask some questions. Can you give me fifteen minutes or so?"

"If you come to my office before nine tomorrow . . ."

"It would be better right now, I think."

"What's it about?"

"Baither, Arnstead, Perris."

"You were very insistent about not being involved in the Baither matter in any way. Do you want to change your story?"

"No. But things come up which puzzle me, Sheriff. If we talked them out, it might be of some help to you, and you might let me leave that much sooner."

"I can't see how you could be of any help to me."

"When you find Lew Arnstead, if you haven't already, get him checked for stimulants. He's a speed freak. When they go over the edge, the condition is called paranoid psychosis, and it would be more comfortable to be around a kid playing with dynamite caps."

"Result of an amateur investigation, McGee?"

"I wanted to find him and scuff him up, and I turned up a few things while I was looking for him, and I decided there was no point in being emotional about what he did to Meyer—who, incidentally, is all right."

"I know. I made inquiry."

"Then I keep wondering how Henry Perris fits into the Baither killing, and what the association was between Perris and Arnstead. And right now Mrs. Betsy Kapp seems to be missing, and my amateur investigator guess says that she's gotten herself into the middle somehow, where it wouldn't seem to be a healthy climate."

The stern hero face looked up at me from under the pale brim of the expensive hat. "Come around the car and get in, Mr. McGee."

When I was in, he put the clipboard on the seat between us, unhooked his mike, and told his people he was leaving the hospital and would call in from his next stop.

"There'll be too many interruptions if we go in," he said. "How about your motel room?"

I drove over in the Buick. He was waiting and as I unlocked the door to 114, he said he had told them where to reach him.

He sat in the armchair, put his hat carefully on the floor beside the chair. I moved over and sat on the countertop where Betsy had sat, eating her sardine sandwich.

"I had a report from Deputy Cable," he said. "So I know you went and talked to Cora Arnstead. I had a report of your conversation with Deputy Sturnevan. I know you spent the night with Mrs. Kapp at her home on Seminole. I was glad to hear you had not left the county. If you had, you would have regretted it. My responsibility is to enforce the enforceable laws and ordinances. Deputy Cable suggested to me that Mrs. Kapp be picked up and charged with public fornication. There is an old ordinance on the books. I have not been able to understand why Billy would want to waste department time on that sort of thing. He is usually a more reasonable officer. I do not wish to make any moral judgments about Mrs. Kapp. She has always seemed to me to be a pleasant enough woman, and she seems to run that dining room well. She would seem to be ... selective and circumspect in her private life."

"Billy Cable went after her a year and a half ago. He'd had a few drinks. She turned him down flat. Last fall she had an affair with Lew Arnstead."

"I knew about the Arnstead affair. How could you know about Billy? How do you know it's true? He has a wife and three children."

"They had a very rough little scene right here in this room this afternoon. Billy asked for bad news, and she gave it to him."

"So at five o'clock he makes that stupid suggestion about arresting her. I'll check it out. I don't like it. An officer should not use his position for personal vendettas. I'm disappointed in Billy Cable. You say Mrs. Kapp is missing. Tell me about it."

"She was here most of the afternoon. Then she went in her car back to her house. I was supposed to meet her there. She knew I'd be over about seven. I went over and she wasn't there. She'd told me where the key was. I let myself in. She left a note telling me she was going out to find out something about this ... whole problem which got me into one of your cells, Sheriff."

"Find out what?"

"She didn't say. I waited until ten o'clock and then I came looking for you."

He went over and sat on the bed and looked up her phone number and dialed it. While it was ringing at the other end, I had a closer look at him under the light of the bedside lamp. His dark suit was wrinkled, his shoes unshined. His knuckles and wrists were soiled, and there was an edge of grime around his white cuffs and around the white collar of his shirt. The light slanted on a dark stubble on his chin. It did not match my prior observations of the fastidious officer of the law.

"No answer," he said as he stood up. He went back to the chair and looked at his watch. "Ten past eleven.

Maybe, Mr. McGee, she decided not to see you again. Maybe she went to stay with friends, waiting for you to give up and go away."

"Not a chance."

"Where is the note?"

"I threw it away. I assure you it was . . . affectionate."

"You told Mrs. Kapp all about the reason why you and your friend were suspected of being in on the Baither murder?"

"Sheriff, she lives here and she works here. She knows a lot of people. I told her everything I know, including your theory about the money truck, and Baither using Raiford State Prison as a hideout. And I built a little structure of supposition, based on little hints, guesses, inferences. I haven't tested it on Betsy yet. I planned to. One way to go at these things is to build a plausible structure, then find facts that won't fit and tear it down and try again."

He looked at me through a steeple of soiled fingers. "Let me hear it."

"Baither put it together. He used two outsiders, pickup talent, possibly from out of state. He had the contacts, apparently. The fourth man was local, and without a record, gainfully employed. Henry Perris, now working as a mechanic down at Al Storey's station on the Trail. The other two men we know only as Hutch and Orville. Baither needed Henry Perris because Henry had access to a wrecker and knew how to operate it. They also used Perris's stepdaughter, Lillian. She was the young waitress in the blond wig at the drive-in across from the track."

"Pure fantasy!"

"May I go ahead? Thanks. After a big score, the people involved watch each other very carefully. I don't think Frank could have slipped away with the money unless Henry and the girl helped him somehow. This would be the deal. Frank would hide the money and take a fall at Raiford. Henry and the girl would sit tight and wait it out. Frank wouldn't let Henry know where the money was because he would be afraid of another doublecross. A three-way split, if you count the girl, would be a lot better than five ways."

"Why Perris?"

"Because Lilo Perris and Lew Arnstead were or are paired off. It started several months back, and with Baither up for release, it would be good sense to have a pipeline into your department, Sheriff. She's apparently a very rough kid. Then you have Henry Perris in a position to pick my envelope out of the trash at the station, and you have Lilo ready and willing to decoy Arnstead into that shack in back of the place. But it was a bad impulse. People get bad, tricky ideas when something has gone wrong. They get nervous and they don't think things out. Manufactured evidence backfires. So Perris and company was suddenly up against the very dangerous situation of having vital and damaging information lodged in the mind of a speed freak. If you went after the name of the woman who decoyed Arnstead into Baither's shed, you could probably shake it loose. And to have it be the stepdaughter of the mechanic at the station where I swear I discarded that envelope makes everything a little too tight. Have you located Lew?"

"Not yet."

"There's a chance, a reasonable chance, that they had brought Lew all the way into the picture. Maybe they needed the kind of help he could give them. Nine hundred thousand is a lot of persuasion. The girl could make certain he wouldn't be thinking clearly. The girl and the amphetamine, and something a little warped in his mind before he even started downhill. If they did, what's your chance of finding him alive?"

"Facts will tear down your structure, McGee."

"If you have them."

"There were three men working at that station all day Friday. Albert Storey, Henry Perris, and Terrance Moon. They submitted to interrogation willingly. There was a period of about two hours and fifteen minutes, starting at the time we drove away with you and your friend, when their actions are important. None of them left the station at that time. No phone calls were made. They were interrogated separately. The customers who stopped during that period were strangers—tourists and commercial traffic on the Tamiami Trail. The men talked about Frank Baither being killed to each other, but not to anyone else. I am left with the remarkable coincidence of someone unknown to those men stopping for gas, seeing that envelope in the trash barrel, picking it out and taking it up to Baither's house to leave it where we found it later."

"And you can't buy that and neither can I."

"Then you dropped it in Baither's place."

"You know I didn't."

"What choice do I have, McGee? And, of course, your evaluation of Lillian Perris is total nonsense." There was a force in his voice, an animation in his face which surprised me. "The girl has a lot of spirit. She should have had a lot more discipline. She's been in scrapes, but nothing serious. Considering the environmental and social factors, I think she has done remarkably well."

"I was only—"

"Forget any idea of her having any part of it."

"Okay. And Henry Perris is a pillar of the community and a lay preacher?"

"All I know is that he has no record."

"Let's concentrate on Henry for a minute, Sheriff. Just for the hell of it. Let's say he was in on the Baither murder, and it went wrong and he was shaky. He comes to work late. He gets our names and the reason we're being picked up from Al Storey. He goes to put something in the barrel and sees the envelope with my name on it and he picks it out when nobody is looking and puts it in his pocket."

"But I told you that—"

"I *know* what you told me. He had to leave that station soon after we left."

"But he didn't."

The message on his face was clear: Don't pursue further.

"What could Betsy Kapp have remembered that got her into trouble?" I asked.

"*If* she's in trouble."

"Are you going to look for her?"

"Missing persons reports have to be filed by the next of kin."

"I don't think you always go by the book, Sheriff."

He smiled for the first time. "If I did, I would have you back inside, McGee."

He phoned Betsy's house again, with no results. He looked troubled. "I'll put the word out."

"Thanks, Sheriff." I walked him out to the car and asked him if he minded if I looked around.

"Inside the county, Mr. McGee."

"Of course, Sheriff."

So I began my blind quest, because anything was better than going back to her empty house to sit and wait.

FOURTEEN

CRUISE THE AFTER-MIDNIGHT STREETS of the sleepy city, checking the lots, and driveways, the on-street parking for the distinctive shape of the VW bug. Hard to tell gray from tan under the street lamps. Then remembered the thing she had affixed to her radio antenna, handy way to find the car in the jammed-tin wasteland of the shopping center parking rows—a plastic sunflower, big as a saucer. Easier to eliminate the look-alike VWs.

Stopped once in a while at the bright upright coffin of a pay phone, listened to ten rings, got the same dime back every time. Aware finally of hunger pangs, and I turned back to a place where I had seen the all-night drive-in. No car service after eleven. Very bright inside. Big table of teen-agers, whispering and haw-hawing at delicious private nonsense, making a point of excluding the square grown-up world from all of it. A few night-people spaced along the counter. Plastic radio with a burr in the speaker playing muted rock.

The waitress was a plump, pretty girl, hair bleached to a coarse pure white and hanging lifelessly straight. Blue nylon uniform. DORI embossed on the name tag. A smudge of tiredness around her eyes. Mechanical smile, presentation of the grease-spotted bill of fare.

Here they called them a MaxiBurger, and they came on a toasted bun with caraway seeds. Very little taste to the hot meat. Bits of gristle. Much better coffee than I expected. Munched the meat, sipped the coffee, wondered why the girl looked so familiar.

Had paid, left, started the motor before I realized why she might look familiar. Got out the Polaroid shots, sorted them under the interior lights, located Dori. Different hair style. Same face. Same plumpness. Startled expression, one hand blurred by movement.

I replaced the other pictures, put hers in my pocket and went back inside. She came over with the mechanical smile and the menu and then realized I looked too familiar.

"Oh, you were just in, werncha?"

"Decided on another cup of coffee."

"Well, I'll forget you went out and come back, so you get the seconds free anyways."

She brought it and I said, "Thank you, Dori. When you've got a minute, I want to ask you something."

"I got a minute right now. Like what?"

I slipped the picture out and held it low so that only she could see it. I watched her face. She swallowed and bit her underlip and looked warily toward the other girl. She leaned toward me and said, "Look, this is some kind of a mixup. Put that away, huh? He must have got confused or something, honest. He was supposed to have tore those up, mister. Go find him and tell him Dori said he should ought to be more careful."

"He didn't seem to be confused."

"What kind of a car you got?"

"White Buick convertible."

"Look, you drink your coffee and go sit in it and wait, and I got a break coming, I'll come out and explain. Okay?"

In a little while Dori came walking quickly across the blacktop, the white lights strong behind her, yellow cardigan around her shoulders. Yellow straw purse in her hand. I leaned and swung the door open for her. She tugged it shut, pushed the dash lighter in and got her cigarettes out of her purse.

"It would have to be some kind of foulup, because it was always part of the deal he checks with me first, for obvious reasons. And he wouldn't let go of a picture. That's kind of rotten. And what he always did was tell me where to be and when, instead of sending somebody to where I'm working. Way back we made the deal, and I told him then that okay, so I was in a box, I'd go along with it, but only until my husbin got back from the service and then I couldn't take any kind of chance like that. So Fred got back seven months ago and I was nervous about if the deal would stand. But it did. Look, mister. Six weeks ago, maybe two months ago, a guy came in by accident and I'd had a date with him over a year ago, and he is a little bit smashed and thinks he can get fixed up right now. He started to get loud and so I got hold of Lew and he came by and took the fella out into the parking lot and bounced him up and down some and he went away. So it looks to me like something is going on I don't like. Now you tell me how you got that picture and what it is you've got in mind."

"Did you know he was fired?"

"I heard about it. For beating up a prisoner and for goofing off when he was supposed to be watching the house where Frank Baither got killed. I thought maybe he'd come in but he hasn't."

"Nobody has seen him, Dori. There's a pretty good chance he's dead."

She sucked the final half inch of cigarette down to the long filter, the red glow illuminating her small frown, her hollowed cheek. "Something was going bad for him. He was getting so jumpy he looked flippy almost. I cry no single tear, baby. That was the meanest son of a bitch I ever knew or ever want to know. When I know Lew is surely dead, I'll sleep a little better. Anyway ... who *are* you? Some kind of a cop?"

There was new anxiety in her voice. "Not exactly. I was picked up with a good friend of mine, the one Lew pounded. It looked like we knew something about the Baither murder but we didn't and they let us go, but I have to stay in the county. I let it be known I wanted to find Arnstead and beat on him. Now I'm worried about how I'm going to make out if they find him in a field or behind a warehouse tomorrow, beaten to death."

"They could make out a long list, mister."

"You don't blame me for trying to protect myself?"

"Not if you don't get me involved."

"I happen to have a little picture gallery that belonged to Lew. Never mind how or where I got hold of it. You looked familiar so I came out and looked at the pretty pictures and found yours."

"Just don't get me involved."

"Dori, put yourself in my shoes. Suppose he is dead and Hyzer tries to make me for it. The only thing I *can* do is spread out my picture collection and tell him to check it out. He'll find out that Lew had this sideline going, and probably as long as he was an officer of the law, nobody wanted to take the chance of putting him out of business. But he lost his immunity with his job. So check out all the husbands and all the boyfriends. Why should I leave you off the list?"

"I swear to God, cross my heart and hope to die, Fred hasn't any idea at all what went on. I love the guy. It would kill him, it really would. And he might kill me. He's got a terrible temper. Give me the picture, please.

Don't you have enough without me? How many have you got? I always wondered how many there were of us."

"Fourteen, counting you."

"Jesus! I was thinking six or seven. Don't you have enough to make your point without me in there? I swear, he hasn't tried to set me up one time since Fred got back, and that's been seven months. What's your name, anyway?"

"Travis McGee."

"Trav, be nice. Please!" She looked toward the restaurant. "I've got to get back before Carolyn gets really scalded."

"When do you get off?"

"I've been on since five. I get off at two."

"Does your husband pick you up?"

"That's my wheels over there on the back corner."

"Can you come over to the White Ibis when you get off?"

A snort of disgusted laughter. "Oh, boy. The same old crap. Be nice to me, baby, and I'll be nice to you. I must lead some kind of charmed life. Every time old Dori gets boxed in."

"Just talk. I want to get an I.D. on as many of the pictures as I can. I want to know how it operated. Can you do it?"

She looked at me, skepticism in the tilt of the silhouetted head. "I guess. Fred will be asleep on account of he has to get up at six to go to work. I hate this shift every time I pull it. I try to sneak in without waking him up, and he tries to sneak out in the morning without waking me up. Then when he gets off work he comes and eats here and leaves me the wheels and walks home. What's your room number?" I told her and started to explain where it was. She stopped me. "I know the layout. I've been there before. I just didn't expect to have to go back again."

She trotted back and went inside. Through the expanse of glass I saw her, sweater off, standing talking to the other girl, shrugging and gesticulating.

I had something better than forty-five minutes to continue the dogged search for the plastic sunflower. I tried her number again. Nobody heard the ringing except Raoul.

As I drove I thought of what I had said to Hyzer, about facts toppling structures built of supposition. You want facts to simplify and clarify. But this one I had stumbled on merely deepened the murk. What I had thought were trophy shots were in truth a salesman's sample case. Pick your pleasure, sir.

It is a useful and profitable sideline practiced by venal, underpaid, crooked police officers in every urban area of the nation and the world where police administration leaves enough room for improvisation. A certain number of females are always going to get into trouble with the law. A certain percentage of them are always going to be physically attractive. The investigating officer can make a deal that is mutually advantageous. Play ball or face a conviction, honey. The procurer cop has advantages denied the free-lance pimp. He can more safely strong-arm the unruly customer. He can protect his string from arrest, and at the same time keep them in line with the threat of arrest. If he is careful in his selection, they will never fink on him because they, in turn, have too much to lose by any public exposure of the relationship. And he has a handy source of special favors for politicians and administrators. Tonight, sweetie, you got a date with Judge O'Harran. Here's the address. He'll be looking for you about eight o'clock. This one is a freeby.

It was a big-city sickness I had not expected to come across in a small city in the central flatlands of Florida. And it puzzled me that Deputy Arnstead could operate his string right under the cool nose of a man as diligent and professional and subtle as Norman Hyzer. And it bothered me that Betsy Kapp had been in the sample kit. Maybe a very useful talent was fading, my ability to sense what people were after—what made them struggle and what made them give up. That talent had kept me alive a few times when the odds were against it. And I could think of no game Betsy could play which would enable her to turn a little hustling into some kind of romantic dramatics, into a sentimental eccentricity.

I was waiting when Dori parked. When I opened the door for her, she came scuttling in, furtive until the door was closed and she had tugged the center gap in the opaque draperies shut. Then she was at her ease. Saw that all I had was gin and Scotch, said gin and Coke would be fine if I could get some Coke, so I got a bottle out of the machine when I went to get more ice.

She wanted to talk. She was all full of her plump and pretty animation, bouncing around in the chair, gulping at her drink, sucking her cigarettes, brief skirt of the waitress uniform at midthigh, exposing the fine skin texture of her pretty legs. Lots of gestures and animation. She had been aching for a chance to tell somebody about the enormous, heartbreaking tragedy which had befallen poor Mrs. Fred Severiss, and had no idea that it was a drab, tiresome and ordinary little story, because she knew it had happened to her, and she could not feel commonplace, nor can anyone in their unique little time around the track.

She had always been "fantastically stupid" about money, and she had been a salesgirl at Garnor's Boutique at the Woodsgate Shopping Center, and Fred was far away and she missed him and she had this thing about buying clothes and shoes to cheer herself up, and she had charge cards, and besides she had this "wonderful crazy girl friend" and they would go whipping over to the east coast and go to the dog tracks, and she was absolutely true to her Fred etc., etc. So she got in a terrible money jam, and the credit people started getting very ugly, and she missed car payments and she didn't know what she would do if she lost the car, because how would she explain it to Freddie? So she had eighty dollars and she and her girl friend had gone over to the dog track and she thought that if she could build it into three or four hundred she could get out of the jam, but she lost it all and fifteen dollars more she borrowed from her girl friend. Then she started clipping the cash sales at the Boutique, saving the halves of the inventory tickets, thinking of it as "just sort of a loan, actually, on account of I was going to live quiet as mice and pay it back before Mrs. Garnor took inventory May first. That was the season before last." Then Arnstead had showed up at night at her little studio apartment, and it was the first she knew that the thieving had been detected, and Mrs. Garnor had asked the law to find out which of the five clerks was doing it. She had tried to deny it and Arnstead had broken her in about five minutes, and she had, at his direction, written her confession about it being a little over six hundred dollars taken over the seven weeks. Then he said he would take her in and bail would probably be about five hundred, and the least she could expect for grand larceny would be eighteen months in the state prison for women. Blubbering and begging and pleading for mercy had done no good. And when she was in total despair, he had given her the little hint that she was so pretty that maybe he could delay it, see what he could do, and she had lunged at that like a starving bass, taken him into the narrow Bahama bed, telling herself it wasn't like cheating on Fred actually, because what she was really doing was saving their lives and their marriage from absolute wreckage, and she had vowed "to just be a thing, and go through the motions with my mind a thousand miles away." But the deputy had kept seeing her and he was persistent and she had been alone for months and months, and couldn't help herself really, and got so she responded to him, and got to "needing him in a crazy way even though I didn't like him." Then he wanted her to be nice to a friend, and they had a terrible battle about it, and by then, of course, he had taken some pictures of her, and had the confession which he said was good for seven years, and he could mail a picture and a xerox of her confession to dear Freddie if that was the way she wanted it. So she had slept with his friend in a motel over in Everglades City a couple of times, and then there had been others, and Lew would bring her fifty dollars, or twenty, or seventy-five, depending. And once, a year ago last July, he'd sent three of them to Naples and they'd gone cruising for four days on a big company boat with a hired captain and three sort of vice-president-type people, and that time it had been a hundred twenty-five from Lew and fifty that the man she was with had put in her purse like a bonus or something. She knew there were other girls, and she had only run into three of them altogether, the two others on the cruise, and one on a kind of double date right here in this motel.

She counted, frowning, on her fingers and said that it had all lasted maybe fifteen months, and she could not remember the number of affairs, or the amount of money. Maybe twenty or twenty-five dates. Lew promised it would end when Fred came home. She had finally realized that Lew knew he could control her, but Fred was something else. Fred would try to kill him and would surely kill her. She'd been terrified that Lew wouldn't keep his promise, and she'd been terrified that Fred would somehow be able to tell what she'd been up to, but it had worked out all right.

By then she had worked her way through the second gin and Coke. She was flushed and her articulation was not quite as distinct.

"I'm just damn lucky I got out of it, Trav. I'm just lucky it's over. I keep telling myself that. But it's funny . . . I don't know. I'm different somehow. I mean I feel I'm sort of faking the happy little wife bit. One time I got to fussing at Lew until he got sore and grabbed my neck and shoved me over to a mirror and hurt my arm and made me look into my eyes and say dirty things about myself. Things like: 'I'm a whore. I peddle my ass. I bang for a living.' Things aren't like what you always think they're like, I guess. It's not real different from dates, where if the guy is sweet and fun you have a good time, and if it's some old fat guy, you just get it over with. I don't know. Sometimes I think of standing on my feet in that place and how long it takes to make fifty, and how long it took to make fifty on my back. Fred is a great guy, really. I think that maybe somebody will come in and look at me and say let's go, baby, and I'll get in his car and never come back."

She lifted her wrist and peered at her little watch. She shifted in the chair, ran her tongue along her lips, took a deep shuddering breath. In a huskier tone she said, "Like now. If you should want it, honey. Like on the house."

"Let's look at the pictures."

She came out of her sensual glaze. "Oh, sure. Jesus! I don't know what's wrong with me lately, I really don't. Yeh, let's look at them and then I got to get going because Fred could wake up and get worried and wonder what the hell and phone the place and find out I've been gone forever."

I laid the pictures out on the countertop under the lamp, one at a time. She came and stood beside me. Thirteen of them.

"That's Donna Lee something. She was on that cruise. She's a real fun kid, real lively, and she's got a real cute body as any fool can plainly see. She works in a real estate office. Up over the bank. Associated Realtors, Inc. No, I don't know *this* one at all. I don't remember ever seeing her around town anyplace. I *have* seen this girl somewhere. Let me think. I think she works in the courthouse. I'm pretty sure. *This* one I know. Sort of. Her name is Brenda Dennis? Dennison? Denderson? A name like that. She was on the double date with me. She's sort of quiet and hard to know, and she isn't built very good, is she? She works at Elian's Stationery, but I haven't been in there in so long I don't know if she's still there. I've seen *this* girl someplace I think, but I don't know where. This one is older, huh? I never saw her before as far as I know."

When I turned the seventh picture she gasped and said, "Holy Maloney! It *can't* be! This is Miss Kimmey, for God's sake. She teaches third grade and sings in the choir at our church. She's got a real nice soprano voice. The kind of clothes she wears, you'd never guess what a great body she's got. Now how in the world did Lew ever nail her? Boy, would I like to find out."

She drew another blank on number eight. But she knew number nine. "That's Linda Featherman. I nearly dropped my teeth when she turned out to be number three on that cruise. I mean there's lots of money there. Big ranchlands and grovelands in the northeast part of the county. At first I thought she was going to spoil that cruise by acting as if she was so much better than Donna Lee and me. It was her car we went to Naples in, and she drove and hardly said a word all the way. She took darling cruise clothes along, worth like a fortune. But then she was okay after the first day, a lot more human. Poor gal, I couldn't believe it when I read about it."

"About what?"

"She got killed a little while ago. Let me count back. Two weekends ago, I think. The state police said she had to be going at least a hundred miles an hour, heading back out to the ranch at three or four in the morning, about fifteen miles north of here, and they said she probably fell asleep because there weren't any skid marks. She just went right off a curve in a straight line and right into an enormous pine tree and broke it right off and hit the next one sideways. They say it took hours to identify her for sure."

Number ten was one Jeanie Dahl, and on seeing the picture she remembered Lew saying that Jeanie was in the club. She and Jeanie had both been in the Miss Cypress City contest when they were in high school, and Jeanie had been second runner-up and Dori had been third runner-up. Jeanie had been married and divorced, and lived with her mother who took care of her little kid while Jeanie worked in the office at Kramer Building Supply.

Eleven was an unknown. Twelve was somebody she thought she had seen often around town, but had no idea where.

I had adjusted them to leave Lillian (Lilo) Hatch (Perris) until last. She actually recoiled from the picture, and made a little coughing, gagging sound and turned away.

"What's the matter?"

"Her name is Lilo Perris. I don't want to talk about her."

"Why not?"

"Give me a minute. Fix me a drink. That made me go cold all over. That girl is crazy. I mean for real crazy. That girl is a maniac."

I made her the third drink. She was back in the chair. When she settled down she told me.

"It was about the fourth time Lew sent me to meet somebody. He was a spook. He wanted things I didn't want to do. So I wouldn't. He got mad and I got mad and it broke up fast and I went home. I was waiting for Lew to come around so I could tell him not to send me to spooks like that. He sent Lilo to see me. That girl is crazy! She hurt me so bad I fainted, I don't know how many times. After she went away I kept throwing up. I was so weak I stayed in bed two days. Then Lew came around and said the spook was a very important man in Tallahassee, and I was going to have another date with him. He said if I didn't want to make the spook happy, he'd have Lilo come to visit me again. I think I would really rather die than have her start doing things to me again, smiling at me and giggling and calling me love names and saying how much fun it would be to really kill me. She's as strong as a man, and she knows every way there is to hurt a girl. She's absolutely insane, Trav."

"How long ago was this?"

"Maybe . . . a year ago last June. Look at me. Look at the goose bumps on my arms and legs just thinking about her. I used to get nightmares about her and wake up bellering and twitching around."

"Do you know of anybody else who was in on it, where I don't have a picture here?"

"Gee, I don't think so. I can't think of anybody."

"Possibly Mrs. Betsy Kapp?"

"In the dining room at the Lodge. The old blonde with the huge boobs. No, and I can tell you why I'm so sure, even." She started to say something, then closed her mouth and looked guilty.

"What's the matter."

"Well . . . I guess I lied a little. But only about one of the gals."

The truth came out. She had lied about Jeanie Dahl, about only remembering Lew mentioning Jeanie when she saw the picture. She saw quite a bit of Jeanie, as a matter of fact. Why shouldn't old friends see each other? As a matter of fact, Jeanie was the crazy friend who'd go with her to the dog tracks, and Jeanie had gotten in as bad a jam about money as she had. And as a matter of fact once she'd started having affairs that Lew lined up, she had some drinks with Jeanie and told her all about it, and how it was, and what the payoff was, and found out Jeanie had been clipping a little bit now and then from petty cash at Kramer Building Supply and was scared of getting caught. So she had asked Jeanie if it was okay if she told Lew that Jeanie might be interested, and at first Jeanie said no, and then she changed her mind. And it was nice to have a friend who knew the whole score, and was in it with you, and you could talk to them the way you couldn't talk to anybody else in the whole world, and compare notes, and tell about the weird things that happened. So because of Jeanie's mother and the kid, they had set it up for Lew and Jeanie to meet at Dori's apartment while Dori was working, and when she got off work Jeanie was still there, alone and asleep, and said she and Lew had made the deal, and sealed it with a lot more than a handshake.

"I kinda sluffed over Jeanie's picture because ... maybe I felt a little weird about getting her into it all, too. But when you're in a bind, you wish somebody you knew was in it, too. At least I warned her about that Lilo and told her she better not ever get choosy about anything if she got set up with a spook. Since Freddie came home seven months ago, I go have lunch with Jeanie whenever my shift works out right. It's like ... resigning from something and you want gossip about what's going on since you left. She took a whole week off from work last January and flew to Jamaica free, and her date was there waiting, and it turned out to be ... well, never mind who. Anyway an important businessman in this town. She came back with a marvelous tan and brought me some fantastic perfume, and she made five hundred dollars!"

"What about Betsy Kapp?"

"Oh. Lew came by when Jeanie was getting off work one day, last November, I think, and he drove her out into the country someplace and parked and he came all apart. She said he cried like a little boy. She said he cried on her shoulder and she held him, and she said it was funny to feel kind of warm-mother toward him, knowing all the time what a mean son of a bitch he is. He finally told her he had beaten up a woman who'd done him the greatest favor any woman could ever do a man. It was all some kind of crazy thing about how he fell in love and he all of a sudden couldn't get it up, and the doctor he went to told him it was a common thing, a guilt thing, feeling unworthy and all that, and gave him shots but they didn't help. And the same thing happened with other girls then, and then the wonderful woman had helped him and he could again, and then he had beaten her up and he didn't know why. Jeanie finally found out it was Mrs. Kapp, and so she just naturally asked him if Mrs. Kapp was taking on customers for him, too. Jeanie didn't mean anything by it at all. But he reared back and gave her such a clout on the side of the head her ear rang day and night for a week, practically. He said Mrs. Kapp was a fine woman, not some cheap little piece of ass like Jeanie. So I guess Mrs. Kapp never had any part of the action. Jeanie said he acted strange, and he had been acting strange, and after that he got more weird. Jumpy acting."

"When did you see her last?"

"This is Sunday. I mean it's Monday morning. Let me see. We had lunch a week ago Friday. We talked about Linda Featherman, mostly. And she said she hadn't heard anything from Lew in three weeks and she was wondering if he was sort of easing off. She said she was getting nervous about keeping up payments on things because she'd figured on the extra money. She said, just joking, that maybe the two of us ought to go over to Miami Beach and see if there was any action. But she was joking. Lew made it awful plain to me and to her, too, that if we did any hustling on the side, he'd find out and we'd be the sickest, sorriest gals in Florida. Anyway, it would be stupid to try to work a place you don't have any protection. The cops pull in the free-lance gals, because that's part of the deal they get paid for by the people who have the action all sewed up. If Lew happens to be really dead, like you think, it's going to be rough for Jeanie to make out. It comes to maybe a thousand or twelve hundred a year, according to what I was making and what she was making, without any tax on it. Part time, like moonlighting, but there has to be somebody like Lew to set you up and do the collecting ahead so no bastard can afford to try to cheat you. We used to try to figure out what Lew was making, guessing how many of us were working for him. So it had to be what? Fourteen to sixteen thousand a year? But I guess he had to split that somehow, to keep himself out of trouble."

She stood up, yawning. "Do I get my picture back?"

I handed it to her. She looked at it and said, "I can just look at a piece of pie and gain a pound." She tore it into small pieces and took it into the bathroom and closed the door. She came out after a while and said, "You've got any of the other pictures of me?"

"No."

"I wish I knew where they were. I'd feel better. It was some sort of game, I thought, the camera on the table and he'd set a little thing that started buzzing and hop back in with me and then the flash would go off. It was one of those he was going to mail to Fred. He cut it so it was him from the chest down, but there I was, clear as a bell, laughing my fool head off. If you come across those?"

"I'll destroy them and let you know."

"The wrong clown gets those and he can put me right back in action. I wouldn't have a choice. Poor Freddie."

"Can I talk to Jeanie?"

She looked secretly amused. "How could I stop you? Why ask? You are a nice guy, Trav. You really are. I'd like to do you a nice favor for being a nice guy, but if you wanna know the truth, seeing the picture of that Lilo really blew out my fire. Going to be around awhile?"

"I guess so."

"Maybe we can work something out. You know where to find me. You wouldn't have to worry about anything. I mean I'm a healthy girl from head to toe. 'Night now. Take care."

FIFTEEN

YES, INDEED. TAKE CARE. I FINISHED the notations on the backs of the thirteen photographs. Six names.

Courthouse, third grade, building supply, real estate firm, stationery store.

Arnstead's Irregulars. Sorry little part-time hookers, each one thinking herself such a very special person, able to play the dark and nimble role, yet remain essentially her own true beautiful self.

There are no hookers with hearts of gold. Just lazy, greedy, dull-minded girls whose greatest joys are the clothing rack and the mirror and the makeup table. Such a simple little task, to take that ever-familiar tumescent rigidity into the slippery muscular depths, and brace tight, and hip-smack it into its brief leapings and sagging flaccidity. Simple task, sometimes pleasurable enough to incite an inner matching clenching, hidden explosion, and sighing release. Then say it was beautiful, tell him he's special, tell him it hardly ever happens like that for you. Give him the mirror-practiced expressions, and use the familiar ways to ready him again, because the better you work him, the more chance of a tip, and the thirty-dollar blue sandals are on layaway, and they are darling.

So simple a task it soon has no meaning, and then there is no meaning in being a woman, in that sense of being a woman. The only meaning left is in the ever-changing adornment of the body, that thing they buy. It is like the mercenary who sits alone, smiling, and with oil and stone, puts an ever finer edge on the combat knife, hoping that the next sentry will die so quickly there will be that little feeling in the belly of professional satisfaction, and a feeling almost of fondness for the unknown sentry because it had worked so well.

No evil in either hooker or mercenary. Just laziness, a small familiar greed, a mild anticipation of unimportant sensation, and the ever-challenging problem of what kind of pretty to buy with the fee.

Poor Freddie. Why did she leave and where did she go? She's going, soldier. One day soon. She'll leave because, no matter what the uniform, the mercenary blade always pierces exactly the same heart, stopping it over and over again. Only the angle changes. Until all hearts become the same target. And the hooker receives from all customers exactly the same plum-taut glans, slaying it in the same rocking lubricious clench of inner muscle ring, clasp of outer labia, pumping it to its small jolting death, welcoming it ever again, affixed to the loins of another stranger, but always the same in its greed for death. Only the duration changes. Until all erection is the same, including the husband one, all equally meaningless except for the chance of pleasure-feeling, and the money.

I thought of Betsy and her silly, touching, romantic conviction that each episode was unique and meaningful and full of glory. Faith and conviction made it so, and a stereo at cost and free tapes were gestures of friendship, and a hard man could understand a little of this, and weep for having beaten her.

It was nearly four-thirty in the morning, and again her phone did not answer. I tried the sheriff. He was not available. I stretched out to think of what to do next, how to fit the parts together, and suddenly it was bright morning outside, the room lights still on, my mouth stale, and my eyes grainy.

The phone rang just as I was reaching to turn on the shower. It was Sheriff Hyzer to tell me they had not located Mrs. Kapp or her car yet, but that they had found Lew Arnstead's black jeep hidden in the yard of an empty house four doors down Seminole from Mrs. Kapp's cottage. Maybe I'd like to stop by.

I didn't ask any questions. I hurried the shower, and it was twenty after eight when I got there. Hyzer's cruiser was in Betsy's driveway. He seemed to be alone. Fresh suit, shirt, tie, shoes. He'd nicked himself twice shaving.

We walked up the street. The chain was unhooked. A deputy was dusting it with professional care and deftness, lifting fragments and sections of prints, making notations of location.

"It made me wonder, Mr. McGee, if Arnstead had hidden this here yesterday evening, gone to Mrs. Kapp's house and taken her away with him in her car."

"I suppose that could have happened."

"Not when you see this. Come here." He took me around to the front, pointed to a brown object fastened to a protected place under the headlamp. "Mud dauber," he said. "Fresh. They turn pale when they dry. They don't work at night. This nest is nearly done. You wait a minute you'll see her come flying in with another mud ball. She had to start yesterday morning to get this far. She had to build it up to a certain point then go find the right kind of spider and paralyze it with her stinger and shove it in there. Soon now she'll have just a little hole left. She'll lay her eggs in it and then seal it up, and when the young hatch they'll have spider meat to live on before they break out."

"Very interesting."

"So it was left here Saturday night, probably. You spent the night with her. Hear anything?"

"Not a thing."

"We had a telephone report of an altercation at three in the morning in this neighborhood."

"I didn't hear that, either."

"It doesn't make sense, at least not yet, for him to hide his jeep here and walk away from it and not come back."

"Meaning he couldn't come back."

"Or somebody abandoned it here to leave a false trail. Tom, don't forget to dust that Dr. Pepper bottle on the floor."

"No sir, Sheriff."

"Getting anything usable?"

"Too many smudges. A few pretty good partials and right here at the top of the windshield, one real good one of the whole heel of a hand. Could be a woman's or a child's from the size."

"Call Johnny's to come tow it in when you're finished, and get those vacuum bags to the Bureau fast as you can."

As we walked back to Betsy's drive I said, "You're a very thorough man, Sheriff."

"We try."

"I imagine you must be aware of everything that goes on in Cypress County."

"All I need to know, I hope. We put through a consolidation a couple of years back, absorbed the city police into the county and put all the law enforcement under the Sheriff's Department. Cuts duplication and expense."

"Excuse me, Sheriff. You seem more amiable toward me today."

"I like to be fair. You said Perris had to leave that station Friday morning. I tried it once more. I phoned Al Storey this morning and asked him if Henry Perris had left the station for any reason whatsoever, business or personal. First he said no, just as he did before, and then he remembered that Perris had finished a brake job on an Oldsmobile and had taken it down the road to the customer, a man named Hummer. It was a combination road test and delivery. Hummer had then driven Perris back to the station. To get to Hummer's road, Perris had to pass a little roadside park with a public phone booth. Can you fill in the rest of it, Mr. McGee?"

"Make a phone call to someone to pick up the envelope he hid in the phone book."

"Perhaps. Storey did not think of that in the same sense as actually leaving the station. Leaving involves personal business. A delivery is work time. I told Storey not to talk if Perris was nearby. He said Perris was late again, as usual. I told him not to mention the conversation to Perris."

"Are you going to pick Perris up?"

"Not yet. I want him to feel safe. I want to have more to go on."

"Now will you admit the girl is implicated, too?"

His stare was like stone. "If evidence should show at some future date that she is involved, knowingly, in any criminal activity, then she will be arrested and charged."

End of amiability. End of conversation.

I drove down to Johnny's Main Street Service. Miss Agnes had been taken off the line. I found her on blocks in the body shop, with a big sweaty Ron Hatch wielding a rubber mallet and some curved templates with comforting skill.

He came out and said, "Hi, Mr. McGee. Some of it isn't as bad as I thought. But, Jesus, they used some kind of gauge metal in her." I borrowed the broken fitting from him and made a call from the office to my mechanic friend in Palm Beach. I told him what it looked like and where it went. He had me measure it, and had me hold the phone. He came back on the line in about two minutes and said he had it and where and how should he send it. I had him ship fastest means direct to Ron Hatch at the garage. The operator came back with the report of charges, and I gave the exact change to the office girl and she put it in the petty cash box just as a man in his late forties came in. He was trim and held himself well, and his hair was a little too thick and dark to be entirely unaided. He had a golfing tan, and an elegant sport shirt, and a gold-and-black wristwatch with three or four dials and a lot of gold buttons to push.

"McGee?" he said. When I said I was, he said he was Johnny Hatch, and invited me back into his office. Small, paneled, cool, windowless, and private. Golfing trophies and trap-shooting trophies, and framed testimonials about his civic services. A color portrait in a silver frame, showing a very lovely young woman smiling out, her arms around a little boy and a little girl. She looked young enough to account for his trimness and his hairpiece and dye job.

"Thanks for treating the kid right on the work he did on that old Rolls truck of yours. It set him up pretty good."

"He's a nice kid."

"Not much you can do with them these days. That Liz Taylor haircut of his makes me want to throw up every time I see it. He won't go back to school. He's a car nut. I'll say this. He'll do the job right for you. Now I got a second litter coming along, and it makes you wonder what kind of problems they're going to be."

"I wasn't exactly eager to put any more money into your operation, Mr. Hatch. It seemed to me like you took me pretty good."

He shrugged. "I could show you the books. We don't get rich on county business. We have to bid it. We lose on some and make out on the others, and hope to end up the year ahead. Don't tell me a fella who can afford Lennie Sibelius is hurting for a little garage bill."

"Word gets around."

"Small town. You know how it is. Everybody hears everything. Trouble is that when they pass it along, they add a little to make it more interesting."

"Then you know Arnstead is missing?"

"I heard about it."

"And Betsy Kapp is missing, too."

He was startled. "The *hell* you say."

"She had a seven o'clock date last night and didn't keep it and hasn't been seen since."

"That's a weird one. That isn't like old Betsy. I tell you, it would take a lot of pleasure out of having lunch at the Lodge if anything happened to her."

"I understand she and Arnstead were pretty close. Maybe they took off together."

"Hell, I can't buy that. They had something going, I guess. But that was months ago. Funny, she'd fool around with Lew."

"Maybe it was a business relationship, Johnny."

He leaned back, watchful. "What's that supposed to mean?"

"I knew the name was familiar, but I didn't connect it up right away. I remembered that a year, year and a half ago, somebody told me that if I ever got stuck in this neck of the woods, I should look up a Deputy Lew Arnstead, and he could fix me up with something real choice, that it would cost, but it would be worth it."

"Do tell."

"You're the one who told me it's a small town. I guess if it was true, you'd have heard about it."

"I think I heard somewhere that Lew had an extra girl friend or two he'd hire out."

"I guess he'd have to be pretty careful about it, working under a man like Hyzer."

"Mister Norm sees what he wants to see and believes what he wants to believe, just like everybody else."

"He doesn't impress you?"

He shrugged. "I vote for him."

"So it's a nice quiet place, with a very quiet little newspaper."

"There's no point in scaring up trouble by printing a lot of things that agitate people."

"Was the car Linda Featherman was driving brought in here?"

"What the *hell* have you got on your mind, McGee! I asked you in here to thank you for the way you played fair with my boy. I didn't know I was going to get some kind of third degree."

I smiled, stood up. "I'm just curious about your nice little town, Johnny. No offense. I admit I am a little curious about your first litter. I like Ron. He's a good one. But from all reports his sister is as rotten a little tramp as you can find anywhere."

His face turned to a brown mask, and he did not move his lips when he spoke. He spoke so quietly I could barely hear him. "Understand this. Nobody mentions her in my presence. She is absolutely nothing to me, and the sick sow that bred her is nothing to me. I don't care if they are alive or dead. I don't care if they roast in hell or find eternal bliss. Now get out of here."

I got. That much hate is impressive, no matter where you find it. It makes you want to walk on tiptoe and breathe quietly as you get out of range.

I found breakfast and then flipped a coin. Heads was Deputy King Sturnevan. Tails was Mrs. Jeanie Dahl. Had it landed on edge I was going to try Miss Kimmey, in the third grade. It was heads.

King had some reports to finish. He said to wait around. Twenty minutes later he came out and walked over to the Buick. He leaned in and shook his head sadly. "You gotta talent, man. Billy Cable catches you jaywalking, he'll club your head down between your knees."

"Get in, and I'll tell you about it." I told him. I was at the wrong place at the wrong time, and witnessed Betsy chop him down.

King nodded. "I knew he wanted to get into that. But I didn't know he was damn fool enough to go after it that way. If Mister Norm heard he tried to use his badge to get her onto her back, he would be out in the street. Seems like she didn't fight you off much, McGee. That's the way she is. She will, but not often, and she has to do the picking."

"She picked Lew Arnstead."

"I know. Surprised folks. The Betsy-watchers. Not her type. But you can't tell."

"King, how much can we trust each other, you and I?"

He shifted his big belly around and beamed at me and winked a scarred eye. "You can't trust me one damn bit if it's something the man ought to know."

"I have a crazy question which has been growing and growing, and I have to ask. Make it hypothetical. Could and did Lew Arnstead get away with things that Hyzer would have fired anyone else for?"

I watched him make his slow decision. "It bothered me a long time, pal. Tell you the truth, it surprised hell out of me when Hyzer did boot him out and file charges. And I saw Lew's face when it happened, and I think Lew was as surprised as me."

"Do you think Hyzer knew Lew was pimping?"

"You get around good. That wouldn't be easy to come by. I guess Lew started four years back, about then. I think maybe Hyzer decided that if a broad was going to peddle it, it's better to have somebody keeping it under control. He had to hear about it, but as far as I know, he never looked into it. And Lew never turned up rich enough to ask for an investigation of where and how he got it."

"Could he have been handling it for Hyzer?"

"I am going to forget you said that, pally. Because if I remember it one minute from now, I am going to pull you out of this pretty car and see if I can rupture your spleen with a left."

"Sorry I asked. I apologize."

"It just couldn't be, believe me."

"Now you know and I know that a cop builds his own string. He doesn't start off with old hustlers. He starts with girls who've gotten out of line and he scares them into making a choice his way. He's usually smart enough to try it on the ones who will take to it without much fuss, or he isn't in business long. He breaks them in himself, then puts them to work."

His broad face was unhappy. "I guess if Mister Norm looked into it and found that was the way it was being done, he would have had to get rid of Lew. So he didn't look into it. I know the score, pally. I remember there was an immigration officer in Miami who put the heat on for whether girls got a renewal or got shipped back to the crummy villages they came from. Then one of them, as I remember it, wrote her kid sister not to come to the States and told her why, and the kid sister gave it to the old man, and he flew up on the money his daughter had been sending back to Peru, and put a knife into that civil servant. He put it in about forty times, starting just above the knees and working his way up. Somebody could have known about Lew and didn't make the move until Lew was no longer a law man."

"I just happened to tell Hyzer about how Billy went after Betsy Kapp a year and a half ago."

"How can one man make himself so popular so fast? You going to run for mayor?"

"I don't know. I think of lots of questions and look for answers. Question: Would somebody kill Arnstead in order to take Hyzer off whatever hook he was on?"

King thought it over. "He doesn't act like anybody with the pressure off. He's pushing harder than ever. I thought over what you said the other night about Lew. He had to be way out on speed. It fits. So how and why does a speed freak get clobbered? Who knows?"

"King, what was the verdict on Linda Featherman?"

He snapped his head around, completely puzzled. "Verdict? What do you mean? Accidental death. One-car accident. Excessive speed. Fell asleep, maybe."

"Insurance company pay off?"

"What the hell are you talking about? Murder? Suicide? What?"

"What if you were absolutely positive she'd been hustling for Lew Arnstead for at least two years?"

"Aw . . . come *on!* The Featherman girl? You're out of your tree, buddy boy. If anybody tried to muscle her, she'd go to Dale Featherman and say, 'Daddy, somebody is bothering me.' And daddy would go skin Arnstead and salt down the hide after he scraped it clean, and tack it on one of the stables out there at the ranch. He might saw off the top of Lew's skull and use it for an ashtray. No, sir. That's four generations of Florida money, and senators from Washington and bankers from New York come down in a Featherman jet and land on that private strip. You're way off, my friend. She was a very pretty girl and she drove too damned fast."

"Brothers or sisters?"

"Three of each, I think. She was somewhere in the middle. Got back from college three years ago, I think. There were plans for a wedding, but it got canceled for some reason. There's no lever to use on a girl like that. She could buy her way out of trouble, or have the muscle put out of business."

"Unless the leverage was on somebody else, and that was the only way she could protect them."

He studied me. "Okay. We're trusting each other. I just might take your word for it. Are *you* positive?"

They have a badge and they swear an oath. So whether or not something is off the record depends on how much they value that oath. So when you see the cop-glint way back in the eyes you back off, just a little.

"King, let's say it's a pretty fair assumption."

"Then you're wandering around out in left field, McGee. Let's say Lew wasn't all too bright, and let's say he was running women. He wouldn't be so dumb he'd try to muscle Miss Linda Featherman into it, pretty as she was."

"Can you come up with any names?"

"I wouldn't want to try, because I might name some it would turn out they were only close friends of Lew's. If he was setting up every woman he'd been out with in the past four years, he'd have to run the operation with IBM cards, and take home the money in a wheelbarrer."

"Wonder what he was doing with what he was making?"

"Salting it away. Slowest man you ever seen when it came to reaching into his pocket to pay for a beer or a cup of coffee. He bought himself some good guns, and one good horse, but that was about it. Had a pretty fair automobile that he bought half wrecked and had Henry Perris put in good shape, Then he was too cheap to pay collision, so it was a total loss when he racked it up. He kept his business affairs, and just about everything else to himself. Close mouth and a close pocket. It isn't smart for any cop to have a safety-deposit box. I'd guess Lew'd pack it in fruit jars and bury it in the ground."

"Think he dug it up and left?"

"Not if he could still make more than enough to live on around here. I think he's dead."

"Do you think he had guilty knowledge of the Baither killing?"

"Let's you and me stay friends, pally." He opened the door, slowly pulled his bulk out, flipped the door shut, mopped his forehead. "It's going to get way up there before this day is over. See you around, I suppose. Glad to hear your friend is doing fine."

I arrived at the Kramer Home Building Supply headquarters at eleven-fifteen. It was a mile and a half out of town on the airport road. Big lumber warehouse with truck loading docks, a cement block operation with about two acres of decorative block stacked gleaming in the sun, a retail store with everything for the do-it-yourselfer, and a clerical office at the end of the building which housed the retail outlet. It was a bright brisk operation with that neatness of floor displays which reflects a comforting operating net. Old men were browsing through the hand tools and cupboard latches, spray cans and wallboard just as, in the world of long ago, they had prowled the candy store to find out how best to spend the hoarded dime.

There were two middle-aged women and one young one behind the waist-high fence. The young one was the Jeanie of the picture, looking slimmer in a short fuzzy pink skirt, a white blouse with a fine vertical red stripe, dark auburn hair chopped to urchin length. One of the other women started toward me, but I smiled and pointed at Jeanie, who was running invoices on a big Burroughs accounting machine. The woman shrugged and looked a little less hospitable and spoke to Jeanie. She turned and looked at me, first a green-eyed speculation, and then recognition. She turned her machine off and came over to the fence, angling so that I had to drift over toward the corner, and we ended up at the maximum distance from the other two women.

Delicate little features, face wide across the far-set eyes, fat little mouth over the pointed chin. "Your name is McGee, huh?"

The piped music, which always seems to be Montovani in places like that, made our conversation private. I nodded. She made a head gesture and said, "Those old crows got ears that come to points, believe me. Dori said a big tall guy, kind of battered here and there, with a lot of tan and real pale gray eyes. But she didn't say how tall and how big. I could tell from her voice she's turned on about you. She called me after Fred was gone, like seven this morning, and she sounded a little plotzed. She was scared I'd be sore she'd told you about me. She said you're okay, so if it says that in her book it says it in mine. I like to dropped my teeth when she says fourteen gals. I would have said ten at the most, the very most." She looked over her shoulder at the wall clock. "I can switch lunch hours with the girl over there on the register. She hates going at eleven-thirty. That's ten minutes. We can't talk so good here. I can feel Mr. Frandel looking at me through that glass right now, boring a hole in the back of my head with his eyes. Look, you mind buying something? It helps. Then I'll be coming out that door there into the back parking at eleven-thirty."

I joined the browsers and came upon something I had been wanting to add to the tools aboard the *Flush*: a compact, lightweight electric screwdriver, variable speed, reverse, a goodly batch of interchangeable heads, all in a tidy aluminum case for $26.95. No reason why Lennie shouldn't buy his bird dog a little present for the boat. The only flaw in the rig was that some idiot, through cynicism or indifference, had specified steel pins in the aluminum hinges and a steel latch on the case.

So by the time I paid and got out of there, Mrs. Jeanie Dahl was standing in the shade, leaning against the building, ankles crossed, elbow propped in the palm of her hand, cigarette down by a third. She smiled and pushed herself away from the wall and followed me to the convertible. I turned the air high and, when we turned onto the highway, I ran the power windows back up.

"Where do we go?" I asked.

"Right down there where the sign is on the right. Bernie's. There's kind of a crazy grove behind it and you can take stuff out there. I'd like a cheeseburger and a vanilla shake."

I carried our food in a cardboard box out to cement tables and benches in the shade of big Australian pines. We were the only customers in the grove. The other five tables were empty. A pair of Florida jays flew down and landed on the end of the table, hopped cautiously toward us. She held her hand out, arm flat on the table, crumb in her palm. The bolder of the pair, after much inspection, grabbed it and flew to the nearest table to eat it. She continued to feed them as we ate and talked.

"I think he had some kind of protection, sure. But he didn't say anything real definite, right out like. More like saying to me a couple of times there wasn't a thing to worry about, because I live with my mother and my kid, and I said to Lew a couple of times that my mother would make my life hell on earth, and my lousy ex still wants the kid and it could be a chance for him to get Davie away from me, I mean if there was some kind of raid or something like that."

"So if somebody was in with him, it would be logical for that somebody to pick it up where Lew left off, if Lew is dead."

She wiped her vanilla mustache off on the paper napkin. "McGee, I was thinking I wouldn't exactly be eager to go along with Lew on anything if he shows up again. I mean having him be a deputy makes it one kind of thing, and having him be out on bail, waiting for a trial in circuit court is something else. You know? Maybe if he lost his protection, they might want to charge him with this other thing, too. And if I got a subpoena, believe me, I think I'd go out of my mind. I guess the best thing to do is sort of keep my fool head down for a while. If nothing happens, maybe in a couple weeks or so I can set up a date with a local man I just so happen to know, and I've got the idea it could turn out to be a permanent kind of a thing, and he's so turned on about me, I ought to be able to get like a regular allowance, if he isn't too chicken to try to set us up a place right here instead of going way off somewhere. I don't want to lose the stuff I bought on time, like the color TV. My mother and Davie would be lost if we had to go back to that crummy little black-and-white Sears. Look, what is it you want to know, anyway? She said you'd probably give me back my picture like you did hers. It's better it shouldn't be floating around if something happened to Lew."

"I'm puzzled about how he operated. Certainly he wasn't contacted out at that ranch, or at the Department. He must have had some other base of operation."

"Why would he have to? I don't know about how it was when he started it, but by the time I got in, it was on account of one fellow telling another fellow who to get in touch with. Then Lew would meet the fellow someplace, like at the Adventurer bar in the afternoon and size him up and if he looked all right, or there were two or three and they looked okay, he'd tell them the rules, all night only, and no heavy drinking beforehand, and cash on the line in advance. Then they'd pick out who they liked and Lew would phone and say where and when and who to ask for, and if you couldn't make it, the guy made another pick. He tried to steer away from any gal having any regulars. He said that could turn into trouble. There was some locals, not many, and that was pretty much set up for out of town someplace. The next day or a day later, Lew would get the money to me. It was ... easier, I guess, not to have to take the money from your date yourself. And it was more like a date that way, even though you'd know and the guy would know it was paid for ahead. What you were supposed to do was tell Lew if you got any kind of a bad time, like a fellow getting mean and slapping you around, or having a friend show up for a spare piece. Then Lew would take the guy off the list for good. I don't think I'd want to be set up by anybody else unless they kept it under control like Lew did. But lately he was getting careless, like the guys weren't such a nice class of people, and he took longer coming around with my share so twice I had to remind him. And the last time I saw him, a month ago anyway, he called the house about eight at night and told me walk down to the corner and meet him. So I did and he picked me up in a police car and drove out into the country like a maniac and wouldn't tell me what it was all about. It started to rain and he took me off to some crazy little shacky place at the end of nowhere and took me in there and liked to ruin my clothes yanking me out of them, and he shoved me onto a cruddy old bed and he was so rough it scared me, and it wasn't ten minutes, I swear, before I was back in that car, sniveling, scared to death of the way he was driving. He let me out at the corner in the rain, and thank God my mother was too hooked on the television to take a look at me when I came in and went to my room."

"Where was this shack?"

She looked startled. "Hey, that was sort of what you were asking before, wasn't it?"

"Sort of. Was it locked?"

"With a padlock, yes. It was just one room, a pine shack with a crooked old floor, set up on blocks instead of pilings. It had electricity. I remember I saw a hot plate on some packing cases by the wall. There was a little narrow hall to a back door, with a little room with a john and a sink off one side of it, and a storeroom like off the other side."

"Where was it?"

"It was dark and raining and I couldn't find it again in a thousand years. I know we started out Cattleman's Road because I remember wondering if we were going to his place, but it didn't seem likely because he said that if I ever called him there ever, he'd spill my teeth all over the floor. And he would, too."

"You went a long way out Cattleman's Road?"

"A long way. Miles and miles and at a hundred and something miles an hour. Then he turned left, skidding on the corner like a racing driver. We must have been out of the county, or almost. Then he turned right and the road was so narrow the bushes were rubbing on the sides of the car. It went around a lot of curves and the lights shone on the shack and big trees around it and on the rain falling down hard. I asked him where we were and what he wanted. But he ... I was going to say he didn't tell me anything, but he did say something that didn't make any sense. I can't remember."

"Please try."

"It was something crazy. He said it was his birthday present. I don't know whether he meant me or the house. Then he was running me through the rain to the door, pulling me by the wrist, and mud was slopping up on the backs of my legs and my hair was getting soaked, and I had begun to wonder if the crazy bastard had taken me out there to kill me. I think part of my crying all the way home was relief."

"Did he say anything else?"

"No. Oh, when he reached across me and opened the door to let me out on the corner, I started to get out and he grabbed me by the shoulder and pulled me back. He dug his fingers into my shoulder so hard I had marks for a week. He said I didn't remember where I'd been, and I didn't want to tell anybody about being anywhere with him or he'd give me a face that would turn my kid's stomach. I wanted to laugh. I didn't know where the hell I *had* been."

She looked at her face in her handbag mirror and told me how this year she was going to get a really good tan. She said she had better be getting back to work. She asked where the picture was. She studied it and started to tear it, then instead put it in her purse, snapped the clasp.

I drove her back and before she got out she said, "Dori told me to tell you maybe she'll be in touch. Look, she's a crazy wonderful kid and she's bored out of her skull. Fred is a nice guy. It's been too long since she's had any kind of fun. You'd be doing her a favor, and you shouldn't miss out on it anyway, because she's a really fabulous lay, and she loves it. It isn't a sales pitch, honey. It's a freeby, because she likes you a lot."

"And she's bored."

"I told her they should have a kid, but they keep taking tests and nothing happens. Freddie works hard, but, Jesus, if you tell him a joke, you gotta spend a half hour explaining to him where he should have laughed. Anyway, she's maybe my best friend, so don't get turned off because she's a little on the chubby side, okay?"

"And if you remember anything more about the place, call me at—"

"I know where you are. Thanks for the lunch, McGee."

"You're most welcome."

"And the picture. Say, I didn't get to see the others,

dammit. No time now. Maybe I'd know some she didn't."

"I'll get back to you."

"You *do* that! Bye now." Knowing I was watching her, she wagged her little pink skirt all the way to the door, turned as she tugged at it, and blew me a small kiss with her pocketbook hand.

I wrote mental ads as I drove into town: Girls, do you want extra pocket money? Have you ever thought of part-time hustling to supplement your income? Just a relatively few hours a month in pleasant surroundings. Opportunities to travel. Tax-free income. Must be between twenty and thirty, amiable, reasonably pretty and well built, and able to devote time and effort to your second occupation. Do you like people? Are you truly interested in meeting new people of means? Earn as you learn.

It would not be such a nifty little sideline for Jeanie and Dori and company if one of the syndicate operations moved into Cypress City and took over Arnstead's list and picked what looked useful enough and moved them out and put them on the circuit, broke them to total obedience. I remembered the time long ago when Miguel and I forced our way into the circus in Juarez one night, thinking to find the Australian with Miguel's money among the spectators. Four soft paste-white women of indefinite years under the blue spotlights, sweating with the effort of working their circus routines with the black, the dwarf, the burro, and each other. We brought it to a halt when Miguel hit the room lights, knife ready. No Australian among the eight men and three women spectators. As Miguel made his eloquent apologies to the cold-eyed management, easing their indignation with a gift of pesos, one of the performers, a dead-eyed woman with a curved knife scar from forehead to corner of the mouth, which had nicked the eye and turned it milky, padded over to me, her sweat coppery-sharp in the stifling room and said, "Mister, didn't you used to live in Dayton, Ohio? Weren't you a young kid selling cars for the Buick agency in Dayton, Ohio?"

I had time to tell her no. Sorry, no, lady. Then the room lights went off and the dwarf stung her across the rear with his little whip and she yelped and leaped and then went tumbling back onto the mattresses under the blue spots, tumbling back into the interrupted performance. We left, and found the Australian a week later.

It has always bothered me that I could just as easily have said yes.

SIXTEEN

I WENT TO THE OFFICE OF THE COUNTY clerk and put on my most affable and folksy manner and asked if they had any alphabetical list of the taxpayers on the *ad-valorem* tax roles. They sent me to the assessor's office, and a girl there sent me to the central records department, where they sent me back to the clerk's office. Finally I settled for a look at the big book of aerials of the entire county, and by using the line drawing on the front as a guide, I was able to find the pages covering the northern half of Cattleman's Road to the Wagner County line.

I found three places where a northbound car could turn left. Each seemed to have quite a few places where a car could then turn right onto private land. Each photograph had a transparent overlay bound into the book with property owner's names, and the number of the book of deeds and the page in the book which covered the property.

Hullinger, Reiter, Rench, Dowd, Albritton, Eggert, Alderman, Jenkins, Hyatt, McCroan, Featherman. Lots of Featherman land, and lots of Hullinger land.

So on the second aerial of the last road, I found on the overlay an irregular oblong, far smaller than the surrounding parcels, and it said: "Arnstead—3.12 acres. Book 23, page 1109."

I could make out the faint track of entrance drive, and part of the shape of a roof hidden by the pines. I measured the scale and found that the entrance was almost exactly two miles from the turn at Cattleman's Road.

The spectacled girl showed me where Book 23 was. I found the old quit-claim deed to Lewis B. Arnstead, a minor child, from his father, for the sum of one dollar and other valuable considerations.

Often when you are the most hopeful, nothing works. Then you try a long shot and come up with it.

Before I left I used a pay phone and tried Betsy and got my dime back.

There was no breeze and the sun of early afternoon was hazy and hot. As I passed Cora Arnstead's place, I saw the black horse standing in the shade near the pond, grazing. The geese were asleep on the grass by the pond, one sentinel sitting with his head high. The stunted cattle were at the far end of the pasture.

I had no trouble finding the turn, nor finding the driveway two miles west of the turn. The brush touched the sides of the white car. An armadillo stared me to a stop, then went trundling off into the thicket.

It was, as Jeanie Dahl had called it, a shack. Old black cypress siding on a hard-pine frame, with a tar-paper roof, gray-white with age, patched here and there with black tar. Holes in the window screens. Curtains yellowed by age. The stout padlock on the door hasp had been broken. I pushed the door open and went into the sickening oven-heat of the interior. It smelled as if lions lived there. The old swaybacked bed was out from the wall, mattress slashed in a half dozen places, soiled old sheets and blankets on the floor. Interior wallboard had been pried loose. Sections of the flooring had been ripped up. Chunks of the Celotex ceiling had been torn down.

Somebody had gone through it with utmost thoroughness, and had given the same attention to the toilet room and the storeroom. I saw some places which I thought at first could have been overlooked. But then I found the hiding place someone else had found first. It was the hearth in the shallow brick fireplace. It was of fire brick resting on a cement slab. Brush the ashes away and take out the fire bricks on the left-hand side, and the top of a mail-order cylindrical safe was exposed. A hole had been chipped and drilled down into the poured concrete, and the safe let down into it and cemented in. The dial had been prybarred off and then the prybar had been inserted in the hole behind the dial, and the cheap hinges had torn loose. The top was in the fireplace. The interior of the safe, about the dimension of two number-ten tins end to end, was empty.

I sat on my heels and looked at the heap of black charred fragments of paper on the right side of the hearth. Photographic paper burns in a distinctive way and leaves a recognizable kind of ash. With a splinter from the torn floor I carefully shifted the pieces of ash. There were some small fragments of a different kind of paper which had not burned completely. They were apparently sheets from a notebook, torn, but then burned in small packets so that the outside sheets were blackened but the inside ones were merely brittle and yellowed. Fragments of names, portions of addresses, dates, amounts. I could not find matching bits from any one page, but found enough to conclude that it was a customer list, with the girl indicated by initials, DLA, LF, DS, BD, LP, LF, HA.

The ledger accounts and advertising and probably the insurance documents of a very small business enterprise. Insurance in the form of confessions, photographs, letters. Cottage industry, bankrupt due to unforseen circumstances. Proprietor found himself in a hole.

Suddenly I had enough of the oppressive heat, the lion-cage stench, dusty cobwebs, dead bugs, and old ashes. I stood up and started out toward the relative coolness of outdoors, and saw on the wall a cheap gaudy electric clock of the type which makes a sudden appearance in cut-rate drugstores at Christmastime. Dangling cord, unplugged. Small gilt face with a radiating array of black metal spikes.

I moved back and found the position of the lens. The peanut can ashtray was on the floor near the corner. Yes, the table had been there, the end of the bed there, Lilo Perris standing there, her head in the way of the clock face.

Confirmation of partnership. The chunky, brawny little sunbrown girl with all the contradictions in her face, who worked as Arnstead's enforcer, so suited to the occasional chore that even after a year and a half, the photograph of her could turn Mrs. Freddie Severiss cold-pale and sweaty, her throat bunching to swallow the sudden bile.

Then I went out, my shirt sweat-pasted to my back, out of the plundered lion cage into the dusty dooryard, into that midday silence when the birds and insects are still, with no breeze to hiss through the pines, or make rain-sounds in the fronds of palmetto.

I walked around the edge of the area, footsteps silenced by the brown cushion of old needles. A track led off to the side, portions of old car tracks in dried mud. I walked twenty feet down that shaded place, and was about to turn back when the angle of the sun made a single bright silvery glint through a line of brush.

So I went further, and saw it, the plastic sunflower growing in alien country. Circled the brush and found the tan VW, sitting there with the brute endearing patience of all small ugly machines. She was not in it.

She was forty feet from it, standing there against the trunk of a tall old pine, her knees slightly bent. When she had tossed the skirt and blouse on the bed and taken her shower, she had put on lime-colored slacks and a tailored lemon-gold shirt.

This was another of the games that Betsy played. Add rose to blue and the color can be a strange and memorable lavender. They had taken the ends of the length of galvanized fence wire, and twisted them together on the far side of the big tree, tightened them enough with pliers. She had stood erect then, perhaps. But later as the wire bit ever deeper into her throat, she sagged, the knees bending. Bulging clown-face in a long lavender look, eyes popping, vein-broken and yellowed, fat black tongue thrusting from the lips in permanent grimace. A game. Fright mask to tease the children. Look at me. Do I scare you? Just a little? I really don't like this game very much, dear. I've dirtied my pretty slacks and I've begun to smell frightful, and the steak I promised is still in the freezer, the wine cooling. But I was delayed. By a game I don't like very much.

I found myself over by the little tan car, my eyes smarting, and I saw my fist in slow motion move six inches, jolt against the side window in back, saw the radiating cracks from the point of impact. Looked at my fist, saw how quickly the flesh was puffing. Idiot woman. Silly, sentimental, pushover broad, trading a tumble amid her gift-shoppe decor for the sound of the ancient worn-out words—love, fate, kismet, eternity, meaningfulness, affection.

Pull back, McGee. You are grown up, you hope. And you spread bad luck where 'ere you go. Somebody gave her the final game to play, and maybe it was quicker than it looks. And why don't you look at that shovel and that hole and start thinking logically, and keep yourself from looking at her, and breathe through your mouth when you are near her.

Old long-handled shovel, rusty and with a dull edge. It leaned against the same tree. I saw where the grave had been started too close to the tree, and there had been too many roots. So the shoveler had moved over to the side and had dug out an area five feet long and a yard wide, and about two and a half feet deep at one end and eighteen inches at the other. Not a good shoveler. The dirt removed had not been piled neatly and handily, but had been thrown too far. Hasty, frantic shoveling. Wear yourself out too quickly. Perhaps trying to finish before having to be someplace, or trying to finish in the last of the daylight. Then, perhaps, reconsideration. What's the big rush? She's not going anywhere and nobody is coming here. Don't move the car yet. Come back and tuck her down into the loam and stomp it flat and spread the needles. Then the risk of moving the car is less.

Whatever you remembered, Betsy Kapp, whatever you tried to check out, it was the wrong thing. And there was no director to step in and stop the drama. Did you come here, or did you go to someone who brought you here?

"What a crazy day," she had said. "What a weird kind of a day?"

I studied the moist bottom of the unfinished grave. A lot of footprints in the deeper end. Size ten probably. Broad. Maybe a D. Small crosswise corrugations, like on the composition soles of work shoes, but worn away in the center, under the ball of the foot. A triangular nick out of the heel of the right shoe, on the outside toward the back, half an inch long.

I walked back to the shack area, back to my car. I fixed the front door precisely as it had been. I reviewed everything I had done. The only evidence that someone had been here was the star cracks in the side window of the VW, and I could not undo that. It might not be noticed or, if noticed, someone might think they had not happened to see it earlier. It went with the scalloped edges of the fenders, the dinged bumpers.

Run breathless to the Man and say, "Sher'f, my God, I found her and she's stone dead, plain and pure murdered to death."?

And get patted on the head and reminded I am a civilian, and be told that I would probably find out in due course what happened.

I was going to stop playing it their way. They had this big poker table working, and they had let me take the empty chair, provided I played my cards face up on the table and played by their rules. If I was naughty, they would deal me out of the next hand.

No more earnest efforts to please. No more defensive play. No more letting the house man deal. As of now, it was intensely personal, time to kick over the table, scatter the chips, break out my own deck, deal my own game—without explaining the rules.

The handle they use on you is your wistful need to pick up your life again right where it was interrupted, to be allowed to go in peace. When you decide that you do not give a damn about your own continuity, then you can even win a hand, and sometimes you can break the house.

I went roaring out of there, and on the way south on Cattleman's Road I found myself bumping the heel of my sore hand against the rim of the wheel, and humming a tuneless hymn of anticipation.

"Sorry to keep calling you up like this, Sheriff, but I tried Betsy's phone again just now and didn't get an answer. Have you found out anything?"

"Nothing yet. But we put out an all points hold on the car."

"I was thinking about her cat. Okay if I go over there and feed it and let it out in that fenced yard awhile?"

"You can get in?"

"Sure. I've still got that key I told you about."

"No objection, Mr. McGee. I heard you were in the courthouse looking up some property. What was that all about?"

"It was just a wild idea that didn't work out."

"It might be better if you just have some patience. Our investigations are proceeding."

"It must be quite a work load, Sheriff."

"How so?"

"Murder of Frank Baither. Disappearance of Lew Arnstead. Disappearance of Betsy Kapp. I'd heard this was a quiet county."

"It has been, and it will be again. Incidentally, I questioned my chief deputy about the incident with Mrs. Kapp. His version differs in certain particulars, but there was enough substance for me to give him an additional warning. I wouldn't want to lose him. He is a very valuable man, and the department is shorthanded."

"I think I better stay away from Billy."

"Until he has a chance to calm down. Yes."

"Well, thanks, Sheriff. I'll be in touch."

Had Raoul been a little kid, he would have been standing crosslegged and moaning. When I opened the door he went at a humpbacked lope to a grassy corner, squatted and with a dreamy distant stare, emptied the inflated feline bladder. He came strolling back into the kitchen, stared into his empty dish and said, "Raoul?" I opened the cupboards until I found his canned glop, whined one open on the electric machine, tapped it into his dish. He ate a few hungry gobbles, then looked up and walked out of the kitchen. I followed him into the living room and into the bedroom. He looked in the bathroom and turned around and came out again, saying, "Raoul?"

"Not here, furry friend. And she won't be."

He sat down and began to wash. When in doubt, wash. I opened the lower left drawer of the dressing table and took the weapon out. Still loaded. Untouched. In Florida you can have one in the house, or in your car, but not on the person. I thought it would be nice to have it in the Buick. I poked around until I found a small, brightly-colored, rubberized beach bag with a draw string. I dumped a dozen extra rounds into the bag and put the revolver in carefully, making certain that I knew its exact position in the opaque bag. I placed the bag on the passenger seat, toward my side, making it look entirely casual, yet so placed that my hand would fall on the grip naturally and without strain or obvious effort.

Before I locked up, I asked the cat what the hell I was going to do with him. He seemed to have an amber-eyed confidence that I was going to make every effort to maintain him in the comfort to which he had become accustomed . . . and to let him out oftener.

I remembered the Shell Ridge Road turnoff from the long nightwalk I had taken with Meyer. It was not far from the south line of the County, slanting off to the right, southwest.

Rural mailboxes. Small frame houses on fill, with the wet marsh behind them, some cypress and live oak hammocks. All of them were on the right side of the road. The left side was fenced wetlands, posted at the proper legal intervals, the wire and posts new. Hounds and banty chickens and little kids and swamp buggies and campers. White dust behind me off the crushed white shell of the limestone road.

Read the signs on the boxes. Stane. Murrity. Floyd. Garrison. Perris.

Perris was a one-story block house painted a pale, water-stained green, with a roof of white asbestos shingles. There was a gnarled and handsome oak in the front yard. There had been white board fencing, but it was rotting away. There had been river gravel in the drive, but most of it had rain-washed away. Some dead trucks and cars sat out to the side of the house, hip deep in the raw green grasses of spring. There were parts of other dead vehicles strewn around. There was a big frame building behind the house, with both overhead doors up, so that I could see into it as I turned into the drive, see a litter of work-benches and hoists and tools. A dainty little baby blue Opel with a savage little snout was parked under the spreading shade of the live oak out in front, its slanting windshield spattered with the grease of the exploding bugs of high-speed travel. When I parked beside the slab porch and turned the engine off, I could hear the muttering hum of a big air-conditioning compressor at the side of the house, and a tinny resonance of the sheet metal housing.

It was three-fifteen when I rang the doorbell. I waited and as I started to ring it again, Lilo Perris pulled it open and looked out through the screen. She wore what I think is called a jump dress, a kind of mini-dress which is shorts rather than a skirt at the bottom. It was a vivid orange, deepening her tan, whitening teeth, bringing out the healthy blue-whites of her eyes. There was a little flicker in those eyes as she looked at me, then glanced beyond me and saw the white convertible out there. No alarm, no surprise. Just a little click of recognition, identification.

At first she was just a girl with a blunt little face, twenty-two or -three. Brawny little chunk of a girl. Then came the extraordinary impact of a total, driving sexuality. I could remember only two other women who had exuded that degree of psychic musk at close range—one was a successful film actress who could not act and had no need to, the other a woman who, before her thirtieth year had married and divorced three fortunes, cutting herself an ample slice of each. It was arrogance and availability. It was posture and look that said, "Here it is, baby, if you're man enough, and I don't think you are, because nobody has been man enough yet." But not that kind of presentation alone. Two other things with it. A total health, the kind of health you see in show dogs and race horses. Glossy pelt, glistening eyes, blood-pink membranes, with pulse and respiration infinitely slow with the body at rest, preparing it for explosive demands. In addition, a perfection of detail, the natural eyelashes like little curved and clipped bits of enameled black wire. No dentist would have defied reality by making teeth that perfect.

"If you were selling something, man, nobody wants to buy if you get the house heated up." Deeper voice than expected, but without huskiness. A clear, flexible contralto.

"So ask me in, Lilo."

She came out and yanked the door shut and let the screen slap shut. She went down the single porch step and across the front yard, certain I would follow her. She picked up a sandspur on the tough sole of her bare right foot, and hardly breaking stride, licked her fingertips, brought the knee high and plucked it off. I saw the velvety bunch and flex of muscles in her brown back as she did so. The jump dress had a deep V back.

In the oak shade she turned and braced an orange haunch against the front fender-curve of the Opel and said, "I'm kind of a car freak. I like to fly this thing, but there's a shimmy up front over eighty and that bastard Henry can't find it. I told him he finds it or I strap him to the goddam hood and wind it up and let him see for himself."

And that was the last ingredient, a flavor of total and dangerous unpredictability. One could never feel at ease with her unless she had been welded into a steel collar, and there was a short length of chain fastened to a heavy eyebolt in a strong wall. And even then you'd take care to see that there was nothing within her reach that she could use to hit with or slice with, or throw. It was the same feeling as the time the pretty lady came aboard *The Busted Flush* with her ocelot, unsnapped his chain, and told him to stay on the yellow couch. He did, and watched every move I made, with pale-green eyes that never blinked, with an occasional ripple of muscles in back and flank. He seemed to smile at me, as if telling me that we both knew he could rip my throat open before I could say "Pretty kitty." It made us very aware of each other in a feral way. If she wanted to strap Henry to the hood of the Opel, she would do so. And if she wanted to wind it way up and then bang the brakes to see how far ahead of her down the highway she could propel Henry, she would do that, too.

I could not use her unless I could appraise her well enough to find strengths and weaknesses. She was so unlike what I had expected, I had to discard all plans, including the wild one of getting her out somewhere where I could thump her unconscious and let her wake up wired to a tree facing the horror of Betsy Kapp. One cannot make any impression on an ocelot by showing it a dead ocelot.

"Nice little car," I said.

"The name is McSomething. Somebody told me."

"McGee."

"McGee, what you are doing is boring me. Can you think of anything to build this up a little? Maybe you get your kick out of memorizing me or something."

"It's like this, Lilo. Hyzer said stay around. So I was killing time until he said leave. But maybe there are some things lying around that could be interesting."

"Depends on what freaks you, Mac."

"The lush life, and so it is always a question of financing it, isn't it?"

"You want to cut yourself in on how I've got it made, living here on my big estate, with all the swimming pools and the billiard room and all that?"

"Maybe it's just that you have talents you're not getting

the maximum return from. You made one hell of an impression on Dori Severiss."

A sharp look of renewed interest. A merry, hearty, crinkly laugh. "Now how *about* you!"

"You could go around drifting and dreaming, girl, and never get loose from this big estate of yours. Lew Arnstead was making a dollar."

"Maybe your idea of a dollar, not mine, Mac. Lew had a nickle-dime way of thinking. He had some ass on call, and he shook some people down here and there, but it was too big a risk for what he was taking out of it. I told him. I told him forty times, honest. I told him he oughta contact somebody in the big time and wholesale those pigs of his for cash and have somebody come and get them before he got in a mess and Hyzer threw him out."

"And you'd know all about that?"

"A few years back, Mac, I used to go on trips with a friend. You keep your ears open, you learn how things are."

Not at all a dull-minded girl. A shrewdness about her that was impressive.

"But didn't you take on some risk when you helped him straighten out Mrs. Severiss?"

She made a face. "I was stupid. I get bored and I do stupid things and get in trouble. I shouldna. He was telling me his problems and I said let me handle it, and he said go ahead. Just that once with her and once with his schoolteacher, what's her name. Geraldine Kimmey. She got herself in a bind by groping some little kid, and then after Lew dated her up three or four times, she wanted to bluff her way off the list, so I had her sing me a lot of soprano where nobody could hear the high notes." A sudden, merry, ingratiating smile. "A shrink could have a picnic checking me out. When I get all edgy and uptight and mean-acting, making somebody scream and sweat works just like a charm. The better they yell, the more warm and friendly I feel toward them. I like to fell in love with Geraldine. It's like I was helping them get past something, or over something. I wonder sometimes if it's got anything to do with being so strong."

"You look healthy enough."

"It's more than that. I'm some kind of freak. Wanta see?"

"Sure."

She looked into the blue car and reached in and took out a beach towel and shook the sand out of it. She went to the front bumper and used the towel to avoid the bumper edge cutting into her hands. She braced herself, back to the bumper, torso erect, knees flexed, shifted her grip and her stance, then took a deep breath, let it out, then snatched up the front end of the car, stood with her knees locked, holding it. Under the thin layer of fat beneath the skin, a female attribute, the sculptured muscles bulged in thighs, calves, shoulders, and arms. Thick cords bulged in her throat as her face slowly darkened. She turned her head slowly and smiled at me, a strangely provocative and knowing smile. Then she lowered it quickly. She wiped the sudden sweat from her arms, throat, and face. I had felt an unexpectedly savage surge of absolutely simple and immediate sexual desire for her, a brute impulse to fell her where she stood and mount her. And she knew it, and had deliberately caused it. There is a perverse streak in all of us, an urgency to experience the unusual. She was totally feminine, and sometime, somewhere, she had discovered that a demonstration of the unusual power of her body would provoke the male. Such physical strength is a rarity, a kind of genetic aberration which could be a throwback to prehistory, to a primitive construction of muscle fiber quite dissimilar to our own. It is more common in men than in women, is quite often coupled with a low order of intelligence which leads to the sideshow career of bending horseshoes, driving spikes barehanded, and folding coins with thumb and forefinger.

She tossed the towel into the car and said, "I can put most men down arm-wrassling. Not very girly-girl, huh?"

"You seem to be all girl, Lilo. I had the idea you were probably on Lew's list."

"Peddling it? Hell, no. I'm not on anybody's list. Lew was on my list, you could say. No matter what anybody says, it's a short list, Mac. With Lew it was sometimes, when he had hung around so long looking like a hound dog it got on my nerves, or when there was something I thought he knew that he wasn't planning to tell me. He always told me."

"Past tense."

"Dead, isn't he?"

"What makes you think so?"

"Because he isn't hanging around me, Mac. And that's the only thing that would keep him away. And because he was going bad fast. He was popping those pills like candy and they were scrambling his brains. He was seeing things, hearing voices, forgetting what he did last, and no idea of what he'd do next. So I guess somebody had to kill him before he spoiled somebody else's fun and games. Somebody tucked him into a swamp. What kind of games are you trying to play with me, Mac?"

"I've been interested in you since last Thursday night when I came within an inch and a half of killing you."

"Me? What the hell are you talking about?"

"The only reason I can come up with why you ran in front of my car was because there was somebody out there in the night you wanted to have see you. But you cut it too close."

Three seconds of silence, then the jolly grin again, and a wink. "I sure did, friend. What happened, my foot slipped coming up that bank, but I thought I could still make it. Then all those headlights were close enough to touch. I felt the breeze from that fender on my bare tail. I didn't mean to put you in the canal though. Sorry. Sure, I wanted somebody to see me. I wanted somebody to see that it was a girl not a man, because they were after Frank Baither."

"Who?"

"Somebody who wanted to kill him and did. Frank was the first and the only real man I ever did know. Some kid stuff before I met him, but after that nobody touched me but Frank, until they jailed him and then sent him up north. He's the one I went on trips with. We were gone four months when I was sixteen one time, and he made thirty thousand dollars and we spent twenty of it."

"What did he knock over?"

"He and two other guys took a casino in Biloxi for ninety on a three-way split. No, it was a hundred, because I remember he had to give ten to the cop who set it up for Frank because the casino was shorting the cop on the insurance money they were paying. Then we went out to California because there was a payroll thing Frank wanted to look at. He decided he didn't like it, and later some other people tried it and one got killed and the other two ended up in Q."

"Who came to kill Frank last Thursday?"

"Two men who'd been in on something Frank never told me about. He said their names were Hutchason and Orville. He said they thought he'd given them a short count on a split. The way it happened, I was practically living there from the time he got back, because he had a lot to catch up on. He heard something outside and woke me up and got his gun and told me to go on home, sneak as far as the road and go like hell. One of them followed me, or both of them. I thought they would think it was Frank and shoot me. So I ran across in front of your car so they'd see me. I went on home. It's only about three and a half miles from here, about. I went back early in the morning and saw the county cars and found out they'd killed him. I just . . . just didn't think anybody could ever kill Frank. You know, I didn't think you'd have a good enough look at me for long enough to remember me."

"If the sheriff knew there'd been a girl there with Baither, wouldn't he know it had been you?"

"He might think on it, but Mister Norm doesn't fuss with me much."

A back country silence, standing in shade. She stood against the big trunk of the tree, one knee flexed, bare foot against the rough gray bark. She idly scratched the rounded top of her brown thigh, and I could hear in the silence the whisper of her nails against the skin. The animal hunger she had awakened with that odd display of strength had not died away. She caught and held my eye and read it, and built it back again with but a slight arching of her back, softening of her mouth.

"Could be," she whispered. "It just could be."

"Think so?"

"Like part of whatever game we're playing. Saying one thing, holding other things back. We can go someplace, try us out. You'd be thinking I'd say more. I'd be thinking you might say more about what you know, or think you know. That would come after the edge was off. I'm not like this often, Mr. Mac. Could be more than you can take on?"

"I manage to totter around."

She said, "I got to go in a minute, see if that damn Nulia has got the old lady cleaned up right this time. Last time she got through the room still stank, and I had to whop her old black ass and make her do it over right."

She grinned, shoved herself away from the tree, and thumped me on the biceps with a small hard brown fist, a considerable blow, and ran to the house, fleet as a young boy.

SEVENTEEN

SHE WAS IN THE HOUSE OVER TEN MIN-utes. She came out and beckoned to me and headed toward my car. By the time I got to it she had jacked the driver's seat forward and turned the key on. I got in the passenger seat and put the rubber beach bag on the floor.

"Easier than giving directions," she said. "I don't want to drive mine until Henry gets that shimmy out of it. Okay with you?"

"Sure."

"Pretty bag belong to a nice lady?" She backed out onto the unpaved road, and headed southwest.

"Friendly lady name of Jeanie Dahl."

"Mmmm. That's where you found out about me and Dori Severiss."

"And Lew's sideline."

She was driving more conservatively than I had expected. "Thought you were getting the scoop from ol' Betsy Kapp, knowing you wasted no time moving in on those giant titties. Never knew just how much Lew talked to her. Never could figure out how they got together in the first place. He had a funny soft spot for that fool woman. I told him once he ought to sign her onto his little team. Even offered to go convince her, but he told me if I ever went near her, he'd club my head right down between my knees, and I think he meant it."

I saw the sign indicating we were leaving Cypress County. "Hyzer asked me to stay in his jurisdiction."

"Right now, mister, does that mean a hell of a lot to you?"

"I wouldn't say that it does."

"We aren't going to be out of it long, honey. Right turn coming up, before we come out onto the Trail, and it swings back into Cypress County. Car rides nice."

"Seems to. Where are we going?"

"A place a friend of mine lent me when he went in the Navy. It's real private."

And it was. It was a fairly new aluminum house trailer of average size, set on a cement-block foundation on a small cypress hammock in marshy grassland. Limestone fill had been trucked in to make a small causeway between an old logging road and the hammock. A flock of white egrets went dipping and winging away through the cypress and hanging gray moss when she parked by the trailer.

She squatted and reached up and behind a place where a block had been left out for ventilation purposes, and pulled out the keys. She went over and unlocked a small cement-block pumphouse and tripped a switch that started a husky gasoline generator.

"Now we've got air conditioning and, in a little while, ice cubes, Mac, honey."

"Can I object to Mac?"

"You can ask for anything your evil heart desires, man."

"Travis or Trav or McGee."

"So I settle for McGee."

"You do that."

She unlocked the trailer and stepped up into it. "Hey, let's open this thing up until the air conditioning starts doing something."

We opened the windows. It was tidy inside. It had the compact flavor of a good cabin cruiser, with ample stowage. She checked to make certain there was water in the ice-cube trays. She turned on a little red radio and prowled the dial until she found some heavy rock and turned it up far enough to drown out the sound of the generator and the whine of the refrigerator and the busy whackety-thud of the compressor on the air conditioner.

She reached around herself and undid the few inches of zipper that reached from the V back to the base of her spine, and said, "Can you think of anything special we're waiting on, McGee?" She shrugged it forward off her shoulders, lowered it and stepped out of it and flipped it aside. I noted with a remote objectivity that her breasts were a slight quarter-tone lighter than the rest of her, and that the bikini band around her hips was as white as in the photograph.

She was as totally at home in her naked hide as any animal. She moved without either coyness or boldness, walked over to the bunk bed, knee-walked toward the wall, rolled over onto her back. "As any jackass can plainly see, I am all the way ready. Whyn't you close the other windows, but let's leave this here one open the way it is? You're sure in some terrible rush, huh? Gun shy, McGee?"

I closed the windows with all deliberate speed. It had to be a setup. Though Meyer might try to argue the point, young girls do not make a habit of suddenly propositioning me, driving me off to a hideaway, peeling off their clothes, rolling onto their backs, and breathing hard.

But just how was I being set up? Strong as she was, I couldn't see her doing much bare-handed damage to me. If there was a weapon, where was it? Down behind the mattress? There were no cupboards she could reach. As I unbuttoned my shirt, I noticed that the two little hooks which held the aluminum screen in the window were undone.

Setup. Phone call from the house. Lots of noise. She had opened that window, so she had unhooked the screen. She had moved over to the far side of the bunk bed, under the window. We were expecting a visitor. Maybe he had arrived and was squatting under the window, awaiting the sounds of festivity. She was certainly powerful enough to hold me or anyone motionless long enough, and perfectly positioned.

She was obviously in a state of sexual excitement, her face slack, eyes blurring. She was rolling her hips slowly from side to side, and her breasts were swollen, nipples thrusting, belly muscles twitching and rippling.

"Come on," she said in a petulant smothered tone. "Come *on!*"

So I fumbled with buttons long enough for her to roll up and crawl toward me, reaching to help, and when she was positioned correctly I thought of the way Betsy's face looked, and I hit Lilo Perris as hard as I have ever hit anyone, and as perfectly. I reached up as though getting my hands free of the shirt buttons, then I dropped my hand. It traveled about eight inches before it hit her on the left side of the chin, and kept going another foot and a half after it knocked her mouth open. Sensing a reluctance to hit a female, I had told myself to hit through the target and beyond, not hit at it. When you hit at something, you pull it. When you hit someone in the nose, you try to smash an imaginary nose on a person standing directly behind him. That gets the back into it.

She dropped immediately and bonelessly, face down, head hanging over the side of the bed, one arm dangling, legs splayed in frog posture. I put my fingertips against the pulse in her throat and it was fast but strong.

Now, honey, we get ready for visitors. Try the cupboards. Nothing. Nothing. Hmm, an extension cord. Box of Kleenex. Nothing in the next one. There now! Nice fat roll of black plastic electrician's tape.

Roll you over in the clover. Feel the jaw, shift it about a little. No looseness. No gritty sound of bone edges. Didn't even chip a pretty tooth. Beginning to puff and darken right there on the button, though. Thumb the mouth full of tissue, and draw a black X with tape across it. Bring your arms in front of you, and hold your elbows so they touch, and wind the tape around and around. A nice binding just above the elbow, another around the forearms, a third around the wrists. Now clasp the loose hands together and . . . around and around like this. An awkward attitude of prayer, dear girl. Up with the knees, close together. One binding just above the knees, one just below, and one around the ankles. Now, my muscular darling, we roll you up into a ball, into fetal position, and we put the extension cord around your legs under your knees, thread it up between your upper arms and breasts, and we tie it right here, at the nape of your neck, just firmly enough. Comfy? Special treatment for a very strong girl.

Radio blasting away. Sound protection works both ways. Stay down, so you won't be seen by anybody looking in the windows, McGee. Careful with the door. Bit by bit. Nothing. Step down. Strategic window on the other side. Ease around the end. Nothing. Now up to the last corner, lie flat, stick head around the corner made of block.

And by God, what do you know, there is broad, brown Henry Perris, master mechanic, wife-stealer, and Sunday pronger of the stepdaughter, standing very tense, squatting below the window next to a handy pile of block. What has good old Henry got in his hand? Why, he has what looks like a short section of hoe handle with a short sharp piece of metal sticking out of the end of it. Head bent in attitude of listening. Fingertips against the aluminum love nest. What are you waiting for, Henry? A signal? Why, of course, how logical. In extremis, the lady yells to the unwary chap in the saddle, "Now! Now!" And good old Henry stands on the blocks and lifts the screen out and leans in the window and sticks that sharp piece of metal right into the back of lover boy's head, right where the base of the skull fastens onto the neck, and for a lady who gets her jollies out of hurting people, if her timing is right, that must, indeed, be a memorable thrill. Same thrill as the lady spider devouring the mate while they are still coupled.

One might, in fact, suspect that Hutchason and Orville both met this same fate in this same place at these same hands, because there was no time to set up anything so complex in the time she had on the phone.

I eased back and stood up. Insight is perhaps what pops to the surface of the mind after subterranean processes of logic have taken place. If Perris and Lilo were two of the team of five who took the money truck, then Frank Baither went to Raiford knowing they would stay right in the area, waiting for the division after he got out. And if Hutch or Orville showed up, they could not make Henry or Lilo tell them something they did not know. And it would be the assigned chore of Henry and Lilo to quietly take them out of the scene. Baither would certainly know that Lilo was, by inclination, a competent executioner. Unless Frank were out of reach, she could have no chance to get them off guard, to get close enough. And then, of course, the lie to Frank when he came back. They never showed up. Maybe something happened to them. They never showed up, Frank.

Then the dead men had been used to decoy Frank Baither. To send him clattering around in the night in the old pickup, so that they were in position for him when he came back.

Out of the delusion of their own irresistible male

charm, Hutch and Orville, one at a time, had clambered so eagerly onto the deathbed, coupled with the strong brown spider. I realized that had I not found Betsy's letter to Lew, had I not seen the sweat and pallor on Dori Severiss's face when she told me of Lilo, I could have been less on guard. I could have bought her rationalization about it. "You'd be thinking I'd say more."

No problem to phone Henry at the station. And he could scoot west on the Trail, turn onto the far end of Shell Ridge Road, be there before we got there. She had driven slowly. He could drive beyond the little causeway to the hammock, tuck his car away, come back under the cover of the noise of generator and rock radio.

I had revealed too much to her. But maybe it did not have to be very much, if she was that twisted. "It's like I was helping them get past something or over something." Helping them get over the problem of living, of breathing. And Dori saying, ". . . smiling at me and giggling and calling me love names and saying how much fun it would be to really kill me."

Thoughts roaring through the mind like a train racketing through a tunnel, while another part of my mind flipped through the possible ways of taking Henry Perris. I did not know how well he would move. I knew he could be as powerful as he looked. And I knew he had a useful weapon in his hand.

Estimate the triangle. Henry was fifteen feet from me. The white convertible was parked twenty feet in back of Henry, and perhaps thirty feet from me. Burst out in a full run and I could almost be at the car before he could react. She had turned it around and parked it heading out. Driver door was on this side. Beach bag on the floor on the far side.

So run around the hood, yank door open, pick up bag, find shape of gun through the fabric, and come up with it with a very good chance of taking one step to the side and firing across the hood through the fabric. If he was too close, there'd be no time for shoulder or thigh. If he was far enough away, one into the ground at his feet might do it.

One and a two and a three and go, McGee. Don't lose your stride by looking at him. Not until you round the hood. Now look. And he is down off the blocks, and he is yanking the bright rubberized beach bag open in fumbling haste, and you should think a little better, McGee. Your thinking is spotty. You work one thing out and get overcome with your goddam brilliance, and forget that she parked the car in a blind spot, where it could not be seen from any window of the trailer, and so he had to use that angle as his approach, and it would be natural to check the car, heft the bag, finger the distinctive shape, bring it along.

All the shots are going to do out here is startle the egrets and puzzle the brown girl, if she is awake yet. And unless you get smart very fast, they are going to make some very final and very ugly holes in a fellow you have often felt kindly toward over the years.

Fact: It is not accurate at any long range. Take a quick look into the car. Fact: The keys are gone. Fact: He has the gun out of the bag. Fact: It is too damned long a run for cover, if you want to get into that cypress. Probability: If you stay by the car, he will angle out to the front or rear, stay fifteen feet from it, and pot you in perfect safety.

I dropped and looked under the car. Coming at the predicted angle toward the rear end of the car. Not running. Better if he was running. Plodding along. Patience and good nerves.

Find place with best clearance under the thing. Okay. Onto the back. Pull yourself along under it like a cat playing under a sofa. Out the other side, roll up onto the feet and into full speed for the first few steps, then sacrifice speed for that crouching zigzag, like long ago, when they'd put the old tires on the practice field. Absolutely ice-cold traget area in the middle of the spine. Corner of the trailer apparently receding into the distance. Not coming close very fast. Bam. No impact. That thing would hit you like a small sledge. Bam. And you are around the corner, skittering, skidding, the comedy runner, sliding to a bulge-eyed frantic stop, yanking the door open, plunging into the trailer, falling to hands and knees, spinning, yanking the door shut, taking the wheezing breaths, feeling the tremble in the knees.

The red radio is hollering about "a little help from my friends." Sidle to a window and try to spot him. Sudden silence. Music chopped off. Dying wheeze of the air conditioning, fading whir of fan. Methodical fellow. Taking his time and thinking it out. Avoiding mistakes.

I crept to the galley area, opened logical drawers, found a flimsy carving knife, a dull paring knife, four rust-flecked oyster knives, steel blade and handle, rounded tip. Tried one. It balanced precisely at the juncture of handle and blade. Each was forged out of a single piece of mediocre steel. One in the right hand, handle outward, blade flat against the underside of the thumb and the heel of the thumb. Provided a little amusement that time I spent holed up with Miguel in the Sierras. He had the single throwing knife. Tree target. Basic lessons. Always the same motion, a long forearm snap. Always the same force. Let it slide away from the thumb, naturally. Useful only at reasonably exact distances. Make a half turn and chunks home at fifteen feet. Hold the handle end and get a full turn at thirty feet. Hold the blade and get a turn and a half at forty-five. Got arm-weary throwing it and foot-weary trudging up to yank it out of the tree and going back to the mark. I held the other three oyster knives by the handle in my left hand. Miguel said a man who tries for the target at thirty feet, when it is an important target, is frivolous. Fifteen feet is so much more certain. At the slow rate of spin, it will be blade first from twelve to eighteen feet, enough to slash at the outer limits of the range. At ten feet or twenty it will strike flat. Do not try to adjust. Throw always for the right-angle impact at fifteen feet.

A rattle of small stones under the nearby footstep, beyond the aluminum. "McGee?" Hoarse voice. No urgency. Calm and reasonable. "Want to do some dickerin', McGee?"

I backed away from the side of the window, then leaned a little forward, cupped my hand to confuse the point of origin of my voice. "What are you selling, Henry?"

He was selling gunshot wounds. Not bam this time. More like braing. Hole at chest height a foot in from the window edge and an exit hole high on the far side. I thudded both feet on the carpeted flooring and moaned and backed away.

"No good, you tricky bastard. I heard it go whining off, tumbling. Couldn't have touched you. What did you do to her?"

Lilo answered. She squalled behind the packed wad of tissue, a sound of pure animal anger, muffled, like a cat in the bottom of a laundry hamper.

"Tied and gagged, eh?" Henry said. "That would take some doing. That I would like to see. I really would. Getting warm enough for you in there?"

No point in answering him.

"I've figured out something, McGee. I think what I'll do is go around and turn off the bottle gas for the stove at the tank and cut the tubing and shove the end back into the hole and turn the gas on again. Good idea?"

Yes, it was a splendid idea. Simple and effective. After a while he could figure some way of igniting it, if I didn't come choking and stumbling out. It was such a good idea, that it did not seem logical that he would stand around and chat about it. He would go do it. So there was a factor that kept him from doing it. And that was most probably the serious effect it would have on the health of Miss Perris.

I moved back to the galley, put the knives down, and in one surge slid the small refrigerator out into the middle of the work space and crouched behind it.

"Henry, at the very first whiff of propane, I am going to take one of these dull kitchen knives and saw that throat open on your little pal. You had better believe it."

"Now why should that make any difference to me?"

"I wouldn't know. The abiding love of a stepfather for a high-spirited girl, maybe. It's the only thing you left open that I could try, Henry."

"Go ahead and cut away." Just a little too much indifference.

"Henry, you could try to smoke me out. Or you could get a piece of rope or cable and fasten it low on one side of this thing, throw it across the roof, hook it to the Buick, and roll this thing over. Let's see now. You've got a car here. You could swing the Buick around and get a good start and just run the hell into this hunk of aluminum. But if I smell smoke, Henry. Or feel movement. Or hear the Buick. Or hear anything else I can't understand, I am going to start sawing."

In the long silence Lillian made muted bleating noises, and even tethered as she was, managed to snap and flex enough muscles to bounce herself around on the bunk bed.

"She tied up good? Can't get loose?"

"Guaranteed," I said. I moved as quietly as I could, over to the bunk bed and sat close to her, and put the oyster knives on a shelf above the foot of the bed, blades outward. "Matter of fact, Henry, I'm sitting so close to her that if you try any more trick shooting, you can just as easily get her as me."

I looked down at her. She was on her left side in her curled position, her feet toward me. She looked at me with a ferocity that was an almost physical impact. Then her muscles bulged and her eyes closed as she strained to stretch or break the tough tape. I could hear little poppings and cracklings of joints and sinews. Then she let her breath out and relaxed, snuffling hard. I reached and gave her a friendly caress along the flank, a little pat on the brown haunch. She snapped into the air like a shrimp on a dock, eyes maniacal.

"We can work this out, McGee," he called.

"Now just how do we do that, Henry?"

"The thing you want to do most is stay alive."

"I guess I'd give that the number one priority."

"I could trade some time, maybe. I don't know how much time I'd need with her, or how much time I'd need after I get through with her. If I back off, far enough, and get the car keys to you, you could get away from here.

But there'd be the problem of you going straight to a phone and messing me up."

"And you can't take my word."

"I wouldn't think so."

"And I can't take yours, Henry. Stalemate."

"What?"

"It's a chess term. Neither player has any way to win."

"Oh. By God, I sure messed up when I tried the idea of using that envelope. I guess I was edgy. I thought you were some dumb-dumb who'd look good to Mister Norm. Lilo told me it was a bad idea, but I told her to do it anyway."

"You left the envelope in the phone book in the booth when you went to deliver the Olds, eh? Then she picked it up and took it to Baither's place."

"I guess you just fixed it so there's no way I can leave you go now, McGee. Sure. Lew let her into Frank's house to see where it happened. Gave her a chance to drop the envelope when Lew wasn't looking. All she had to do was promise Lew a quick piece. Lew was so hooked on it, he'd have chopped up his old mother and sold her for cat food for a chance to get into Lilo's pants. She kept that boy on short rations."

Lilo was trying to tell me something with her eyes. Pleading. Working her mouth around. I leaned and got an edge of the tape with my thumbnail and ripped the X off her mouth. She tongued the spitty mass of Kleenex out and swallowed several times.

She said in a low voice, "I know where a lot of money is. He wants to make me tell him. If you kill him, I'll tell you. We can take it all and go away."

"Killing is something I charge high for."

"Your end would be four hundred and fifty thousand. Right down the middle. No tricks. I wanted to leave him out because he's stupid. You're not. I need somebody like you to help me with it."

"No tricks."

She smiled her happy smile, her pretty and disarming urchin grin. "No tricks, honey. Ever."

"So tell me right now where it is. You know. Give me a motivation."

"Afterward. I promise. Get this tape off, huh?"

Henry shouted from a new position outside the trailer, "Having a little talk, are you? She trying to sell you something, McGee?"

"She's trying to sell me you, Henry."

I saw her face contort, and I put my finger to my lips before she could join the conversation. I reached and heeled her jaw shut and put the old X of tape back on, tore some more strips and sealed her off, and once again she tried the bonds, in a convulsion so violent it seemed possible she might break bones in the effort.

"You know what she is?" Henry called.

"I've got a pretty good idea."

"What she was doing to Frank kept making me sick to my stomach, McGee. I was over at the window, gagging, when he finally told her, his voice so weak I couldn't hear it. She had that ice pick into his heart before I could take half a step. She wanted to make sure he wouldn't say it twice. You want to trust her?"

"I don't want to trust either one of you."

Again he had changed his position. He was moving quietly. "It's that word you said before. Stalemate?"

He was back near the pile of block under the window above the bunk bed. I could guess the chance he was thinking of taking. Crouch on the block then come erect and fire through the screen. The window was three feet square, and the bottom sill was about twenty inches above the level of the bed. I debated the idea of backing off and then taking a dive out the window. The unhooked screen would swing out. But I would have to hit it hard enough to carry all the way through, to get my legs high enough to clear the sill. I would overshoot him and land sprawling and rolling away from him, giving him the perfect shot, because he would have time to recover from surprise before I could reverse direction and get back to him. If I waited until his silhouette popped up in the window, I'd give him a wing shot.

The last thing he would expect would be for me to come

back outside where he had the considerable edge. I slipped my shoes off and leaned closer to the window. "Henry, if you are thinking of taking a pot shot through the window, I've got her right in front of me. Think it over."

I gathered my four oyster knives and went toward the door as quickly and as quietly as I could. He would think it over for a few seconds, and realize his best move would be to suddenly yank the screen off and stand up and cover me and the girl at close range. He could come in over the sill and have it all his own way, because he could get so close I couldn't use her for cover. She was too small.

Out the door and down, and quickly around the front of the thing. Heard the tinny clatter of the falling screen as I rounded the last corner. Henry leaning in the window, fifteen feet away. Miguel's voice from long ago, speaking inside my head. "The elbow, *amigo*, should point toward the target, and it should not move until after the release. At the release the arm is straight, then it moves down so the hand ends up to the rear of the right calf of the leg. Throw strong, but never hurry it. The left foot is ahead of the right, both knees bent. The knife is close to the right ear before the throw. The wrist, it is locked. It does not move. The aim is to the center of the body. If it is an armed man, finish the throw with a dive to the ground, and then roll to the right, if it is a right-handed man, because he must then swing the gun to fire across his body, which is more difficult, no?"

So, squinting in the dazzle of sunlight against bright aluminum, I threw strong, and plucked the second blade from my left hand and threw strong again, and dived forward and rolled hard to the right, found the third blade as I came up, heard the close-range shot, felt the sting of gravel against my thigh, knew as I released the third that I had hurried it too much and was off target. Nearly dropped the fourth, fumbling for it, snapped it back into position, and held it there as Henry in a crooked crouch showed me his white grin, fired directly down into the ground, and tumbled off the block, lifting his arms to break the fall. He rolled onto his back and over onto his face, an arm pinned under him. Both legs quivered and kicked and leaped about, like a dog asleep in a dream of running. Then he flattened against the packed earth in that unmistakable stillness, that death-look which changes the clothes into something stuffed with cold ground meat.

I had a sudden chill which chattered my teeth. I approached him. His left arm was flexed, hand over his head. Right hand and gun were somewhere under him. The first one had to be the one socketed into the left armpit, hitting when he was still leaning in the window. Another lay on the ground by the blocks, unstained. A third was hanging by the tip from a long groove it had sliced in the aluminum side, under the window. There wasn't much blood on the coveralls near the protruding steel handle. It had to have done a mortal damage in there, in the arteries above the heart.

"So a knife is ogly, Travees? I know. And a gun is ogly and death is ogly. Sometimes there is only a knife to use. And the difference is the knowing how to do it. We are here for a time. So? Why not learn from one who knows, to pass the time?"

Thank you, Miguel. Thanks for the lessons. Without them both of us would be dead, instead of only you. Sleep well.

EIGHTEEN

I WENT BACK INTO THE INCREASING oven temperature of the trailer. She had wormed herself around so she could watch the door, sweating so heavily in the heat she looked oiled. I could see the momentary astonishment in the lift of black brows. She had no reason to believe the shots had not gone into me.

And if I could walk in, the stepdaddy had to be dead. The upper half of her face changed, showing that she was trying to smile under the black tape. If I took it off, she would tell me that all is well, lover. We bury Henry in the marsh. Half the money is yours. We'll be a great team.

I sat on the corner of the bed and looked at her. Making someone dead is a game for the unimaginative, for someone who cannot ever really believe they, too, can die. The curse of empathy is to see yourself in every death, and to see the child hidden in the body of every corpse. The local box score was sick-making. Hutch, Orville, Baither, Lew Arnstead, Betsy Kapp, Henry Perris. Might as well add Linda Featherman. Meyer came close to being on the list.

I don't know what she read in my face, but it took the smile-try away. Her eyes turned watchful. Glossy black hair was sweat-matted, and droplets slid down her cheeks, her ribs and breasts and belly, darkening the faded blue spread.

I got up and opened the other windows so some breeze could come through. Her eyes followed me. I stopped by the bed and said, "Somebody will come after you, Lillian."

Violent negative shake of the head. Grunting attempts at speech. She doubled further, grinding her mouth against her round knees, trying to wipe the tape off.

I took a last long look at her. "I wouldn't want to hear anything you could say. I wouldn't want the whole score, if you were part of the deal. Or double the score."

I put the screen back on and went inside and hooked it. I made sure the other screens were all hooked. I locked the trailer and put the keys in my pocket, sat on the low step outside and tied my shoes. I had to touch Henry's body to get the keys to the Buick.

After a quarter mile I rolled the windows up and turned the air on full, aiming the outlets at me. My shirt was unbuttoned, and the chill air dried my sweaty chest. I found my way out to Shell Ridge Road, and turned back on it, heading northeast.

When I came to the Perris place, I turned in and went to the door. An elderly woman, tall and stringy, opened the door and looked at me without expression. She was saffron-brown, the racial mix of Seminole and black in her face.

"Are you Nulia?"

"Yem."

"Miss Perris asked me to stop and tell you that she won't be back tonight, and neither will Mr. Perris."

"Fixing to go on home now, back to keer for my own. No way I can stay on. She *know* that."

I found one of Lennie Sibelius's fifty-dollar bills, damp with my exertions. I handed it to her and said, "Please stay on and look after Mrs. Perris, Nulia."

She looked at it and would not let herself be impressed. "Some bad thing going on, cap'n?"

"You could say that."

"I pray to the Lord ever living day of my lifetime for

the devil to come a-crawlin' up out of hell, huffin' fire and stompin' his clove hoofsies, and claim his own, and snatch her back down to the black pit and the eternal fire." She put the fifty in her apron pocket. "I'll stay take keer, but working for you, cap'n, not her, til you come tell me stop. Much obliged."

Twenty after five by the bank clock when I got to the center of town. Temperature: ninety-two degrees.

Parked beyond the patrol cars. Went inside. Business as usual. One of the brisk ones behind the high counter said that the sheriff was busy. I said I wanted to see him right now. It did not sound like my own voice. He looked at me and read something in my face that made him go into a point like a good bird dog.

A few minutes later he took me to Hyzer's office and stood behind me. I said, "I want to tell you some things. You ought to have your tape rolling. I would like to have King Sturnevan here to listen to it."

"He's off duty."

"Can you call him in?"

Hyzer found a number on a list under the glass on his desk, dialed it, and in the silence I could hear the burr of the rings at the other end. He hung up after the eighth. "Will Billy Cable do?"

I thought it over. It had to be one or the other of them. It couldn't be both. I nodded. Hyzer told the desk man to tell communications to call Billy in.

I sat in a chair six feet from the desk and waited. Sheriff Norman Hyzer continued with his desk work, in faultless concentration. In seven minutes by the wall clock, Billy Cable knocked and came in. He looked at me with hard-faced antagonism.

"Can you have him sit over there beside the desk, so I can watch his face, Sheriff?"

"What kind of shit is this?" Billy said.

"Sit over here, Cable," Hyzer ordered. "The tape is on, McGee."

"Sheriff, did you ever hear how one of the planets, one way way out from the sun, was discovered? Nobody had ever seen it because not enough light hit it, and they didn't know it was there and didn't know where to look."

"You called me in off patrol to listen to—?"

"Keep your mouth shut, Billy."

"They measured the pattern of orbit of all the other planets, and they found out that the pattern wasn't quite right, that there had to be some gravitational attraction they hadn't found yet. So they worked up the math and figured out where to look, and found it. I know the patterns aren't right. I can't make them fit. So somebody else has to be in this. Somebody has exerted force and pressure to distort the patterns, Sheriff."

"What sort of things have impressed you as being . . . a divergence from the norm, Mr. McGee."

"You diverge a little, Sheriff. You have this great air of efficiency and high moral rectitude. People seem to believe that you know everything that goes on in your county. Yet you let one of your deputies run a call-girl operation right under your nose, using his badge to muscle them into the operation."

"Sherf, do you want me to—"

"You are going to listen to this with your mouth shut, Cable, if I have to have you bound and gagged."

"Yes, sir."

Hyzer was looking at me attentively. I said, "You also took the risk of demoralizing your own troops, Sheriff, by letting Arnstead get away with acts which would have gotten another deputy tossed out. When you finally did bring charges against him and threw him out, it surprised him."

"Go on, please."

"And I cannot understand your appraisal of Lilo Perris. There are enough people in this county who know that she is a sick, vicious, twisted, dangerous, rotten animal so that somehow some of the information should have filtered back to you. You did a nice job of reconstructing the money-truck job as being Baither's project. You must have known the previous relationship between Baither and the Perris girl. She would be the logical one to have played the part of the young waitress in a blond wig. But you either have a blind spot, or you want to sell others that blind spot by calling her just a healthy, high-spirited young lady. So that either puts you into the middle of the scene, Sheriff, or it means that somebody has a kind of leverage they can use on you which can prevent you from doing the kind of job you pretend to do."

"She may have foolishly placed herself in a position where—"

"Sheriff! Here is a letter I have been carrying around with me. I had it hidden in the car. Betsy Kapp wrote it a few months ago to Lew Arnstead. As a practicing student of human nature, I think you will agree that it has that perfect ring of truth. It illustrates one of those . . . positions she foolishly placed herself in." I leaned and flipped it onto the desk, saying, "I suppose you could bring in Roddy Barramore and get a confirmation."

He read it to himself, and it made the skull-shape show through the flesh and skin. His face seemed to shrink and dwindle. He cleared his throat and, in a flat voice, read it into the record. I could see that it cost him, but I could not understand why.

He said, "When Mrs. Kapp is located, I will want to get further confirmation from her that she wrote this letter."

"Mrs. Kapp was wired to a tree sometime Sunday evening. The wire was around her throat, and she is very very dead."

Hyzer picked his hat up and stood up. "You'll take us there right now."

"When I'm through. A little delay won't make a damned bit of difference to her."

After a long hesitation he sat down. "Where did you get this letter?"

"I found one of Lew's little hidey-holes." I reached into the front of my shirt and heard Billy's hand slap at his holster, and I quickly pulled out the packet of pictures. I tossed them onto the desk. "Arnstead's sample case. Arnstead's Rent-a-Broad. I know who some of them are. Lilo Perris, for example. Geraldine Kimmey. Linda Featherman."

Billy hitched his chair closer, leaning to peer at the photographs as Hyzer examined them.

"Jesus H. Christ!" Billy said.

I said, "Don't act as if you never knew he was in the business, Billy."

"Hell, I knew he had some hustlers working. But Miss Kimmey! And the Featherman girl? Hell, no!"

"Sheriff, Betsy Kapp's body is not far from the place where Lew Arnstead had his number-one storage place. Somebody tore the place up and found his barrel safe under the fire brick on the hearth and tore it open and had a bonfire. I think that's where he hid the items that gave him the most leverage over the women. Special pictures, written confessions, assignment lists, date, time, price, and place. So somebody very interested in removing all evidence regarding some specific girl could have gone there and burned the records on all of them, and taken the money he kept there. They could have known or suspected Lew was dead, and wanted to keep somebody else from picking up where he left off. Or they could have thought he was still living, and wanted to put him out of business, or get one specific girl off the hook. Or maybe they didn't want anybody to ever be able to prove that one of Mister Norm's deputies had been running a string of women."

"Lots of possibilities, Mr. McGee."

"Try another one, too. Lew and Betsy Kapp had a special relationship that was different from the setup he had with his other women. He could have told her about that place, and she could have gone there at the wrong time, when somebody was cleaning it out."

"Shall we go now?"

"After some more possibilities and some things I know are true, Sheriff. Five people on the truck job. Baither, Perris, Hutch, Orville, and Lilo. Hutch and Orville came into the area, probably quite a while back. I think I know where you should look for the bodies. About that envelope. Lilo got into the Baither house before she let Lew take her into the pump house. The previous night she worked on Baither until he told her where to find the money. Henry was there. But it had made him sick and he

had walked away from it and didn't hear it. So she put the
ice pick into Baither so he wouldn't tell it twice."

Hyzer folded his hands and rested them on the edge of
the desk and sat with his eyes closed.

The phone rang. He picked it up. "Sheriff Hyzer. Yes,
King. Go ahead. What! All right. Go back there and stay
there. We'll be along."

He hung up and pinched the bridge of his nose, eyes
closed, scowling. At last he looked at me and said,
"McGee, as long as we're putting the cards face up, I'll
tell you that Sturnevan wasn't off duty. I got permission to
let him work in the county to the south of us. I'm the only
one who knows that. The call I made to his home was just
some misdirection. I had him put a beeper on Henry
Perris's Rambler and hook up the directional equipment
in his own private car. He just phoned in to say Perris got
away from him, and he had to spend a lot of time cruising
back roads until he found the one that would finally take
him in the right direction to locate the car. He found
Perris and the girl. They're dead."

I hadn't worried about fingerprints, or the tire prints of
the Buick. And Nulia would talk about her fifty dollars.
"The girl was all right when I left the trailer," I said. "But
Henry wasn't. He was dead. I killed him. I came here
from there."

Cop eyes. Suddenly you are on the other side of an
invisible fence, and they stare across the fence at you, like
a rancher would stare at a sick steer.

"I left the gun under him. He fell on it. Henry was very
determined to kill me. I threw an oyster knife into him.
I'll reenact it at the scene."

Hyzer stood up and said to Billy, "Make sure he's clean
and we'll bring him along. Have Wallace and Townsend
follow with their gear. Make sure they bring the flood-
lights. I'll radio Doc on our way down there."

Back over the same roads, riding in the same cage
where I had ridden with Meyer, in the same faint stink of
illness and despair. The second car was close behind us
when we pulled up to the trailer. There was a big sunset

224 JOHN D. MACDONALD

beginning to take shape, tinting the aluminum trailer a golden orange.

They got out and left me in the cage. King was standing by an old green-and-white Dodge sedan, in much the same off-duty uniform he had worn when I met him at the Adventurer, cigar in the corner of his mouth. They talked for a little while and then Billy came back and let me out.

"From the beginning," Hyzer snapped. "A short version. No oratory. We can fill in the details later."

So I gave them the bones of it, including where the gun came from, how he had nearly gotten me out by my car, how I had gone inside and gotten out again, and where I had stood, and the condition of the girl when I left her.

They took me in for a look at her. She was still trussed up. She was on her side on the rug beside the bunk bed. The rug was soaked. There was a blue plastic bucket on its side on the rug near her head. The tape had been pulled off her mouth. Her hair was soaked. Her face was dark under the tan, a strange color. The light was going fast. Eyes half open. Foam caked in the corner of her mouth.

"Somebody held her head in that bucket," Billy said, "pulling it out to give her a chance to talk and shoving it in again when she wouldn't. So finally she did and McGee shoved her head back into the bucket and held it there until she drowned for sure, then let go of her. She fell over on her side just like that and he walked out."

"Billy," I said, "you are a hundred-and-ten-percent jackass."

"Sher'f," he said, "you think he would have said anything at all about this if King hadn't called in when he did? You know damn well he wouldn't."

Hyzer did not answer. He kept staring at the body of the girl.

King said, "You don't make good sense, Billy. Why would he come in at all? No, sir. I say somebody come here after he left and before I could find my way to where that damn needle kept pointing."

There were too many big men in that trailer. It was overcrowded. The girl lay dead at our feet. I felt faint.

Hyzer pushed by us and we followed him out. The doctor arrived, the ambulance following him in. By then they had to hold lights on the bodies, but they were short examinations. No enigma as to the cause of death.

"On the man," he said, "it got just deep enough to slit the arch of the aorta, I'd say. Death in eight to ten seconds. Visible petechial hemorrhages in the girl's eyes and characteristic darkening of the skin. Death by drowning or suffocation. Need the time pinned down? I took the temperatures. At least one hour, possibly two."

"There's another one for you," Hyzer said.

"Another one! What the hell is going on?"

"I'll get in touch later."

They had taken the pictures for the record. I watched them slide the two meat baskets into the ambulance and take off into the dusk at leisurely pace. No hurry anymore.

I walked over to where Hyzer stood and said, "On my way back I stopped at the Perris place and gave the woman there some money to stay with Mrs. Perris. I told her the girl and Mr. Perris wouldn't be back tonight. I thought the girl would be in custody. I didn't know she'd be dead."

He looked at me. "What?"

"I said I stopped and gave . . ."

"Yes. Yes, I heard you. Cable, Sturnevan, stay here and help them finish up. Billy, you ride back in with King. No. Have King show you where Perris's car is and you bring that in. I'll take McGee back with me. Come on." As we approached the car, he said, "You can ride in the front."

"Thank you."

He drove badly. The car wandered and he would slow down and speed up for no reason.

I saw in the reach of headlights the blue Opel under the big tree, and then he swung into the driveway and stopped.

"Come on," he said and I followed him to the doorway of the lighted house.

Nulia opened it and said, with a pleasure that surprised

me, "Evenin', Sher'f Hyzer. Evenin'! Y'all keer to come in the house?"

I followed him in. "How is she tonight, Nulia?"

"Well, you know. Nothing much changes."

"I think the best thing to do is tell her right away. They're both dead, Nulia. Henry and Lillian."

She held her clenched hands against her chest and bowed her head, closed her eyes, lips moving silently. "Amen," she said. "Best she should know. What in the world will happen to her now?"

"I'll see that she gets care. McGee, you wait here."

He went through the living room with assured step and into a hallway.

Nulia said, "Sher'f comes to see Miz Wanda sometimes. Calls me to my own place, asks me to call him when I'm sure they's both out for a spell. She like a ball of soft bread dough. Cain't move one finger. Sure needs a heap of keer. For talking, she blink her eye. One time for yes, two times for no. Closes them entire when she don't want to talk no more."

He was in there fifteen minutes. His face looked weary when he came out. "She taken it okay you think, Sher'f?"

"I guess so."

"Shouldn't want to cry no eyes out for them two, her or anybody else. I'm all fixed to stay here the night. My eldest brang me what I need."

I went out and got in with him and he drove better. He slowed down and put a spotlight on the side of the road, then made a careful turn over a short private bridge over the drainage canal and drove into a yard.

"Baither place?" I asked.

He said it was, turned off the lights and motor and got out. He leaned against the door on the driver's side as if suddenly taken ill.

"You all right, Norman?"

"He had two weeks before he set himself up for my jail and his guilty plea and Raiford. He could reasonably figure on two, three, or four years, because he was going to go after a perfect record up there. He did all the little maintenance chores necessary when you are going to leave a house vacant in this climate through the hot seasons, through the chance of hurricane. I used to come out here and try to think like Frank Baither. I think he set up a meet to make the split, set it up far enough from here so he bought the time to tuck it all away. It was bulky, you know. I got the track deposit list. Twenty-three thousand in ones, for example. They're counted by weight. Ninety-nine bills on the scale or a hundred and one, and the pointer swings way off center. Automatic banding. A hundred and fifty-one five in fives. Three hundred seventy-three eight in tens. One hundred eighty-eight three in twenties. Ninety-six thousand in fifties. Eighty-eight thousand in hundreds. Nine hundred and twenty thousand six hundred dollars. Take just the tens. Over thirty-seven thousand pieces of paper. Two hundred and forty pounds or so. The whole thing could go into six heavy suitcases."

"How did they get it back here?"

"Just a guess. Al Storey remembers that about that time Henry Perris found some winch trouble on the big wrecker, and drove it to his place to work on it over the weekend. So he would have covered the name on the cab doors with a fake name, changed the plates. When the money-truck crew passed out, he put the hook on it and took it to the rendezvous point where the other car or cars were waiting. After they broke it open, they probably offloaded the money into Baither's car, and he and Lillian drove back here with it, taking a different route than Henry did, bringing the truck back. They could have talked the other two into moving out quickly, into going into Miami and setting up an alibi. We'll meet at the X motel at Jacksonville or wherever. The two pickup specialists would buy it, because Baither had the reputation for never crossing anyone, and for good planning. But he never had one that big before, one big enough to set him up for life. No more risk. So he crossed them, and left Henry and Lillian to take care of the other two when they came around. Frank Baither was making a business investment in setting himself up for Raiford. It took suspicion off him, if anybody ever decided the money-truck job looked like his handiwork. And his insurance was that he was the only one who knew where he hid it. I don't think it mattered to him who killed off who. I think the money is here somewhere. Clean and safe and dry. But I haven't been able to find it."

I whacked at the mosquitoes humming around my ears, and scratched the chigger bites on my thighs that I'd picked up on the night walk with Meyer.

Silence. "But I guess it doesn't matter. It's all over for me here. I'll wind it up. Billy can operate it until they appoint somebody to take over until election."

"Why?"

"It's all turning sour in some strange way. I don't mean in a personal way. I knew in the back of my mind that I was wrong. I kept my eyes shut about ... a personal matter, and told myself I would do such a total and dedicated job in every other way that it wouldn't matter. But it doesn't work that way. The scales don't measure the way they should. One little thing in one side weighs more than ... everything else in the other side."

A fractional moon rode above the dark line of treetops. I could not risk saying anything. He was talking to himself. Yet he was at the same time making a rare offer of friendship. He was asking for help of some kind. A man proud, thoughtful, and troubled.

"It isn't just that I slaved over that tape playback and weeded out almost every trace of the accent of the people I grew up with. And it isn't that I realized and accepted the fact that I have a better mind than I thought I had when I was the high-school muscle man. Those things can isolate a man from his beginnings. But there is something else in the air. The faces of the young ones and the look in the eyes of the old ones. The guidelines are blurred. Are cops pigs? If I operate within a system where juvenile court cannot touch rich kids, where the innocent—meaning those presumed innocent because they have not yet been tried—are jailed with the guilty when they can't raise bail, where judicial wisdom is conditioned by friendship and influence, where there are two kinds of law, one for blacks and one for whites; then if I go by the book, I am a kind of Judas goat, and if I bend the rules to improve—on my terms—the structure of local law, I am running my own little police state. I'd better get out of it because I can't live with either solution."

"Not with a little rule-bending here and there?"

"Like I bent rules for Lilo Perris? And Lew Arnstead?"

"That gravitational influence I was talking about?"

"Do you know what it is? You go around making guesses."

"She was your daughter. She knew it and Lew knew it."

"Is it *that* damned obvious!" he said, his voice breaking.

"Only to a man who mentioned her name to Johnny Hatch, and who was told by Nulia you visit Wanda from time to time."

It was a shabby, ordinary little story, and he felt compelled to tell it in detail, a way of punishing himself. Wanda had been married to Johnny Hatch over a year. She was bored and restless and full of vitality. Norman Hyzer had come home for Easter vacation from college, engaged but not yet married. The Hyzer backyard and the Hatch backyard had a common rear property line, though they were on different streets. She'd asked him to help her dig up a small tree and move it, asked him into her house to clean up afterward, kidded him, teased him, challenged him, and seduced him. Though aching with guilt, he had found himself unable to stay away from her during the brief vacation. Later he could take a more objective view of it, and see how easily she had engineered it, and how little it had meant to her.

But when he came back with his wife and baby daughter after his people were dead, to clean out the house of personal things and ready it for sale, she had come casually in through the back of the house to tell him that he had a very pretty little three-year-old daughter by her, named Lillian. She told him the date of birth and asked him to figure it out for himself. There was a baby boy, Ronnie, she said, definitely Johnny's. But Lillian was his seed.

And they had made love that afternoon on a mattress

on the floor in the upstairs hallway, and again the next morning, and had either still been making love or had finished at about the same time his wife and daughter were crushed to death by the fleeing car.

It was classic Biblical guilt and retribution, sin and punishment. He had come back and had become sheriff. He learned one aspect of Johnny and Wanda's divorce that was not public knowledge. Johnny's attorney showed the judge, in chambers, medical evidence that a man of Johnny's blood type could not have fathered a child with Lillian's blood type when the mother had Wanda's blood type. But there was enough evidence against her without that.

"She was the only person in the world of my blood," Hyzer said. "She was ... maybe a symbol of the little girl who died. It's easy to close your eyes and ears, to say she could not be warped and rotten. Wicked, in the classical meaning of the word. Bend the rules. Let her off with a reprimand. Because she would have that mocking look her mother had. She knew, and knew I wouldn't acknowledge her. Arnstead found out four years ago. He picked Wanda up for drunk, and out of all the babbling and mumbling and weeping he heard something and got her sobered up enough to tell the rest of it, and got her to write it down before she was sober enough to realize he was using her."

Arnstead let him know what he knew, not in a confrontation, but in little hints. Wanda had become fat and coarse and loud, and Hyzer had already let the girl off too easily too many times. A sheriff who is snickered at, loses authority, and elections.

"Balancing it out doesn't work," he said. "Lew didn't push it too hard or too obviously, so I told myself he wasn't doing any actual harm, maybe even some good. I told myself that his girls would be hustling anyway, so it was better to have them kept in line."

"Then he went too far?"

"Beating a prisoner. Neglect of duty. Culmination of months of little things. So I had to. It was go down one way or go down the other way, and in the end you make a choice."

"Now I know why you were so anxious to nail us for the Baither thing."

He thought it over. "Yes. A suspicion in the back of my mind I couldn't consciously admit to myself, and you and Meyer were the way out. That's proof enough I better close it out and move along. Bend the rules and you start bending your own judgment, too."

"Without finding out who killed Lilo?"

"That's part of closing it out. After Wanda had the first stroke, when she could get around, she came to see me. The left side of her face looked dead. She made me promise to look after Lillian, keep her out of trouble. I promised. That was part of it, too, I guess. Then, a little while ago, after I told her, I wanted to know how she felt. Brutal damned question. I asked her if she was sorry Lilo was dead. She blinked her eyes twice. Same answer for Henry. That letter you showed me ... Even mother-love couldn't live through that."

I had to make the guess that he wanted some kind of an answer. "You have a couple of incurable hang-ups, Norman. One is an old-timey hang-up on decency. The other hang-up is thinking too much, trying to separate cause and effect and locate where the guilt is. You are not with the scene, man. Guilt only happens to people who get caught. Sex is a handshake. Man has poisoned himself and he's on the way out, so pick up all the bread you can in any way you can. Enjoy."

"Sure, McGee. Sell yourself first."

"I keep trying, but I haven't been able to get into the spirit of the thing somehow. I keep going back to this role-playing of mine, you know, with the white horse and the maiden fair and the grail and the dragons and all that crap."

One flat and mirthless grunt of laughter from Sheriff Hyzer.

I said, "I do not want to be sickly sentimental, and I know that it is pagan barbarism to venerate the empty flesh when the spirit is long gone, but I think of Betsy out there in the night wired to that goddam tree, and how her face looks, and I keep thinking of how careful she was to look . . . nice. That's the only word. Nice."

He opened the car door. "Show me. I can call the people in from there."

NINETEEN

HE HAD A BIG BRIGHT CAMP-LIGHT IN the trunk of the cruiser. We walked slowly, and he kept the light on the ground so that we could avoid destroying any foot tracks or tire tracks.

I had trouble orienting myself at night. The tan Volkswagen would have been a big help had it been there. But it was gone. And Betsy was gone and the shovel was gone. In the grove we could walk around freely because the soft springy mat of brown needles of many seasons would not hold a print.

"Are you sure?" he asked.

"That's the third time. I am very damned sure, yes. Please stop asking. All right. One of these trees in this area, and it was about the same size around the trunk as that one."

It was Hyzer who spotted a silky lemon-gold thread clinging to the bark of a tree of the proper size, about four feet off the ground. Then in close inspection under the bright beam, I found a couple of blond hairs caught in the bark. That gave me enough orientation to show him where the half-dug grave had been.

I knelt near him and held the light while he carefully brushed away the blanket of pine needles, brushed down to the ground where it had been freshly, moistly stamped flat, leaving the same sole marks I had seen in the dirt in the half grave.

He grunted and began, just as carefully, to brush the needles back over it. "What are you doing?" I asked.

"I'll take the risk of assuming Mrs. Kapp is buried right here. Will your . . . sentimentality get in the way of leaving her here for a while?"

"No. It was the tree part that got to me. This is endurable. What do you have in mind?"

"Knowing something that somebody doesn't know you know is a useful thing in this line of work. Sometimes you don't know in advance how you'll use it. I'll come out alone tomorrow and take a cast of the shoe prints and any tire prints I can find. Let's take a look inside that shack now."

Whoever had come back to the unfinished business of burying her, had done a halfway job of tidying the shack. He had scattered the ashes, put the broken lid back on the barrel safe and covered it with the fire brick. I showed Hyzer the safe.

On the way back into town I told him, without telling him too much, exactly how eager I was for all kinds of publicity and press coverage.

Deputy Billy Cable had drafted an official release and he was holding it for Hyzer's approval. Hyzer sat at his desk and read it and said, "Billy, go and make certain every mouth is closed and stays closed, and then come back here."

Billy was back before Hyzer finished changing the release. Finally Hyzer handed it to him, saying, "Get it typed up again and get somebody to take it on over to Mr. Goss."

Billy read it and looked dismayed. "But . . ."

"What's wrong?"

"You've got it person or persons unknown, and this son of bitch McGee *confessed* he kilt Henry Perris."

"He thought he did, Billy," Hyzer said soothingly. "It was an honest mistake. Could you really believe a man could throw an oyster knife that deep into Henry's armpit from almost twenty feet away?"

"Well, I heard him tell how . . ."

"The way I reconstruct it, it is a heavy piece of metal and it struck Perris on the skull and knocked him out. After McGee left to come here and report it, the next person along saw the opportunity and picked up the knife and thrust it into the unconscious man."

"If that's the way you want it."

"That's the way I want it."

"And you took out the part about Mrs. Kapp."

"Mr. McGee took me to the place where he thought he saw her, but he was apparently mistaken."

"I don't want to upset you, Sher'f, but shouldn't your chief deputy know what the hell is—"

"Come back here after you send that off and I'll tell you."

When the door shut, I said, "Many thanks."

"I'll try to stick with that, McGee. But if somebody goes on trial for killing Lillian, I'm not going to turn over a doctored file to the State's attorney for grand jury indictment. You'll have to go back into the picture, and with that weapon he had to stab you with, and with the photographs of the holes in the trailer, you should be able to satisfy the court that it was self-defense. I will testify that you made immediate confession, but that I kept it quiet for the sake of not giving the killer too much free information. Raise your right hand."

It had a lot of golden ornamentation and an eagle and three shades of colored enamel, red, white, and blue. It said that I had finally finked out all the way, and was a sworn deputy sheriff of Cypress County Florida, with all the rights and privileges pertaining thereto. There was a wallet card with the sheriff's signature and mine. And I pinned the badge inside the wallet, and practiced flipping it open a few times, thinking of how Meyer would laugh himself into hiccups.

Billy Cable came in as I made the final practice flip, and tucked the wallet away. His eyes bulged.

"Norm!" he wailed. "I mean, Sheriff. Him? After all!"

The whip cracked, and Cable came to sudden attention. Hyzer said, "You are the best officer I have, Cable. And in ninety-five percent of your duty assignments you are superior. In the remaining five percent you turn into a vain, stupid, inept man, causing me more trouble than you are worth. Do you know what this flaw is?"

"I . . . ah . . . no, sir!"

"I request you to make a guess, then."

"I guess . . . well, sometimes I maybe let my own personal feelings; . . . Sir, a man can't be a machine!"

"Cable, off duty you will let your feelings and your emotions and your prejudices slop all over your personal landscape. You can roll and wallow in them. On duty, on *my* time, you will be a machine. Is that absolutely clear?"

"Yes, sir." It was a very small "yes, sir." Cable was swaying. Only the most effective chewing can make a grown man sway.

"Temporary Deputy McGee will be privately assigned by me, and will not be subject to your authority or control in any way, nor will you make any mention of his status. Now go and shake his hand and welcome him to this department."

Cable came over. His eyes looked slightly glassy and his palm was damp. "Deputy . . . glad to . . . hope you enjoy your . . ."

"Thanks, Billy. The name is Trav."

"Now you can both sit down," Hyzer said. "We will discuss McGee's theory of gravitation, and the identification of unknown influences. Billy, I made out a schedule of . . . recent events. I checked out the duty cards and duty reports, and I have placed your approximate location and activities in the right-hand column. I see no chance of your having been involved directly in any way."

"For God's sake, Sheriff! If you think I—"

"Didn't we just have a little discussion about emotion?"

". . . Sorry, sir."

"This is a guide, merely to show you how I want a special project handled. You are the sample. I want you to run these six deputies through the same thing, without letting anyone know what you are checking out. I want you to make certain that the deputy cards and duty reports are correct as to the hours involved."

"Somebody in the family?" Billy asked.

"McGee thought it had to be either you or me. It isn't either of us. So let's be certain it isn't *any* of us."

For one precarious moment, full of fellowship and conscious of the ornate badge of authority, I wanted to give them the full report on Lew Arnstead, so it could be added to Hyzer's list of unusual events. Sure, and good old Betsy would swear to every word of it as being the truth. I would bounce about three times right on the place where now the badge rested, and hear the steel door clang.

Hyzer stared with raised eyebrows at Cable until suddenly Cable came to with a start and hopped up and hurried out of the office.

"And that leaves us," said Mister Norm, "with two more places to go. Or three. Lew Arnstead. Mrs. Kapp could have guessed where he would be, could have known about that hideaway shack, gone out there, and found him closing the store, picking up the money, getting ready to move."

"And forgot where the safe was?"

"Or tore the place up after he killed Mrs. Kapp to make it look like a stranger. Relocked the safe and tore the door off."

"Was he that subtle?"

"Any police officer learns what other police officers look for and how they make their judgments. Acquired subtlety, call it. He knew that Lillian had tricked him and left that envelope of yours in the Baither place. So he goes after her. And he finds her."

"You said three possibilities?"

"Somebody trying to either get a woman free and clear

of Arnstead for good, or get even for what happened to the woman."

"Featherman?"

"A possibility. Maybe Mrs. Kapp arrived and found someone there, and Arnstead was there, dead. He could be under those pine needles too."

"The black jeep hidden on Betsy's street doesn't fit that one."

"Or the first one, either. Unless we get too fancy, and jam pieces into the puzzle whether they fit or not. Lew abandoned the jeep there to cause confusion. Or somebody picked him up right there and took him out to his shack."

"Or, Sheriff, Henry and Lillian killed him because they couldn't risk you finding out who engineered leaving that envelope. Maybe Henry and Lillian knew about that shack and they had to make sure Arnstead hadn't hidden anything out there that could tie them into Baither's death. And Betsy walked into that scene."

"That was my third guess," he said. "Save the best until last."

"Lillian knew about the shack. That photograph of her in that batch in your desk drawer was taken out there. Remember that clock on the wall?"

He took them out, found hers and studied it. "Very good, Deputy. Observant."

"When you find yourself in a sling, it's time to start thinking clearly or start running."

He put the pictures back, slammed the drawer hard. "Around and around and around," he said. "The mythological animal that grabs its own tail and starts eating and disappears down its own throat."

"A fifth man in on the money-truck job? Or maybe Henry and Lillian nailed either Hutch or Orville, but not both."

"We're going further and further into the mist," he said. "So we haul it back to specifics. Mrs. Kapp's car might tell us something. There are hundreds of little tracks across that scrubland up there. Tomorrow I call in a chopper for an air search. The biggest specific is the plausible assumption Lillian told someone what she learned from Frank Baither. That bucket technique is efficient. She would probably try some lies. So the technique is to keep at it until you get the same answer time and again."

"Do you have any idea how powerful she was?"

"Yes. I saw one demonstration. I see your point. Either one strong person or two people to handle her like that, even taped up."

"I'd buy two."

Then he told me my assignment. We checked the inventory of confiscated weapons, and I settled for a Ruger standard carbine in .44 Magnum, with a five-round capacity, four in a front tube and one in the chamber. I'd had one aboard *The Busted Flush* for a time and had used it on shark coming after the hooked billfish, until one day I had decided that the shark was doing his thing, and it was bloody and disrespectful to kill an honest scavenger just because he happened to come into the ball park when you are trying to win. From that day on, the rule when fishing from the *Muñequita,* after towing it to billfish country behind the *Flush,* was that the lookout would yell out when he saw the first fin, and you would release the billfish then and there instead of later, at the side of the boat. We do not bring dead meat home and hang it high for the tourists to say *Aaah* over. We take a picture of the good ones as somebody leans down to clip off the leader wire. The stainless hook corrodes out of the marlin, tuna, or sailfish jaw in days, leaving him free to go take the dangling bait of the commercial long-liners, fight his heart away against the resistance of the buoys, and, after the shark have browsed this free lunch, leave his jaw or his whole head on the hook for the deckhands to haul up and toss away on the pickup round.

So I knew it would fire five 240-grain slugs as fast as I could pull the trigger, bust each one right through a seven-inch pine tree, and had a reasonable accuracy for a weapon a yard long overall, weighing less than six pounds.

They had grabbed it off a poacher. Norm Hyzer approved of the choice and gave me a handful of jacketed factory loads. After he explained what I was to do, I asked if I could have another few pieces of equipment. So he drove me to the shopping center and pointed out the hardware store that stayed open late. I bought my junk, and then hit the supermarket and provisioned myself for a forty-eight-hour vigil. Hyzer said he would check me out of the White Ibis after he dropped me off, and put my gear in the rental car and shut it up in his own garage, well out of sight.

It was ten-thirty when he dropped me off at the Baither place, wished me luck, and drove off.

It took longer than usual for my vision to adjust to the night. Priority one was slathering myself with repellent before a couple dozen of the more muscular hummers got together and lifted me up and wedged me into a tree to consume at their leisure.

I checked out the pump house by leaving the flashlight on inside, closing the door, and waiting again for night vision to see how much light came out. It was pretty good. A narrow crack above the knob, and a wider gap at the bottom. I could fix those on the inside by cutting some strips from one of the old blankets inside.

It took over an hour to set it up the way I wanted it. I had bought enough wire so I could take the long way through the brush from the pump house to the old wooden bridge. I turned out my flashlight each time I heard a car coming. In time I located an old gray warped plank with the right gap underneath and enough give to it. I taped my little brass terminals from a dismembered flashlight to the warped underside and to the supporting timber. I brought the buzzer along the road and put it down close enough to hear it from the bridge. There was no way to walk across or drive across without closing the circuit.

For somebody who, for some reason, wanted to come in from another direction, I used the primitive old black thread and rattle-can device. Closed the pump house door, turned on the flashlight, covered the cracks, made and wolfed a pair of thick sandwiches, drank a quart of the almost-cool water. Stretched out on the narrow cot

to find the place to prop the weapon where my hand
would find it with no fumbling, no loss of time.

Turned the light out, opened the door, stretched out on
the cot again. I invited sleep by willing the relaxation of
neck and shoulders. Deputy McGee on duty. It is to
laugh. Or cry.

And I let myself down into that dark turbulence knowing I would find there the dusty-looking eyes of Arnstead,
and Betsy playing her lavender game with stomach-
turning grimace, and a flat steel handle sticking straight
out of a twill armpit, and the foam caked into the corner
of the dead mouth of the mad young girl.

TWENTY

AT FIRST LIGHT I GOT UP AND CHECKED
my warning system, took my thread and tin cans down
and stowed them under the cot. Later, at sunup, I prowled
the area, locating logical access so I could do a better job
of hooking up the dangle-cans at nightfall.

I found a way of wedging the pump house door so it
would appear to be locked if anybody tried it. Hyzer did
not want the seals broken on the doors to the Baither
house. I found a window catch I could slip, and climbed
in over the sill. The wide white tape still dangled from the
armchair where Baither had died, and under the chair and

in front of it were the crusted black places on the brown rush rug where his blood had dried.

I found a shady thicket with a good view of the terrain and settled in, carbine beside me. There was a nostalgia about it. Not the warm kind, with the misted eye and the sad smile. The other kind, that sucks the belly muscles in, and gives you access to the old automatic habits of survival, such as holding half a breath from time to time while you listen to bird sounds and bug sounds, waiting for them to stop in some unseen area. Listening for some little clink or jingle of equipment, or oiled snick of weaponry being readied. Nostrils widen and you snuff the faint movement of the breeze, for taint of alien sweat. You move a little bit from time to time because if you remain still, muscles can lock and when you must move, it might be necessary to move quick as a lizard, or take the hammer blow of unexpected automatic weapon.

At eleven the bridge boards rattled and an old white Mustang came in, packed with kids: two bleached boys in the bucket seats, three limber, noisy, bikinied young girls sitting high on the downfolded top. The driver swung it around the old red pickup so spiritedly, one of the girls nearly fell off. The girl in the middle grabbed her. They stopped and I could hear them clearly from my sun-dappled thicket.

"Tommy! You bassar, you like to kee-yul me, doon that crazy kind of drivin'."

"Not ef you land on your haid, Bunny Lee."

They piled out and went to the house and circled it, peering in every window. I heard the girls saying how spooky it was. They were all telling each other what happened to Frank Baither.

"Let's bust in and get a good look," one of the boys said.

"Hell with that," the other said. "Ol' Hyzer has got it sealed. You maybe want him on your ass? Not me."

"Come on," the first one said. "Look at old Norma Jean here. She's dead set on getting in there and making out with me in old Baither's sack."

"That's grass talking, goddam you Tommy!" a girl said.

The girls were slapping at their bare legs and shoulders. One of them said, "Get me out of here, you guys. I'm about to get et up. There's nothing here. Let's go bug old Dolores."

They ran for the car, piled in and charged out, shrilling the tires when they hit the paved road.

I took another tour. There was a crude patio off the other side of Baither's house, about twelve feet square, three steps down from a sealed door to the living room. It had a low wall around it of block painted pale blue. There were some planting pots with dead sticks coming out of the baked dirt inside. The patio area was paved with solid cement block a little larger than shoeboxes. They had been laid on tamped earth with sand poured between the cracks and watered down. It had been a sloppy job. The rainy season had washed the foundation uneven. Weeds grew out of the cracks. An old redwood chair, bleached gray, with a broken arm, crouched in a corner. Some blocks were missing.

I sat for a little while on the low wall, being scolded by a blue jay. I was thinking of Betsy Kapp in her grave up near the other end of Cypress County. And something in the back of my mind was looking at more immediate things, and finally sent the message upstairs that it seemed odd that some of the blocks looked paler and newer than others.

So I squatted and lifted one out and turned it over and replaced it and had the answer. Hyzer had directed a thorough search. So the blocks had been taken up and they had done some digging, or some probing with sharpened reinforcing rod, and had then replaced the patio floor. They had not taken the time or trouble to replace them all the same side up as they had been before. So the ones which went back in upside down looked a little newer. They had not had as much time to weather.

In fact, they had not even taken the trouble to put them all back. Four were missing from the far corner.

Everyone has their own fund of small idiotic compulsions. There are people who have to have their papers perfectly aligned with the edge of the desk. There are

picture straighteners, and compulsive cleaners of ashtrays.
I am a jigsaw freak. If I find myself in a room where there
is a partially completed jigsaw puzzle, I find myself circling, then hovering, then finding the piece that goes here
and the piece that goes there. Small triumphs. I cannot
stand the sight of a fishrod rack that will hold five rods
and has only four rods in the clips. I go through life fitting
objects into their obvious and proper places.

So while thoughts moved away from the scene, back to
the trailer this time, Henry circling it, I went scuffing
through the rank grass and weeds, back and forth, around
and around the three sides of the patio, moving further
away from it, hunting for the block that would satisfy my
moronic sense of order and fitness.

I woke up about forty feet out from the patio? No block.
Irritation. What the hell did they do with it?

Pause for thought. Okay. So they searched the patio.
Took up all the block. Piled it out to the side, probably,
but close. No need to tote it an inch further than necessary. Very probably they had piled it on the broad low
wall.

So maybe there hadn't been quite enough block to pave
the patio in the first place, and I was looking for something that didn't exist.

I went over to the corner and gave it close inspection.
No, dammit. You could see the oblong depressions in the
dirt underneath. And here was where one of the vine
weeds had been torn when they had been lifted out. Green
at the root end, and brown beyond the tear.

I straightened up and stood with my mouth hanging
open. I stood in a comic strip, with a big light bulb
suspended in space over my head.

I heard Lennie Sibelius, in that resonant and flexible
voice, " . . . medium height with a bull neck and very
broad thick shoulders. As a kid he had worked for his
uncle who operated a little yard making cement block,
and he had carried enough tons of mix and tons of
finished block to give him that muscular overdevelopment."

My light bulb faded and dimmed. Hold it a minute,

temporary deputy. Wouldn't a brand new patio completed during Frank's two weeks before he went to jail stand out like one very large and very inflamed thumb? And this block looks old. Maybe twenty years old.

But Baither had that old truck and he could take the original block far away and dump it. And he could add stain and dirt to the next mix. I yanked a block out and put it on its side on top of the wall. I yanked a second block out and slammed it down on the first one. It bounced off and nearly landed on my instep. The second smash broke a corner off. The third blow broke it open like a walnut. The meat inside the shell was the right size and shape. It had to be skinned. I got down to two banded packets of ten-dollar bills. Two thousand race-track dollars. It had been wrapped in heavy plastic, tightly taped, then dipped in paraffin. From then on the process could be easily guessed. Pour a layer in the bottom of the greased wooden mold. When it started to set up, put the package on it, well centered, and finish the pour.

One hell of a lot of work, Mr. Baither. Two weeks of it. Off somewhere, probably, where you wouldn't be disturbed. Truck it in and lay it down, trying to make it look as beat as the original block, chipping it, scarring it. You could have added a little rock salt to the mix to get the right pitted effect. You must have been tired, fellow, when you finally got shoved into a cell.

I never would have found it or thought of it had not those four been missing, and had I not seen from the broken weed that they had been taken recently. Somebody would have been in a sweat to make certain that the water treatment had gotten the truth out of Lilo Perris. So they had nipped in and grabbed samples last evening, before Hyzer posted me here.

Dilemma. Turn the whole thing over to Hyzer right now. He had said, "Unless you get a visitor, don't call me and blow the cover. I'll get in touch with you."

Explicit. Follow orders. But first take certain steps which are part precaution, part ugly surprise.

I found a rusty old pickax behind the pump house. I soon learned the force required to pop the blocks open without gouging the cash. I stacked the waxed oblongs on the broad wall. There were one astonishing number of blocks in a twelve-by-twelve space, and I found only seven which were solid all the way through.

I improvised a Santa sack out of a frayed old army blanket from the pump house. I made it in five heavy loads, and I didn't finish the job until four-thirty. I crawled into my thicket, aching and winded and incomparably smug. Some very sneaky thoughts came sidling into my mind. With a little applied intelligence a man ought to be able to tie himself up impressively, and give himself a good thump on the head ... "My God, Sheriff, he must have gotten behind me somehow. I never got a look at him."

It would figure out to about twenty years of splendid living. Untraceable. Spendable. With nobody with an ugly disposition coming looking for it, and you. Maybe.

I remembered Meyer telling me that if I ever scored very very big, I had the natural tendency to turn into a one-hundred-percent bum. "And when you lose that last one percent," he said, "I might find you dreary. Sporadic monetary anxiety becomes you. It keeps you polite."

When the sun was very low, I began to make my preparations for the night. I was near the pump house when the buzzer sounded, and as a wind had come up I could not tell whether it had been a vehicle or a footstep which had done it. I ducked around behind the pump house, and heard the car, looked around and saw the green sedan with the blue flashers on the roof.

So I came out, carbine in hand, a tired and honest man ready and willing to make his honest report to his honest temporary boss man. But it was King Sturnevan who pulled his bulk out from behind the wheel and watched me approach, his back to the round golden sun.

"King," I said, "I hope you're delivering groceries and a cold beer."

"If I'd thought of it, pally, I'd of done just that."

"Then suppose you go tell Mister Norm it would be very nice if he would bring one hot sandwich and one cold beer to the recruit."

"Tell him and duck?"

"Seriously, I have to see him. I want him to get on out here as soon as he can. Would you call in, please?"

"Sure thing." He got into the car again. He fiddled with the transmitter, spoke into the hand mike. "Nine to CCSD, come in. Nine calling CCSD, come in." Nothing. He tried a couple more times, then got out, saying, "I told Red this damned set has got something loose on it. Sometimes it works, sometimes it's like dead."

"There's a window I can slip, and I think the phone in there is working. I'm not supposed to call in. Why don't you use it and just say to him that . . . you want to show him something at the Baither place."

"You got something to show him? You find something, McGee?"

"Yes and no. Look, King. I'm reporting direct. You know how it is."

"Hell, I know you're reporting direct. He just said I could stop by and see how you're making out. So whyn't you tell me and I can run back in and give him a direct report, and keep it off the air and off the phone?"

I wanted to think it over, and I eased over to lean against the side of the car. But he got in the way, a little clumsy on his feet. But he had moved very well in his little shower room demonstration.

So I said, "Okay, King. That's probably the best way. I'll tell you the whole thing. But let's sit in the car. Okay?"

"It's too hard for me to get in and out of that little tin bucket. They make cars too small for guys my size."

"Okay. You stand outside and I'll get in the car."

And when he was still in the way, I knew. And I jumped back a good ten feet from him and put the muzzle of the carbine in direct line with his belly.

"What's with you, buddy boy? You some kind of flip?"

"Put the right hand on top of the head, slowly. Now!"

"Dammit, you're acting like . . ."

The holstered weapon was on the belt threaded through his pant loops. "Now undo the belt buckle with the left hand. Now the top button. Unzip and let them fall."

"But . . ."

"King, you better believe me, I will blow a hole right through the middle of you."

He let the pants drop, and I had him pull them off and move away from them, away from the car, so I could circle and, holding the gun on him, look into the car. I didn't see it at first, and if he had been more casual, maybe I never would have noticed it. He had pulled the mike jack out of the radio panel. The mike was on the dash hook, the connector cord hanging straight down.

"I nearly handed it to you," I said.

"You better start making sense soon. This is King. This is the guy on your side, pally." He really looked upset and distressed. He wore blue boxer shorts. His legs were massive and white and hairless. It made me think of something else. I had him unlace a shoe, take it off, and back away from it. I advanced as he backed up. I picked it up and held it toward the light and saw the serrations across the bottom, the place at the ball of the foot worn smooth.

I took a deep breath and let it out slowly, and took the slight tension off the trigger. "You nearly had it right then, King. It was close."

"Somebody better lock you up before you hurt somebody, boy."

"How are you at grave-digging?"

"Now you wouldn't ask a fella big as me to dig his own hole."

"You don't work very hard, King. Got any fresh blisters?"

He looked involuntarily at his right hand, and, like a little kid, put it behind him. "Worked in my garden lately."

"What did you plant in your garden? A dead lady?"

"For God's *sake*, McGee!"

"And spread the pine needles back neat. But we brushed them away very carefully, and this shoe is going to match the mold Hyzer took. You didn't have any trouble following Henry's car. You hung back and saw me leave and went right in. Held her head in the bucket. You're big enough and strong enough."

"You shove it under the skin, or take it right in a vein?"

"King, I am not going to risk messing around with you. You are too good. Now turn around very slowly. I am going to wrap you up, and when your place is searched, they are going to come up with some chunks of broken cement and some wax and some plastic and some cash money."

It was my intent to get close enough to chunk him in the back of the skull with the butt of the carbine, then cuff him to his own steering post, once I drove the car close enough.

He didn't turn around. "You want to be a boy scout, McGee, go ahead and put one right through the middle. You were close before, you said. Go ahead."

"Why Betsy?"

"Good question. Why not?"

Again I had to consciously ease back on the trigger finger so that it rested lightly.

He said, "She came to check Lew's place about the time I was getting the lid off that cheap safe. She decided I'd killed Lew. She didn't say it. But she showed it. I thought I'd set the two of you up nice. I wanted to know what happened to Lew's body, and after I started digging the hole, she told me. So I twisted the wire tight and I had to leave then to go on duty."

"Why Lew?"

"I thought maybe he found out from Lilo where Frank hid the money. I knew he had some money stashed. I had a good idea where. It was peanuts. Eleven thousand. And a bunch of rotten things. Rotten letters and rotten dirty pictures. I had to burn those. They weren't decent. Linda Featherman treated me right. She spoke to me like a human being, not a fat old boxfighter turned cop. Lew gave me the wink after she was dead, and I knew he meant she was one of his women, and I decided to kill him. I investigated an accident she was in. She treated me fine. Just fine."

"You've been lucky, King. Because basically you are one very dumb guy."

"Do you *know* how much money I shoulda had? Do you *know* the kind of payoff I would have had if I hadn't had bad hands and bad managers, and didn't cut easy. I had everything else going for me. I would have had one million bucks anyway, pally. Right now. I had everything else. Speed, punch, instinct."

"So the money is yours by rights."

"I would have had more even."

I realized he had somehow managed to get too close. As I started to move back, he bounded in low, banging the barrel aside with a forearm, and swinging a big left into my ribs, low on the right side. I felt them go, felt myself float back and down and heels over head, light as this-tledown. Felt myself plucked up and saw him in the red glow, bounding and shuffling, moving in. Saw a fist come afloating, and felt my stomach being smashed loose, saw the sky spin, fell again, and felt cold metal under my lips.

"Come on, pally," he said in a wheedling tone, far away. "Upsy-daisy. Dance with the old King a little."

Hand found the metal. It was too much fun for him his way than any other way. Finger found the trigger guard. I had been broken in half in the middle and the two halves were at least a yard apart. I rocked the right half onto its back, bringing the carbine up, and pulled the trigger as fast as I could, but the little joltings of the weapon came at least five minutes apart. A shark sank in a red-sun-sea, and the red rolled over me, and the further I sank, the darker it got.

TWENTY-ONE

ON A VERY FINE DAY IN MAY, MEYER brought Miss Agnes around to the door of the Lauderdale hospital, and the cheery Gray Lady wheelchaired me down the short ramp and out to the curb. Meyer came around and I pulled myself up, stepped on that obsolete convenience known as a running board, and sat on the seat and swung my legs in.

I thanked the lady and she told me not to hurry back. Miss Agnes looked better than I had ever seen her. Ron had hand-rubbed so many coats of blue that you could see down into the surface.

"She running good?" I asked Meyer.

"Aside from driving like an armored lorry, fine."

The whole world looked bright and new and far too brilliant in every color and outline. A couple of weeks inside can do it. My clothes felt strange. And they were a little large for me.

"Nice to be out," I said.

"For a while there, nobody thought you would be."

I knew that. I had lost quite a few days in there somewhere. The doctor absolutely refused to believe that that damage had been done by two blows from the human fist. He said the muscle cover was tough and hard

250

enough to withstand a blow like that. He said I shouldn't have had three crushed ribs, a rupture of the external oblique muscle, liver hemorrhages, and a perforation from a piece of rib bone in the bottom of the left lung. That's what brought on the pneumonia that they couldn't seem to find the right antibiotic for. I had been in shape, but not in shape for the ring.

"Forget about the trial," Meyer said.

"What do you mean? What happened?"

"Sturnevan died this morning. He was coming along fine. The smashed hip was all wired together and seemed to be healing in good shape. Hyzer phoned me. Said to tell you. He said they told him it was a massive coronary occlusion."

"We should both have died, lain there on the ground eight feet apart and quietly bled to death. But those kids came back to break into the house. Meyer, my friend, our luck doesn't run so good in Cypress County."

"I have no pressing need to return. Oh, and Hyzer said your check will be coming through in another few days. Two and a half percent of the total amount recovered. Something under twenty-two thousand."

"Nobody's luck ran very good in Cypress County."

"Nine hundred and twenty thousand is maybe an unlucky number. Your hands get sweaty and you become accident prone."

"Meyer, did they locate any bodies near that trailer?"

"I told you they did. Ten days ago I told you. You looked like you were listening."

"Who?"

"They don't know. They'd been there too long. A tall body and a shorter body, both male, both with a round puncture hole in the base of the skull. I told you that, too."

"Don't get surly about it. Does it hurt to tell me twice?"

"I'm thinking of the other things I told you I'll have to tell you twice."

"There'll be time enough. We aren't going anywhere. Did I happen to do any talking when I wasn't tracking very well?"

"A certain amount."

"Anything interesting?"

"It was all very dull stuff. You know, the usual run of delirium. Sex and violence. Nothing original."

"Thanks. That light is red."

"Even if I hadn't seen it, I would have seen it when you sucked air through your teeth, McGee. Telling me out loud also is superfluous. I might get angry and run into somebody."

"You're driving. So drive. I'll leave you alone."

"A blessing."

"Did you get anybody for the job, Meyer?"

"If I didn't, wouldn't I get stuck with it myself? Yes, I found a woman to cook and clean. An ugly one. A little bit hard of hearing. In your condition I did you a favor and found an ugly one that reads little books of inspirational poems in her spare time."

"You're too good to me, Meyer."

"Wrong preposition. For."

"The light is green, Meyer."

"Do I do this to you when you're driving? Do I complain when you go running into canals?"

"No. But you keep bringing it up."

So soon we went under the pedestrian bridge and turned left and Meyer eased Miss Agnes into a slot reasonably near the entrance to F dock.

"You want to ride on one of the delivery carts?"

"Let's walk. Slow."

So we walked along to F-18, and there were yelps from far boats, and sounds of welcome from nearby ones. And unkind comment. Are you McGee's father, mister? Meyer, who's the clean skinny old man? McGee, where's your tan? Fall into the oatmeal? Let me give you the address of my ex-husband's tailor, darling.

Have fun, people. All I want to do is get aboard and lie down.

So as I tottered across my little boarding ramp, holding carefully onto the safety cable, I noticed that my houseboat looked almost as good as my ancient Rolls pickup. It gleamed and glistened. It looked so good, it embarrassed me. Why couldn't I maintain it like that?

"Meyer, who is the compulsive polisher?"

"That deaf woman has a lot of extra energy. She asks me what next, and one day I said she could clean the outside of the boat, too."

Meyer helped me into the lounge and down the corridor past the galley into the master stateroom. The bed was crisply made up and turned down. I undressed and got in, and Meyer said I would probably feel better if I had my usual, a nice knock of the Plymouth over ice, and I told him he was a nice man. I heard him tinkling around out there.

The tinkling approached and I put my hand out and opened my eyes, saying, "Meyer, where is . . ."

And Heidi Geis Trumbill put the drink in my hand and laughed aloud in her pleasure at my surprise. She was still the most elegantly textured pussycat of them all, a little older now, not a pound heavier, with more of the awareness of living in her eyes, more of the taste of times and places in the look of her mouth. Elegance, freshly tanned, leaning her perfume close to kiss me quickly and softly on the lips, and then sitting down on the side of the bed, looking at me misty-eyed.

"McGee, you idiot, are you crying?"

"It's weakness, love. This water runs from the eye. Means little. Or a lot. Take your pick. But *how!* The last time I saw you was . . ."

"When I got in the car with the luggage and left you standing there, dear. St. Croix. I looked back. You looked so dejected. And my heart was breaking and breaking."

"You went to find your own life, find that right guy, have fat babies I think you said. Well?"

"I found him, but somebody else had found him first. It was a long bad scene, dear, and I cut away from it six months ago. I've been painting like a madwoman. My show sold out."

"What are you doing here?"

"Don't you know? I'm ugly and hard of hearing and I will read inspirational poems aloud to you."

"Did you clean up this crock boat?"

"Look at my poor hands, dear. Look at my nails!"

"Seriously, how come . . ."

"Travis, darling, a long time ago—maybe not so awfully long ago really, but it does seem way way back—I told Meyer that you had picked up all the pieces of me and put me together, and that if you were ever in need of the same he was to find me, through my gallery, and let me know and if I did not happen to have any compound fractures, I would come to you on a dead run. I got here a week ago yesterday."

"So that's why Meyer has looked so bland and smug and mysterious. Why didn't you come to the hospital?"

"Hate them, darling. Sorry. Wasn't this better?"

"This is as good as anything can get. My God, you look lovely. You are something way out else, Heidi."

"Do you need putting together?"

"Haven't you noticed me?"

"Oh hell, I don't mean looking like sudden death. That's a body thing. I mean putting together."

I looked at her and knew that I did. "Something was going wrong and it went further wrong. I don't know. I lost it, somehow, without knowing what I lost. Some kind of . . . sense of light and motion and purpose. I went ragged around the edges and bleak in the middle. The world seems to be coarsening, and me with it. Everything that happens takes away, and less flows back. And I respond less, and in the wrong way. I still amuse myself but there's some contempt in it now. I don't know . . . I don't know. . . ."

"Darling, there's that water from the eye syndrome again."

"Sorry."

"There's nothing so really wrong with you, you know. It's second adolescence."

"Is that it?"

"Of course, Travis, darling. I had delayed adolescence. Remember your absolutely dreadful analogy of comparing me to that old yellow Packard you bought when you were a child, and finally got running so beautifully?"

"Indeed I do."

"In your ravings you let Meyer know you had promised the cruising month of June aboard this fine houseboat to a lady who, for reasons he wouldn't tell me, won't be able to make it. You may tell me or not, as you wish. But I am substituting."

"That is very good thinking, Heidi."

"The cure for my delayed adolescence was a grown-up man. And I think a grown-up woman can cure a recurrence of adolescence, don't you?"

"Shock treatment, eh?"

"McGee, I am a very grown-up woman, far more so than that grim day we said good-by on that lovely island."

"I think you are. Yes. I would say so."

She looked at me and I suddenly knew exactly what Mona Lisa was thinking about. It was exactly the same smile, though on a face far more to my liking.

"I think, dear, that it is going to be absolutely essential for the health of both of us, and the sanity too, if you will kindly get a lot of lovely sleep, and eat the rich marvelous foods I am going to cook for you, and exercise a little more each day, and take the sun and . . . ."

"I guess it's pretty essential. Yes, indeedy."

"Because we are going to further places on our cruise, darling, than anybody has ever reached before on a boat this slow in one single lovely month."

I finished the drink. She took the glass. She told me later that I fell asleep smiling, and that Raoul, the cat, joined me later, curling into a warm nest against my waist.

SUSPENSE...
ADVENTURE...
MYSTERY...

John D. MacDonald's
TRAVIS McGEE SERIES

TAF-17